TRANSCENDENT

TRANSCENDENT

By J.P. Closser

Charleston, SC
www.PalmettoPublishing.com

Transcendent

First Edition

Paperback ISBN: 978-1-64990-723-3
eBook ISBN: 978-1-64990-227-6

CHAPTER 1

Jensen Atwood lets out a groan as he splashes water onto his face from the sink of a job he can't stand; thankful the day is finally over. Using the mirror, he looks down at the Verizon logo stenciled on his gray polo shirt and pulls it off, replacing it with a green plaid button-up. He runs a hand through his dark auburn hair, putting it back in its place before looking at the bags under his hazel eyes.

"I should get more sleep," he mutters while drying his face with the cheapest paper towels the company could find.

He grabs his gym bag off the floor, slinging it over his shoulder as he heads out the bathroom into the showroom of the job that gives him just enough money to live. This is when Jensen is at his happiest—leaving.

"Off to the tables, Jensen!" his coworker yells from over his shoulder. Nate, that judgmental bastard.

"As always, Nate, I've got to make up for what this company doesn't pay me somewhere. It's either the tables or the corners, and I don't think my ass or your mom's wallet could handle that," Jensen responds as

1

he pushes the two-way door to the store open, heading straight for his motorcycle.

It's not a lie—or a joke either. The job pays almost nothing, especially to live in Atlantic City. He lives in a cheap apartment that sits over a bar and owns an old motorcycle that barely gets him from point A to point B. But what Jensen does have is luck; at least, that's how it feels sometimes. Ever since he's been able to enter the casinos, he's had more than enough luck for one man. For the most part, Jensen always walks out on top. He could never really explain it to anyone, not that he really has to. His parents are no longer in the picture; he could care less about his coworkers and friends, who are few and far between. The only family still left in his life is his cousin Luke, whom he sees probably once a month to hustle a few games of pool with.

Jensen hops on his 2000 Kawasaki Zephyr, and after a few attempts, it finally turns over and starts, spitting unburned gasoline from its exhaust pipe as it tries to warm up. He puts on his helmet for the ten-minute ride to his apartment. Climbing on top of his rusty but trusty black steed, shifting into first, he flies out of the parking lot without a care in the world.

Jensen Atwood races eastbound on Ventnor Avenue toward his apartment and the string of Casinos that sits on the infamous boardwalk of Atlantic City. His go-to place for his additional income is the Tropicana Casino. There is no reason to go here, other than it is two blocks from his run-down apartment—or stumbling distance, if it happens to be a good night.

Jensen pops out the kickstand next to the bar he calls home and starts on foot toward Tropicana. He can't help but let his mind wander as he strolls to make his real income for the month. Nobody, not even he, could explain how his luck has worked or why it only works at craps. Slots are obviously a rip off. Blackjack is a numbers game, and Jensen, barely a high school graduate is obviously not where he belongs. Poker players take life too seriously for his taste. But there is something about craps. It doesn't work all the time; hell, it doesn't work half the time. But it does work out enough that he can nearly double his yearly income by playing craps two or three times a week. You couldn't call it beginner's luck either, since he's been doing it for the last three years, ever since he turned twenty-one. There is no trick, no game plan, no person on the inside. It is just plain dumb luck. He'll just sit on one end of the table, think of the number he wants the dice to come up as, and—boom!—almost half the time, it works. He's never told anybody about his *ability* because, honestly, it sounds insane, even to him. He is very superstitious, though, about his luck. Same table, same side, same bet placements. He never bets when he's tossing the dice and only bets big when someone on the other end of the table is throwing.

I sound crazy. He laughs to himself as he opens the front door to the casino.

The cold air conditioning hits him in the face, and he feels strangely at home. He walks over the faded red and white tile floor of the entrance leading to the water fountain, which sits in the middle of the room, surrounded by the first slot machines out of who knows how many.

"You might as well just toss your money into that fountain," he says out loud, paying no mind to someone's grandma at a slot machine; she looks like she hasn't seen the sun since she arrived in Atlantic City.

He makes his way down the pathway between the endless rows of slot machines on either side—sitting on top of a carpet that looks like it hasn't been changed since the days of prohibition. Soon he arrives at *his* table. Both corners are filled with people; only the sides next to the dealers are open, and that just won't do. Can't mess with a proven system at this point.

Guess I'll grab a drink or two until then.

Jensen continues just past the table to a bar within eyesight of the table so he can see when his spot opens up.

He sits with one elbow on the bar and his body angled to the table, signaling to the bartender with a raised finger.

"Rum and Coke, please. Well rum is fine," he adds as he slides a five to the bartender's side of the counter. The bartender just nods, smiles, and starts pouring.

Jensen shivers, goosebumps running the length of his body, ending at his neck. A small jolt hits him at the base of his skull like someone just hit him with a taser. He nearly jumps out of his seat, spins around to see no one there.

That was strange, he thinks. *I don't think I've ever had a cold chill hit me that hard.*

The bartender slides Jensen his rum and coke and goes to give him his $1.25 change, and Jensen waves him off. The bartender smiles and thanks him. Jensen looks down and notices his name tag: *Chad*.

"Thanks, Chad," he says, picking up his drink, turning to see if his spot has opened. Still full.

The goosebumps are still there; he rubs his arms and neck, trying to warm himself up, looking for the source of where it's coming from. No vent above or below. He takes a sip from his rum and coke as he sees her. It's the third time in two weeks he's spotted her. Dressed like she always is: faded jeans, dark hoodie, light skin complexation, almost like caramel. But it's none of the above that draws him to her. It's her eyes, the brightest, most piercing he's ever seen in person. And she's staring right at him. He tries to think of an opening. He turns to break eye contact to make a coherent thought; his table spot is open.

He turns to get one last glance, but she's gone. "Of course she is," he says as he steps off the stool, stepping toward the table he's so patiently waited for.

He stands where he has stood hundreds of times before and lays one grand in hundreds down on the table for the dealer to turn into chips. He grabs his chips, leaving the minimum bet needed to play just behind the pass line. The button on the table is in the off position. The stickman handles the dice with ease and slides them over to Jensen.

"Of course," he mutters to no one in particular.

He grabs two dice out of the five, shakes them, and gives them a toss to the other side.

"Eight!" one of the dealers call out while flipping the button to *on* and sliding it over top of the eight on the table.

The two dice are then slid back to Jensen, who reluctantly picks them back up and tosses them to the other side. Jensen places small bets at the table. Adds some chips to the six and a few to the field, just to not completely waste his time. Eventually, Jensen finally rolls a seven with a little bit of luck, ending his turn with the dice. He lets out a sigh of relief, probably the only person at the table who does and prepares his chips for the onslaught of betting that is about to occur by pushing them from one side to the other in the cradle built into the edge of the table, creating a hypnotic wave of color.

A man, who looks in his late fifties or early sixties, is directly across from Jensen in a nice three-piece suit and tie, making the rest of them at the table look like bums off the street. He picks the two dice he thinks will bring him the luck he needs, sliding them and rolling them to a specific number just before picking them up and tossing them with a high angle back to the table felt.

"Six!" yells the dealer, placing the button to *on* over top of the corresponding six on the table.

Now the fun begins. Jensen smiles and throws some chips on the field, three chips on eight, and receives some change, which he adds right back to pile next to the pass line.

That's good for now, he thinks.

The old man gathers up his dice and arcs them high into the air, and they land with a thud and bounce off the wall of the table next to Jensen. Ten. *Nice!* The field pays out. The dealer slides over Jensen's winnings, which he, in turn, adds to the nine at the top of the table.

Jensen begins the ceremonious tapping of his right index finger on the table.

Five and a four. Jensen thinks over and over. *Five and a four.*

The dice hit the table, bounce.

"Nine!"

His luck continues.

"Yo!" Jensen says while tossing the nearest dealer a hundred-dollar chip to have it placed on a one-time bet for the dice to land on eleven.

Five and six, five and six, five and six. Jensen repeats while tapping his finger.

"Eleven! That's a yo!" the dealer calls, sliding sixteen hundred dollars' worth of chips toward Jensen.

"Hard eight," Jensen says, pushing two hundred dollars of chips over.

The old man who thinks he's on a winning streak watches as Jensen high fives and shakes people's hands on the other side of the table, tossing the dice again.

"Eight," says the dealer, but it's a three and a five—no hard eight for Jensen, but it stills gets a payout on the table.

"OK, concentrate, Jensen," he says to himself, tossing over two more hundred-dollar chips, motioning to the dealer for the same bet on hard eights. The man tosses again. Finger tapping. *Four and Four, four and four, four and...*

"Hard eights!"

The dealer slides Jensen a pile of chips, making his stack around three thousand. Easy day's work. Three thousand dollars for about an hour of his time. It couldn't get any easier. Jensen keeps all his bets out there on the line, waiting for the old man to run out of steam on his own—without the *luck* of Jensen Atwood to help him out.

Eventually, the roller craps out, and Jensen slides the nearest dealer his chips to have them exchanged for a handful of higher dollar coins. That way, he doesn't have to carry three thousand dollars' worth of small dollar chips to the cashier's cage.

After making his way to the cashier's cage and getting his supplemental income in cash, Jensen walks over to the bar he sat at before and orders another drink from Chad. Jensen sits there, smiling, thinking about his so-called luck. Wishing he knew how or why it works almost every single time. It works too often, which is why Jensen only makes a few thousand and cashes out. No need to be greedy. That's how people in mob movies end up with broken kneecaps and banned for life.

The hairs on his neck perk up again, and he looks around. There she is, the bright blue-eyed angel of his dreams, who seems to have been stalking him. He's lucky, but he's not that lucky.

"Wish she would wear something other than that stupid hoodie though," Jensen says, loud enough for Chad to hear. He looks at the blue-eyed girl, looks back at Jensen; they both have a laugh and the bartender moves on.

"How'd you do out there?" a voice with a strong New York accent says from Jensen's left.

Jensen jumps and turns to see a slightly pudgy guy sitting in the chair directly next to him. "Jesus, you nearly scared that hell out of me. Warn someone next time."

"Oh, sorry about that. Didn't mean any harm by it. Saw you over there at the table. Looked like you were making a dent," the stranger says.

"Yea, I did all right. Been on a bit of a lucky streak here lately," Jensen replies, now turned fully toward the stranger, giving him a once over, catching a glimpse of him in the dim light of the bar. He is a chubby fellow with a thinning combover and about as pale as you could get without being transparent.

"That's good. At least, someone is. I'm Terry, by the way, but everyone just calls me T."

"Jensen Atwood. Good to meet you. Down from New York, I take it?" Jensen says with a smile.

T pushes his thinning combed hair to the left while undoing the remaining buttons on his well-tailored but cheap suit. "Yes, what gave it away?" he says with a slight laugh.

"So, what brings you to Atlantic City, T? Business or pleasure?" Jensen says while waving down Chad for two more drinks.

"A little bit of both but mainly business. I'm a private investigator out of New York looking for a group of people. Can't really get into any details now, but heard they were down here. Haven't had any luck tracking them down and was getting ready to drive back in a few days empty handed when I figured I'd have a little fun before I left."

Jensen takes a drink while sliding T the other glass. "Well, that sucks you came here for nothing, but hope you've enjoyed yourself at least. Try to take in a show or something."

"Thanks, Mr. Atwood. I appreciate the drink. Maybe I'll see you around," T says as he slides out of his stool, extending his arm for a handshake.

Jensen turns to face him, wiping the condensation from his drink onto his shirt, and takes T's hand. "Jensen. Just call me Jensen. Well, if you see me, feel free to say hi."

T turns and walks into the crowd of moving gamblers, and Jensen goes back to staring blankly at the random basketball game on TV.

"I need you to come with me," Jensen hears to his left, where T used to be. Jensen turns, half expecting to see a security guard with one of the casino's pit bosses standing there.

This is it, I guess. They finally realized I always win, and they're here to bust me for some type of cheating or scam or whatever they want to blacklist me for. Only, when he turns, it's not a security guard or a pit boss. It's a blond-haired guy, roughly the same age as Jensen. Blue eyes—not as blue as *hers* though—looking at him with a few scattered pockmarks around his cheeks from his time as an adolescent.

"Yea, I don't think so pal," Jensen remarks, turning a cold shoulder to him. Turning right into the blue eyes that he's chased in his dreams. There she is—bright blue eyes, dark black hair pulled straight down and cut to shoulder length. Her caramel-colored skin completely flawless, disappearing into the darkness of the unrevealing hoodie that he so wishes she would remove.

"No, it would be in your best interest to come with us, and right *now*," she snaps from his right.

"Look, I don't know, nor do I care, who you two are, but I'm not going anywhere. Especially since I still have this drink that I paid way too much for to finish. Here's an idea, though," Jensen says. "How about I buy you two a round, and then afterward, you both can fuck off." Jensen hates the fact that the first words he will probably ever say to her involve the word *fuck*.

"Look man. We don't have time for games," the blond man to his left says as he grabs Jensen by his arm. The woman grabs him by his right, and they somehow pull him straight out of his chair.

Damn! this woman is strong, Jensen thinks as his feet scramble to find their place.

"Get the hell off of me!" Jensen yells as he swings his torso side to side, trying to shake them off.

"Look, you don't understand what's going on. We are here to he-" the woman holding his arm is cut short as the casino's real security guards come out of nowhere to break it up.

They are much rougher with the guy than they are the girl naturally. But soon enough, Jensen is standing in the middle of the walkway between the bar and the table he just won thousands of dollars at.

He watches as the guards drag away the people who apparently are trying to kidnap him—as far as Jensen can tell. He looks down at his pants as a cold feeling spreads down his legs. "God damnit!" he states while wiping his spilled drink from his pant leg. "Can't be lucky all the time." He throws a tip to Chad, who is cleaning up the spilled drink from the bar, and gives a friendly wave.

Jensen makes his way out of the casino with his winnings and strolls toward his apartment. *One of these days, I must get a better apartment, but the amount of money I'm saving to get me out of this hell hole is starting to pile up. Maybe another year, and I'll have enough to leave and start fresh somewhere else*, Jensen thinks.

As Jensen rounds a corner leading up to his apartment, he hears a noise coming from the back alley next to a cheap motel a short distance from the Tropicana. Unable to resist the urge, he changes course to investigate. The racket keeps getting louder and louder. The sounds of a muffled scream rise over the sound of an obvious beating or mugging. Jensen picks up the pace, turning the corner to see two people attacking a helpless individual. Jensen begins sprinting at the attackers, grabbing a two-by-four next to a dumpster as he goes.

"Hey!" he yells, hoping to distract them. Jensen swings with all the force he can muster against one of the attacker's backs. The wood splinters along the back of the assailant, who doesn't seem to even waver from the hit. Jensen, shocked at what just happened, stops in his tracks and begins to backpedal to where he came from. The man on the ground scrambles to his feet; it's Terry!

As Terry moves and builds distance between himself and his attackers, he pulls a pistol from the small of his back. The streetlamps glimmer off the steel coating of the pistol as he points it toward the hooded muggers. The gun explodes and spits fire from the barrel. Terry pulls the trigger twice, sending two bullets whizzing at the perps. One of the hooded perps waves a hand, creating a grayish-blue film in the air. The bullets ricochet off the nearly invisible shield, causing a slight spark to flicker, deflecting the shots into a nearby dumpster. One of their hoods has fallen around *her* shoulders. It's the blue-eyed woman from the casino.

"What the…" Jensen says as he stumbles. T grabs Jensen while still pointing the gun, and they run out of the alleyway.

"Let's get the hell outta here," Jensen says, pulling T in the direction of his apartment. "I have a place we can lay low and call the cops if you want."

"That won't be necessary. Let's just get out of here," T answers.

They slow to a jog, both looking back to make sure they aren't being followed before slowing even further to a brisk walk.

"Thanks for the help back there, Jensen," T says appreciatively as they walk north toward Atlantic Avenue.

"Yea, no problem. What did those two want?" Jensen questions while looking back over his shoulder to make sure they still aren't being followed.

"That may be a discussion for another time," T says, a crooked smile crossing his face. "So, where are we going?"

"There's a bar up ahead that is beneath my apartment. We can lay low there until you feel comfortable enough to leave," Jensen says, still looking back toward the alley. "Did that chick block your bullets?" Jensen questions, not really expecting an answer from T; he follows his gaze toward the alley.

"Oh, you saw that too, huh? You wouldn't believe me if I told you. There are things in this world that just can't be explained. That was part of the reason I'm here in Atlantic City. I was looking for them, but I guess they found me instead," he goes on. "Things that would only appear in movies, books, and TV shows, things that, if the public knew about them, would cause mass hysteria."

"What are you talking about?" Jensen asks as they arrive at the bar he has called his home for three years. Jensen opens the door, holding it for T. The smell of stale beer fills their nostrils, along with the constant hum from the crowd filling their ears. He follows, taking one last glance down the street they came from. No one there. The constant buzzing of chatter illuminates the empty sounds of the road behind them. T orders two drinks for them and slides a ten across to the bartender. "Thanks, Coop!" Jensen yells to the bartender over the racket of the crowd.

They wade through the horde to a table in the back—about as private as they are going to find in a place like this. Jensen and T both take their seats at opposite ends of the table, sipping on their rum and cokes. Finally, Jensen can't hold it back any longer.

"All right, out with it. What in the world was that back there? The same two people that just tried to drag me out of the Tropicana just beat the crap out of you in an alleyway. And then, to top it off, you shot at them—which…why do you have a gun? And then that girl just waved her hand and deflected the bullets." Jensen rattles off the questions in a single breath.

"All right, I'll tell you what I know. The quick, down, and dirty version of it. And I have a gun because I'm a PI, remember? People are crazy out here, especially to people snooping around where they don't belong," T explains. "So, there is this group. They stay completely hidden from sight—underground, you could say. The story dates all the way back to the Middle Ages. Like the 1400s, to be exact."

"What does?" Jensen asks quieter than expected, leaning in closer.

T continues, "I won't get into the details right now. I don't think you have that kind of time. But I found a small group of them back in New York City and wanted to confirm it was the same type of people. But these people have powers, like superhero powers." T uses his hands to emphasize the word superhero. "It allows them to control stuff, like with their minds."

"Wait. You mean like telekinesis? Like a Jedi? You're blowing smoke up my ass, aren't you?"

"No, I swear to God," T promises, continuing, "From what I've gathered, they have some type of gene mutation that makes them different. It used to be very prominent back in the day; rumor is, the black plague was the cause of the mutation, like a way for humans to survive or something. But since then, the gene either has died off or has become dormant and forgotten. Until now, that is."

Jensen sits there, unable to speak; then he bursts into laughter. "Man, T, you're a wild dude. Jedi powers, blocking bullets," he continues, laughing, and finishes his drink. "Damn, that's funny. Next time, Terry, just don't shoot the dumpster; then you won't have to lie to me about your terrible aim."

T just continues to sit there with a slight smile on his face as if he's not quite getting the joke.

"All right. Thanks for the drink and the bedtime story. I'll tell you what," Jensen says. "I'm meeting up with my cousin Luke tomorrow for a few drinks and a round of pool or two at a bar just west of here on Ventnor Avenue. I'll text you the address and time when we figure it out. You should join us if you haven't left already, searching for the Jedi Order." Jensen grabs a napkin from the holder on the edge of the table and jots his name and phone number down before sliding it over to T.

T waves as Jenson exits out the front door, waving goodbye. He turns the corner to the left and heads up the rickety staircase leading to the floor above the bar. He takes it slow, trying to locate the correct key on his key ring, closing one eye to help focus the double vision he has acquired throughout the night of gambling, drinking, storytelling, kidnapping, and attempted manslaughter.

Jensen pushes the key into the rusty, loose doorknob attached to his front door. *The chance of this door protecting me from anything wanting to get in is just as laughable as T's story*, Jensen thinks as he finally gets the door unlocked.

The apartment is as "bachelor" as you can get. It's a four-room apartment, if you consider the closet-sized bathroom a room. A kitchen you can barely turn around in, a living room with a couch Jensen has had since he moved in, a fifty-two-inch TV sitting on a stack of wooden pallets he found out back behind the bar. A bedroom with a queen-sized bed—not made, of course—and a dresser overflowing with clothes he should have thrown out two years ago. It isn't much of a home, but it is his home. It is a place where he can shut his brain off, and it is within walking distance of the business that is going to get him out of this god-forsaken city he has been doomed to live in for twenty-four years.

He kicks his shoes off in an unknown direction as he stumbles his way through the living room to the bedroom. Pulling his cell phone out to make sure his alarm is set just before his head hits the pillow. He is asleep before he even gets his second leg out of his pants and onto the bed with the rest of his body. *Jensen, you're a mess.*

* * *

Early in the morning, the alarm's volume steadily rising, Jensen finally moans and rolls out of bed. He shuts off the alarm, checking the time—0630, one hour before he needs to be at that god-forsaken job.

Jensen slides off the edge of the mattress to the floor, dragging his feet as he goes into the bathroom to relieve himself and make himself look presentable. As presentable as he needs to avoid getting fired. As much as he hates the job, it's easy money for his gambling "job." He heads out the front door, throwing his bag over his shoulder and locking it as he goes. Down the stairs and to his bike—he starts it up, letting it run a little to warm up as he puts his helmet and jacket on for the ten-minute commute to work.

On his ride in, he can't help but think about the conversation last night with Terry. *Telekinesis*, he laughs to himself. *Wouldn't that be cool. I'd be so lazy if I had that power.*

He cuts the power switch to his bike as he enters the parking lot to Verizon, allowing his bike to coast in silence to a parking spot so small only a motorcycle would fit. He looks through the windowpanes and sees his three coworkers, Nate, Zach, and Claire. Nate is the manager and a pain in the ass most days. Zach keeps to himself but is one of those people you just can't find a reason to hate. And Claire—well, if she wasn't so weird, she would probably be pretty cute. *Shame.*

The day starts off as normal as any other day; Jensen helps customers pick out an upgraded phone they probably don't need—but the one they have is a year old. *Kids today*, Jensen thinks. *So wasteful.* But that's the job; one customer at a time, he slowly whittles away at the clock. Today is different; he's meeting his cousin, and together, they love to hustle people at pool. Not because they need the money but for the chance to see the look on their faces when they finally realize they are being hustled. Luke owns a garage just west of where Jensen works—off of Ventnor Avenue in Ventnor City.

He's owned that place for as long as Jensen can remember. He's part of the reason Jensen even has his motorcycle. Bought it from a customer who needed to get rid of it fast and for cheap. Fixed it up for nothing, then turned around and gave it to Jensen when he needed it the most. Luke was always there for Jensen; back when he was seventeen, Jensen applied to be emancipated from his parents. They were drunks who couldn't stay out of the casinos—which is very ironic, given what he does for money now—and all they ever gave him were excuses and bruises. As soon as he was of age, Jensen moved on with life, never looking back. The only one he continued to talk to was Luke. He's been the brother he never had but always wanted.

His phone vibrates in his pocket before causing his smartwatch to vibrate. *I don't recognize that number*, Jensen thinks, continuing to help the customer he's with about what phone color she should get. *Someone, please kill me.*

"The pink one is very popular right now, ma'am," he says through a smile and clenched teeth.

After the girl in her early twenties walks out finally, with her new prized possession, after an agonizing thirty-minute debate, Jensen pulls out his phone and swipes the screen to reveal the text he received earlier.

"Hey, Jensen, it's T. Realized you didn't have my number, so here it is," The text reads. He punches in a few keystrokes from memory, adding T to his contact list.

Right after 2:00 p.m., when everyone is heading back to work from lunch, Jensen finds himself standing around with his coworkers. Everyone is talking about shows they've watched, movies they've seen, their opinions on the Game of Thrones series finale. Jensen had little to no idea what they are talking about; he barely spends any time in his apartment, let alone watches TV.

A TV in the background is playing a local news channel, and he recognizes the building. The tag at the bottom of the screen reads, "Shots fired last night near Tropicana."

"I was there last night!" Jensen claims, talking over everyone else's conversations.

"What do you mean? At Tropicana?" Nate asks.

"No, like I watched the shooting happen; it was wild."

"You should probably call the cops if you have any details," Claire says while looking at her phone, with zero interest in anything anyone else is doing.

"I don't have any details, really. Just watched some guy get his ass beat, get up, and fire two shots at the people kicking him," Jensen says.

"Yea, you might want to think about calling the cops," says Nate.

Should've minded my own business, Jensen thinks, shaking his head and going back to ignoring everyone. He laughs to himself as he pretends to move a pencil lying on the desk. *Like a Jedi*, he thinks, holding his palm out toward the pencil. The pencil wobbles and then rolls an inch before stopping. *Yeah right*, he flicks the eraser end, sending the pencil spinning in its place.

"An unknown number of assailants" is the tag on the news report now.

Well, at least they don't know it was T and me who were there.

The clock finally hits quitting time, and as usual, Jensen heads to the back and removes his Verizon shirt before putting on a button-up, ready to meet Luke. He pulls his phone out right before exiting into the showroom and shoots T a text with the name and time to meet at the bar if he's still interested. Out into the showroom he goes.

"More tables, Jen?" Nate asks, knowing Jensen hates being called that.

"Not today, Nate. Got a date with your sister. She's tired of me ignoring her."

"My sister is seventeen, asshole," Nate comes back.

"Oh, I know," Jensen says, putting his back to the door and slowly pushing into it. "I've got to get her ready for the prom." He makes a circle with his left thumb and index while putting his right index through the circle repeatedly.

"You're disgusting, Jensen," Nate calls, but Jensen is long gone. Already on his bike, heading to meet Luke.

CHAPTER 2

In the back office of an art gallery in Brooklyn, New York, a man sits at his desk, chatting into his phone. A very dapper looking gentleman in his fifties, he wears an elegant suit cut precisely to his body that flows down to his double monk strap shoes. His gray hair and beard are trimmed to perfection, without a single hair out of place. His hair shines bright, almost more silver than gray. His eyes are so dark, it's nearly impossible to determine where his pupils end and where his irises begin.

"Do you understand what I'm saying, T?" the silver-haired gentleman says into the receiver.

"Yes, sir, Liam. I am working on it," T explains.

"Mr. Turner, T. You will call me Mr. Turner. And I'm going to explain the importance of the situation again in case, for some reason, you missed it," Liam Turner says. "There are only a few of us left in existence. Well, there are thousands of us out there, but only so many of us have such a natural ability as me or this Mr. Atwood. I needed him here yesterday. I need to let him know just how important he is to my cause, our cause! The more I can gather in one place and make them aware of who they are, the better our chances are of not being hunted and destroyed when my plan goes into action. So, do whatever you must do get him here, and get him here now. For his sake and mine."

"Yes, sir, Mr. Turner. But so you know, the other group is looking for him also. There were two other Transcendents here. If it wasn't for Mr. Atwood, I think they would've killed me. You have to send others to help, other Transcendents preferably," T pleads.

"Fine. I'll send some help your way. You should use their attack to help push him to us. We can't allow them to get their hands on Mr. Atwood just as much as they can't allow us to have him. So far, so good, T. Get back out there and get him to me," Liam says.

"Yes, sir. Thank you, sir," T stutters. "I'm meeting with him this evening. I'll do everything I can to have him on his way to New York no later than next week," he says as the phone hangs up on Liam's end, leaving the call time blinking for a few seconds before going blank.

* * *

Back in Atlantic City, a bright blue-eyed girl sits in her hoodie next to a blond guy as they shake their heads, arguing with each other about who did what and who made what mistakes.

"Sloan, we should never have approached him so aggressively, especially in such a public place," the blond-haired man says, sitting on a couch across from

Sloan, the caramel-colored, blue-eyed woman that once took Jensen's breath away.

"Shut up, Aiden. We had to move in. T was right there, making his move for him. We cannot let the Empyreans recruit yet another Transcendent. We can't allow them to get even more powerful," Sloan snaps back. "And the fact that we let that simpleton get past us...*us*! Two well-trained Transcendents against that fat simpleton."

"You know I hate that word—*simpleton*," Aiden says, aiming a disappointed look at Sloan. "And it wasn't just him; Jensen came out of nowhere and helped him out. Thanks for blocking that attack, by the way. That would have messed my back up for sure. I should have seen that coming a mile away. Hell, it was Jensen. I should have felt him coming two miles away! That kid puts off as much aura as Mason does, I think."

"No worries. That's what I'm here for—protection," Sloan says, making a bottle of water float an inch above one hand and spinning it with the other. "His Transcendent aura really is something else. No wonder Mason has been talking about it for months. Last week, when I saw him at the Tropicana, I knew it had to be the guy he had been talking about."

"At least, I hope it is," Aiden says, staring at the ground between his feet.

Aiden leans back against the couch, looking around the warehouse. The interior of the warehouse looks like a gang clubhouse from an 80s movie like *The Outsiders*. People sit around all over the place, some watching TV, some playing Xbox; a group of muscle heads in the corner where the gym is located are trying to show off who can pick up more weights. Graffiti lines the walls with designs—like signatures from all the Transcendents who have passed through these doors.

In every corner of the warehouse, the second story of loft-style rooms hang from the rafters visible from the ground floor with a staircase leading to each room. A catwalk runs from room to room about fifty feet up. Each room is usually used for getting some rest, except for one, the one in the southeast corner of the building. That one is Mason Knight's office. That's where he sleeps, but more importantly, that's where he plans. Plans to help keep the Empyreans from rising to power, taking control, and—as cliché as it is—using their power for evil. That's why this place exists now.

First, this place was where people who were different—who found themselves to have certain abilities—came to find sanctuary. A place for them to practice what they were born with, what some think God gave them. But now, it has become a place of planning and practicing for the inevitable. A war that only a few around the country know is even coming—a war like any other war—between good and evil. The only difference is, this one isn't going to be fought with bullets and bombs. It is going to be fought with supernatural powers. And if Sloan and Aiden aren't careful, this war just might get harder for them.

Sloan stands. "Well, you ready to go face the music and tell Mason we screwed tonight up and nearly got shot?"

"I mean, are you asking or telling?" Aiden questions.

"Get your ass up before I force you up," Sloan threatens.

"Easy girl. Geez, you're always so serious," Aiden says, and then in his best Heath Ledger voice, he adds, "Why so serrrrrious?"

"Because one of us has to, and you never take anything seriously; that's why. Now, get your ass up those steps and let's face the music," Sloan lightly pushes Aiden forward and up the stairs toward Mason Knight's room in the southeast corner.

CHAPTER 3

Jensen rides down Ventnor Avenue faster than needed just to meet Luke—but honestly, what's the point in riding a motorcycle if not to enjoy yourself while doing it? Jensen pulls up to the bar that Luke told him about. Chelsea's Pub. It's a fine establishment if you like the taste of watered-down beer and stale peanuts.

Jensen pulls in and parks, adding his bike to an ever-growing line of motorcycles. He walks in and is immediately reminded of the Dazed and Confused's scene when Matthew McConaughey's character walks into The Emporium. He imagines the tune—"Here comes the story of the hurricane"—in the background and just smiles to himself.

He immediately heads to the bar to get a drink and to wait for Luke to arrive.

"Rum and Coke, please!" Jensen shouts to the nearest bartender, who acknowledges his presence.

The bartender slides the drink into his hand, and Jensen slides a five into the bartender's; he turns around on his stool just in time to see Luke arrive. Luke, being his cousin, looks nearly identical to Jensen.

Dark auburn hair (with a fair amount of length you could comb your hand through), hazel eyes, a strong frame with muscle surrounding it standing at around five feet, ten inches. If you didn't know it, you would think they were brothers.

"Hey, Jensen. What's new?" Luke says, sliding over the stool next to him and raising two fingers up at the bartender, who he obviously knows.

"Man, you would not believe the last two days I've had. So, I did my normal craps table thing, right?" Jensen says before getting interrupted by Luke.

"Let me guess. Your lucky ass won like four grand?"

"Well, three. But that's not what I'm talking about," Jensen says while Luke rolls his eyes and takes a drink. "No, for real. It's crazy. So, after I won, I'm sitting at the bar, and I meet this weird dude—I'll get back to him in a little bit. But this chick and her friend pretty much tried to kidnap me. Saying I needed to go with them or something like that. Casino security had to step in and kick them out."

"Should have gone with her; might have been a good time," Luke says, a smile creeping out from the side of his glass as he drinks.

"As much as I would've liked to, something felt off. But anyway, after they got kicked out, I'm on my way home, and I see someone getting their ass beat. I step in, and who is it?" Jensen asks, using his hands as he talks. "The weird dude from the bar getting beat up by the chick and her friend. After I step in, the guy pulls a gun and fires at the two. Missing thankfully."

"So, what makes the dude so weird?

"That's the best part. He says the chick has super-powers or something and blocked the bullets from hitting them." Jensen waits for the reaction from Luke.

Luke chuckles a little. "That's it, huh? You sure he wasn't on drugs or something?"

"I don't know, but you might be able to ask him later. I invited him here," Jensen mentions with a smile.

"Well, you're babysitting if it comes to that." Luke puts his empty glass on the table. "You ready to steal some peoples' hard-earned money and maybe start a fight?" Luke says, scanning the crowd for their next victim.

Jensen and Luke patiently wait their turn to get a table; when one finally opens, they begin their long con for the night. Playing mediocre games, always betting fake money with each other until someone takes notice and challenges them to a game. They aren't going to make enough to pay the month's rent, but that's not the point; they just do it to waste time and ruin others.

Finally, a victim presents himself. A heavy-set guy and his skinny friend, who more than likely, own one of the many bikes outside of this lovely establishment. Both have tattoos that appear to go from their necks all the way to their fingertips. *The perfect type of guys you want to hustle out of their money*, thinks Jensen, but there's no stopping Luke when he gets this way.

The first game goes exactly like they want it to; Jensen and Luke win but just barely. The strategy makes the other guys confident enough that they are willing to play another game. When Luke mentions a friendly wager of a few twenties, it's enough to pique anyone's interest without sounding any alarms. The skinny guy racks the second game, and the hook is set. Jensen and Luke let them win by just a few balls, making the other couple very confident and making the next move the easiest part of the night. The hardest part is going to be getting out of here without losing any teeth.

"Nice game, gents," Jensen says, pretending to put his cue away.

"No, wait a minute Jensen. I want a chance to earn my money back. What do you say, boys?" Luke says, leaning against the pool table.

The men don't look intimated or scared. *This should be perfect.*

"Sure, one more game, then I got to get home. I don't know about him, though," the fat guy says, throwing a thumb in his friend's direction.

"Yea, I'm game for one more at least. What are we wagering now?" says the skinny one.

"I say we pump it up—at least a hundred," Luke says, looking at the three of them in turn.

"Shit. How about a hundred each?" the chubby guy says, chalking up the end of his cue.

Luke lets out a whistle. "Four hundred. I think I can get in on that. What say you, Jensen? You in?"

"I mean, why not? I'm not doing anything else tonight; might as well make some money." Jensen says back at Luke, who now has a smile that rivals the Grinch's.

Jensen grabs the rack from under the table and sets the balls up, preparing himself mentally for what will inevitably happen—just like it always does. The ending Luke and Jensen are expecting doesn't take long. After the big guy misses his third shot, Luke, being the pool player he is, sinks nearly all the solids in one swoop, leaving Jensen to clean it up on the back half.

The skinny guy misses his one and only shot he will get this game; Jensen lines up and sinks the last solid. He gets behind the cue ball aimed at the eight ball, pulls back, but just before he releases, sending the white cue ball on its mission, the eight ball is picked up by the big guy and tossed across the floor.

"You hustled us. Didn't you?" he barks at Jensen.

Jensen holds up his hands in a defensive posture. "Look man, we didn't hustle anyone. We are obviously just better than you two."

The heavy-set guy makes a move toward Jensen. His skinny friend, not wanting any trouble, gets in his way, trying to slow him down. Jensen backs up, leaning against the table, reaching for the cue ball as a weapon, just in case. He reaches and searches, but his fingers can't find the ball.

"What the?" Luke whispers as Jensen finds the ball at last. "Did you just see that?"

"What? This guy you just picked a fight with? Yea, I saw it; now how about a little help," Jensen replies.

Right before the big guy brings all his weight down on top of Jensen, a familiar face steps in.

"Easy, gents. Here is your money back; no need to spill any blood over a game," T yells over the crowd, holding up two-hundred-dollar bills in front of the fat man like carrots to lead him away. "Just start trouble everywhere you go, don't you Jensen?" T says as the guy grabs the money and walks away, his friend in tow.

"Terry! What's up?" Jensen says. "How you been? This is my cousin Luke." gesturing to Luke, who is still staring at Jensen. "Luke, are you just going to stand there? Say hi to Terry. Everyone calls him T. This is the guy I told you about."

"Did...did...you not see that?" Luke stutters.

"See what?" Jensen asks, shaking T's hand.

"The cue ball. It jumped. It jumped into your hand," Luke continues.

"It jumped into my hand? Like, was it more like a hop or a skip?" Jensen laughs while directing the two toward the bar for drinks.

Luke looks over at T, almost searching for a confirmation.

"Don't look at me. I didn't see anything," T declares. "To me, it looked like he grabbed the ball. I mean, he could have leaned on the table enough for it to roll into his hand, I guess."

"Shit, I think I need to get out of here. Maybe I've had too much to drink, or I'm exhausted or something." Luke shakes T's hand and then gives Jensen a hug. "All right, I'm going to go sleep this off. Let me know if you make any more balls float with your hands."

"You'd like that," Jensen smarts off with a smile, turning back to T, who has a drink already waiting for him.

Jensen and Terry are just sitting at the bar making small talk when Jensen gets that same strange feeling on his neck. It's not as apparent or as strong as it was at Tropicana, but it's there. *There's just no way*, Jensen thinks as he scans the crowd. *There's just no fuc...* "Get the hell out of here. There's no way this is a coincidence," he says out loud.

"What's that?" asks T.

Jensen leans in, trying to point inconspicuously toward where he's looking. "It's the smoking hot chick from the casino and her friend. Over there in the corner. And I'm pretty sure they are staring over here. What in the world? What is going on with these two?"

"I don't know, but we should probably get out of here," T says as he stands.

Jensen starts to follow T out of the bar then stops. "Wait a minute, Terry. These are the people that were fighting you yesterday."

"And?"

"We can't just hand you back to them on a silver platter. They would be stupid to attack you in a taxicab. Most have cameras now; hell, most Ubers have cameras now. So, we will get you one, and then I'll leave after you. I rode my bike, and there's two of them, so I'd bet all my winnings they brought a car," Jensen says before continuing. "As soon as you're out of here and I confirm they are following me, not you, I'll take off on my bike and lose them. Once I'm home, I'll text you to make sure you're good, and then we can go from there."

"Sounds good to me," T says, pulling out his phone to order an Uber.

They make their way back to the bar and wait for the Uber app to read, "Arriving."

"All right, T, get out of here. I'll text you in, say, fifteen to twenty minutes," Jensen says as Terry nods and heads outside to get into the Uber.

Jensen glances over his shoulder to see the two mysterious people still watching him. *All right, let's go, fellas. Let's have some fun.* Jensen takes off running out the door of the bar, starting his bike and slapping on his helmet in one smooth motion. Jensen pushes on the gear lever, shifting it from neutral to first, releasing the clutch, and twisting the throttle. The back tire breaks traction for a second right before gripping the road and propelling him forward. He races onto the street, cutting off traffic as he goes, horns blaring. Once Jensen straightens out, he looks back in time to see a vehicle, looking to be a late model sedan, fishtail out of the bar's parking lot.

Persistent little bastards. I'll give them that. Jensen downshifts and rips back on the throttle, so he can thread the needle between two honking cars. The light in front of him turns red, causing Jensen to brake hard and make the next right. Down back roads, up alleys, down to the boardwalk, and back up to Ventnor Avenue. A constant zig-zag all the way back to his apartment.

When he arrives outside the bar, he calls home; he put the kickstand down and races up the stairs to get a better view of the streets around his place. No cars, not even any people. *If they followed that, they deserve an award*, he thinks while pulling out his cell phone to text T.

Jensen sends the message, saying he made it and making sure T is good. As he gets undressed, his watch vibrates, T's name appears on the face of the smart-watch. He grabs his phone and reads the message.

The text reads, "Good to hear. Quick question. I need help with a job up in New York this weekend if you're interested. I need another pair of hands, and I can spare 800 dollars for your time. You will also get away from that chick who's been chasing you for a little."

Jensen types back, "Sounds like a plan. Pick me up at my place in the morning. I'll be ready by seven."

This might be the best option at this point. Damn stalkers. That's a new one for Jensen.

I just have to remember to text Luke when I'm heading up there, so he knows, Jensen thinks as he hits the bed after another crazy night out with Terry.

CHAPTER 4

Jensen is up and ready to go at 6:55 a.m. He heads out the door, making sure to lock it; with everything that's been going on, he can't be too careful. He stops at the top of the stairs right outside his apartment door. He can still smell the stale beer and cigarettes from the ashtray outside the bar, which probably hasn't been emptied all week. He looks around, up the street, then down. Looks over his shoulder to the adjacent street. Keeping an eye out for any vehicle or person that may look suspicious. In Atlantic City at seven o'clock in the morning, though, that means anyone who may be sober.

For two days now, the same two people have either A) had the same plans as he does or B) been following him for some reason or another. Jensen is pretty sure it's the latter and doesn't really know why anyone would be following a guy who works at a cell phone store making ends meet, living in an apartment above a run-down bar. Then to top it all off, those same two people were caught beating on a random guy in a casino full of thousands. What made T or him stand out?

Jensen pulls out his phone and sends a quick text to T about where he's at, glancing at his watch: 7:10 a.m.

"Not a very punctual guy, are you, T?" Jensen says out loud.

Off in the background, he hears the distinct sound of a car rolling down the street. This early in the morning, it's easy to hear the slightest sound on an empty street. Everyone else is too busy sleeping off the drugs, alcohol, or financial loss. Or a combination of the three. What a place to live.

A mid-model Ford SUV with a New York tag on the front comes rolling down the street, heading right for Jensen.

"This has to be him," Jensen says with a wave at who he hopes is Terry.

The tinted passenger window rolls down, revealing T sitting in the driver's seat, wearing one of the ugliest plaid sweaters Jensen thinks he's ever seen. *Would totally win an ugly Christmas sweater competition if it had a sleigh running across the front of it.*

"Took your time, I see," Jensen mentions with a smile as he climbs into the passenger seat.

"There's no rush to get to New York, is there?" T comes back. "We could wait for your girlfriend if you'd like."

"No, I'm good to go. I think I've seen enough of her for a while," he says. "Where in New York are we heading to anyway."

"Brooklyn is where my tip has sent me. Once I get there, I'll know what I'm looking for," T says as he shifts the Ford back into drive and does a U-turn in front of Jensen's place.

Within minutes of making a right off Jensen's block, they begin traveling up Atlantic City Expressway, heading toward Pleasantville.

"So, how was the rest of your night?" T asks, changing to the right-hand lane.

"Well, after I raced home, dodging in and out of traffic, trying to lose that tail from the stage-five clinger I've acquired somehow, it wasn't half bad. Had a nice little buzz and some adrenaline pumping through my veins. Made it a little hard to sleep at first, but I managed. What about you?" he says while casually looking over his shoulder.

"About the same, except for the clinger, I suppose," T laughs.

T makes a right onto Garden State Parkway, which will lead them to New York.

"I should've asked before I got in, but do you have the money you offered me?" Jensen says, looking out of the corner of his eye toward T.

T pats around his pockets, navigating through the traffic in the morning hour. He stops when he reaches what he was looking for. He pulls out a small wad of twenties wrapped tightly in a roll like you would see in a mob movie. "There it is: eight hundred dollars."

Jensen grabs the roll and holds it up, admiring how tightly wound he has gotten it. "I want to count it, but I also don't want to ruin this wonderful job you've done." He pops the rubber band off and starts thumbing through the roll, stacking one hundred dollars' worth of twenties in eight separate piles, making it easier to double check. After he confirms all the money's there, he folds the stack in half while pulling out his money clip, securing his newfound wealth into his pocket.

"So, what's this job you need a second pair of hands for anyway, T?" he asks as he throws himself back into the seat, settling in for the two-hour ride up to Brooklyn.

T doesn't move, except for the minor changes in his hands to keep the Ford aligned in the lane. Jensen sits there for a second, expecting him to say something, anything.

"T? It's not something you need lifting, is it?" he asks, almost knowing the answer.

"Not exactly," T says sheepishly, whom he can feel eyeing him through his peripherals.

"You need me to help with trying to find that group of superheroes," Jensen mentions with a small bit of shock, followed by a lot of sarcasm.

"Just a little. It will be quick, I promise. I know basically where they are rumored to be. I just need to find it, sneak around back, and look for any evidence of their existence," T rattles off.

"God damnit, T. Why didn't you just tell me instead of beating around the bush?"

"I needed your help and didn't want you to say no is what it comes down to honestly," he says, keeping his eyes on the road in front of him. T and Jensen sit there for a minute in complete silence. Jensen contemplates what he wants to do next. Meanwhile, T concludes that he's gone this far, so what's the point of turning around now?"

Finally, Jensen turns with a smile on his face, trying to hold back the laughter. "All right, I have the money you promised me, and I'm off work this weekend. So, fuck it. It's not like I was going to do anything around here anyway. Still wish you would've just told me the truth, though." Jensen laughs. "Superheroes... telekinesis."

At this point, Jensen isn't even trying to hold back the laughter anymore. Even T has got in on the joke.

"Yea, I'm sorry I didn't tell you the truth, but honestly, do you think you would have come if I had?" T questions.

"No, you're right. I probably would've laughed you right out of AC," he answers honestly, wiping a tear from his cheek. "But, like I said, that's OK, man. Maybe it'll be interesting. And if we find their capes early enough, maybe I can do a little sightseeing."

Some time goes by without either one of them talking. Mötley Crüe plays on the radio, drowning out the sound of the tires beating down the road. The wind from the open windows pushing Jensen's hair in his face, causing him to continually push it back like he's in a supermodel ad with a fan on him. Finally, Jensen can't contain himself anymore. He reaches over and turns the radio down, ending Vince Neil's rendition of "Girls, Girls, Girls."

"All right, T. Be straight with me; I have to know. What is the deal with these superheroes you keep going on about? Like what is it that you know? If anything."

"Like you want the history of the Transcendents? Is that what you're asking for?" T asks, looking over at him.

"Transcendents?" Jensen says, annunciating every syllable as if he's trying to learn a new word.

"Yes, the people that have these powers—they refer to themselves as Transcendents. Like as in above or beyond the capability of any normal human experience," he says, looking at Jensen without blinking—with so much confidence that Jensen begins to feel like he is the lunatic in this scenario.

"OK, yea. Tell me about these *Transcendents*. Like everything that you know, how they came about," Jensen says, shifting in his seat so he can look at T. As if getting ready for a campfire story.

"It's a long story, so I guess it's a good thing we have a little over an hour to drive," T says, clearing his throat. "All right. Well, from my understanding, the Transcendent gene was created around the time of the hundred-year war between France and England. Which, if you don't know, went on from 1337 to 1453 over the right to rule the Kingdom of France."

"Dang, T. You're throwing out history lessons in this?" Jensen laughs.

"It's about to get a lot deeper. Just sit back and hold your questions to the end, if you can," T says with a smile. "So, as I was saying, the war went on for about ten years, then the black plague happened. It devastated the land, as I'm sure—or at least, I hope—you're aware of." T shoots a grin at Jensen. "Well, the rumors are that, because of the plague, certain genetic mutations started occurring—you know, as if nature was trying to save the species. That's why most animals mutate—to adapt, to survive. Well, the first person to really find out about this mutation and its abilities was Joan of Arc."

"Wait, *the* Joan of Arc. Like the woman who changed the tide of the war without killing a single person? That Joan of Arc?" Jensen says, surprised.

"Very nice. Correct. That's the one," T says with a smile. "So according to history, Joan heard the voices of St Michael, St Catherine, and St Margaret when she was thirteen in 1425. Now, that's what all the history books will tell you. But what Transcendent history says is that was when she realized she could move stuff with her mind and much more. According to Transcendents, she was very powerful; every now and then, certain Transcendents are just naturally more powerful than the rest. Just like in nature, some are strong, some are weak. So, Joan fought hard to prove to the king of France she needed to be on the frontline to help protect her land. History says they let her do this because they believed she was talking to God. Transcendents believe she showed them what she was capable of doing, and then they let her; she also had the ability to see the gene in others, allowing them to unleash it. So, of course, they let her fight. And England started getting pushed back since France now had these superhuman entities on their side, so naturally they started winning the war."

"T, this is the most insane thing I've ever heard."

"I'm not done yet. In 1430, Joan was captured; that part is in the history books, but what isn't in the books is that, while she was held prisoner..." T sees the question coming and stops Jensen from asking it.

"And I don't know how they kept a superhuman captured without her escaping." Jensen's mouth closes, and T continues. "While she was captured, the king of England forced her to locate and unlock as many gene carrying people she could to fight for England before her execution in 1431. After her death, the war continued for twenty-one more years, with Transcendents on both sides wreaking havoc on one another and the countryside. I'm almost done," he says, holding up a hand.

Jensen smiles. "Good because our exit is coming up in about ten miles."

"So, after France finally won due to England having to retreat for economic issues, everyone who had the gene, according to Transcendent history, didn't want to see their powers used for war again. There was so much death and destruction that they hid it from that point on. Anyone who used the power of a Transcendent was sentenced to death for being a witch or being possessed—or whatever else they wanted to call them. And with no one using the power or practicing with it, the ability and the gene disappeared. I mean, the gene is still in a huge number of people, but unless someone shows them they have it or they figure it out, it remains dormant. Supposedly, Transcendents believe the gene is in one in every five hundred thousand people, compared to the 1400s when it was one in every five thousand. At least, that's what I've heard," T finishes, waiting for Jensen to talk.

"That is one of the most insane stories I have ever heard, T," Jensen says with a chuckle, settling back into his seat to look forward. "Well, if what you said is even a little bit true, this trip is going to be awesome."

They both laugh as they take the exit for NJ-440 N, heading toward Brooklyn.

CHAPTER 5

"**W**ell, that could have gone a lot worse, if you ask me," Aiden says while opening a bottle of water and rolling the window down on the old beat up Buick they are driving.

"Yeah? Is that why Mason had you sitting outside Jensen's house all morning, waiting for him to show his face? Good thing we did too; otherwise, we would have had no idea they had even left town," she says.

Their 2000 Buick Regal rolls down the Garden State Parkway, following the gray Ford Explorer at a safe distance as they try not to have a repeat of last night. Aiden sits back, looking out the window, thinking about how long his night has been. After the conversation Aiden and Sloan had with Mason about Jensen getting away, he ordered both of them to wait on Mr. Atwood until he showed the next morning.

Sloan sits in the car a few blocks away, waiting on the text to come from Aiden. While Aiden sits, nearly invisible to the naked eye, leaning against the wall adjacent to Jensen's apartment.

As Aiden sits there, slumped in his seat, droning down the parkway, he lets his mind wander to the last few years. Learning about his *new* power that he's apparently had his whole life. Getting brought in by Sloan. Trained by Tyler and the other Transcendents. While under the watchful eye of Mason. *What a wild dream...or was it a nightmare? Only time will tell,* he thinks.

"Speaking of Mason." Aiden fixes his posture and turns toward Sloan. "I overheard some of the topics you three were discussing after I was dismissed like an errand boy," Aiden jokes.

"You were not dismissed," Sloan says, glaring at Aiden with her piercing blue eyes. "He just wanted Tyler and I's opinion on some of the things that he's been hearing through the grapevine from the Philly Boys and the DC Charter."

"And?" he asks, dragging out the word.

"Mason is just getting nervous about how powerful Liam Turner is getting. He already has that art distribution company, which gives him not only money but a place to launder all that money while also meeting wealthy connected people," Sloan says, changing lanes to keep the Ford within view while staying far enough back to blend into the background of traffic heading north. "Rumor has it, Liam is planning a political move this coming election."

"What? Like president?" Aiden asks with sarcasm in his voice.

"No, not that high up, at least not yet. Mason thinks it's going to be more like governor or Congress or something like that. The Philly Boys told Mason when he was over there a few weeks ago, they overheard he wanted to get some political power to bring the Transcendents into the public light," Sloan continues.

"And what's so wrong with that? It would be nice not to have to hide these sweet powers anymore. Bet they would work wonders on the ladies," Aiden laughs, shooting Sloan a wink.

"You're an idiot," she says without even looking in his direction.

He laughs and takes a drink. "So why the hell would he want to oust all of us? Wouldn't that endanger him too?

"It would unless he plays it right. He wants to slowly write us into legislature, showing everyone who matters that we're not that big of a deal. That we aren't that big of a threat. And once they can't touch us legally—that's when Mason thinks he'll strike. That's why he's been slowly building an army. Why he's been recruiting us all over the country—hell, the planet. He's got Transcendents up and down the east coast trying to find their way into a political seat to help the cause." Sloan takes a second to catch her breath before continuing. "This is part of the reason Liam left Mason high a dry and started the Empyreans. He believes that there is no reason a group of genetically enhanced humans should be led by simpletons."

"For the love of all that's holy, please stop calling normal people simpletons," Aiden says, rolling his eyes.

"Anyway," she continues as if not hearing him, "he believes that we should be in power; we are the stronger of the species in this world. And the strong are meant to survive. Survival of the fittest and all that."

"OK, I get all that." Aiden raises his hands defensively. "But what exactly is wrong with all of that? We could live openly among the public, free to be who we are." Sloan looks over at him from the corner of her eye; he can feel the daggers in her stare. "Relax, I'm just being the devil's advocate."

"Because. Yes, maybe it would work; maybe we could come out and let everyone know who and what we are. You watch a lot of movies. How often does that happen?" She looks over at Aiden, who's going through the list of movies. *The Incredibles*, *The Batman movies*, *Hancock*, *Superman*, all the DC Comics TV shows— the list goes on. "Exactly," she says, reading his facial expression. "The public doesn't like change, especially change that they can't control. The public threw a fit when Instagram got rid of the like feature for Christ's sakes."

Aiden laughs at the reference. "I see your point."

"It would be mayhem; maybe not at first, but eventually, the people would resist. They always do. It could be nothing, but the more likely scenario would be a three-sided war. It would be us, the Empyreans, and the regular population out there who fear what we can do. The second they see someone move something without touching it or creating a weapon out of nothing or people like you turning invisible, no one will feel safe until we are eliminated."

"Easy. I get it, I get it. Just wish I could tell my family my secret sometimes," Aiden mumbles under his breath. "So, what about this Jensen kid. What are your thoughts?"

Sloan takes a minute to ponder the question. "There is definitely something about him. I didn't believe Mason at first until I felt it for myself. That boy has some natural Transcendent abilities that some of us have probably never even seen before. And if he does, that would totally explain why Liam wants him so badly. It would be the perfect addition to the Empyreans. If what Mason says is true about Liam's abilities compared to everyone else..." Sloan trails off.

"Mason has been training since he was young, right? Like when he was thirteen or something crazy."

"Sixteen," Sloan says. "He trained with his uncle, who had the gene and saw it in Mason. Shortly after that, finding and training Liam. They were just trying to teach people to live normal lives with these powers, and Liam went and got a big head. Mason has never gone into any details but has said that, since Liam left the group his uncle brought him into, they have had to take out a few *rogue* Transcendents. Most likely brought up and trained by Liam. But that's what Mason doesn't want. Violence. Just like with wars, violence only brings more violence. Sure, there's peace for a while, but it will always return. And with people like us, that return is going to be devastating."

"Well, you sold me on it," Aiden says with a smirk. "Let's get to wherever the hell these two are going, rescue the unsuspecting damsel in distress, and get the hell out of there. Hopefully, without anyone knowing we're there. Wouldn't want to use these sweet new moves I've been practicing with the other Translucents now would I?" he says, bobbing and weaving like a boxer in the ring. He makes his forearms go invisible up to the elbow and punches through the dashboard of the Buick.

Sloan laughs a little to herself, then swings a light slap at him. Her hand goes through his transparent wrists and hits him in the chest.

"Hey," Aiden says, allowing his hands to transition back to normal.

"Enough playing around. We have to be getting close to the end of this trip. Is that Brooklyn up on the right? There! His blinker's on; it has to be this next exit," Sloan says while trying to get over to the right.

"Looks like exit 5, NY-27 E. Definitely getting off for Brooklyn," he answers back.

"All right, as soon as they stop, we are going to continue right past them, loop back around, and scope the place out. I want to try and be in and out—no noise, no mess. You got it?"

Aiden lets his head fall back in disappointment against the headrest. "Yes, mother."

CHAPTER 6

Jensen and Terry pull off the highway into Brooklyn, New York. T's taken so many turns by this point, Jensen wouldn't be able to find his way out of New York without using his cell phone connecting to the satellites above.

Jensen feels the Ford slow; the engine settles to an idle as their momentum comes to a halt. Jensen looks forward, seeing a line of high-end retail stores. Coach, Dolce & Gabbana, Prada, Versace—the stores go on and on. The only time Jensen has ever seen any of these name brands is on TV or on some high roller in the casinos.

"You sure we are in the right place? I can't imagine this as a hideout for a group of superheroes," Jensen says sarcastically.

"Yea, I'm pretty sure it's up here on the right. Just past all these stores I can't even afford to look at," T replies.

"Yea, no kidding. Me either. We end up in any of these stores, I'm going to have to charge you extra."

"No promises," T says as he pulls the Ford over to the curb and stops.

Jensen looks out of the passenger window to see a very classy looking art gallery. All white finish up and down the walls. Fake plaster pillars flanking the glass entrance. The windows looking into the art gallery are as big as Jensen's whole apartment. Inside are row after row of paintings and sculptures whose asking price he doesn't even want to know. Right above the glass entrance, in big, bold red letters, are the words "Empyrean Art Gallery."

"Where in the hell are we, T?" Jensen asks, looking toward Terry just in time to see the driver's door close.

Jensen pops out, leaning over his open door, staring at T as he casually walks around the front of the Ford SUV. "Hey! T, what the hell man? What is this place?"

"This is it; this is where my tip said it would be, on this street behind this place. The Empyrean Art Gallery," he says, waving his hand at the storefront. "All we got to do is go around back. I'll pick the lock. We sneak in and look for some evidence of some superhuman shit, and we are out of here. And you're 800 dollars richer. Easy as that," T says as he continues moving toward the alley running down the side of the gallery.

Jensen slowly closes his door, looking between T and the gallery. "Something doesn't feel right about this at all," Jensen says to himself.

"Say what?" T asks, turning around as he reaches the alleyway.

"Nothing, man. Let's just get this over with."

Jensen picks up the pace to catch up with T. "So, how did you find out about this place exactly?" he asks, looking behind him down the alley and back to the street.

"The rumor I heard was they work out of here as a front and, also, it bankrolls them some good income as well," T says, reaching a door that looks like it would open into the back part of the art gallery.

"I guess so, hiding in plain sight and all that," says Jensen.

"Just watch my back while I pick this door, will ya?" T says over his shoulder, pulling out a small bag, which Jensen assumes is a lock-picking kit.

Jensen looks up and down the alley, noting that it looks like every alley he's ever seen on a TV sitcom or movie. The dumpsters, the piles of cardboard boxes, and the stacks of pallets on either side of the door T is trying to open.

"All right, I think I got it," T says, standing up and pushing the door open, revealing only darkness inside.

They both move inside as quickly as possible, making sure no one is on the street watching them. Jensen closes the door behind him as he enters the storefront's giant warehouse, allowing his eyes to adjust to the darkness. He moves slowly with his hands extended, sliding his feet forward, ensuring he doesn't hit or knock anything over.

The lights kick on in typical warehouse fashion, starting from the front and turning on one row at a time—row after row, all the way to the end of the warehouse. Jensen looks around and sees T with his hand on the light switch.

"Lucky guess," T says, falling in behind Jensen, who is still moving slowly, expecting an alarm to sound any moment.

But it's not an alarm that sounds. It's the sound of a garage door opening. Jensen looks left to the enormous retractable door at the warehouse's end, rolling up into the ceiling.

"Shit, we gotta get out here," Jensen says quietly but firmly.

He turns to leave and sees Terry leaning against the door they came in, his hands in his pockets. "It'll be OK, Jensen; Liam is a great guy."

"What the hell is going on, T? And who the hell is Liam?" Jensen says, trying to keep the fear out of his voice. He looks over his shoulder just as the door finishes retracting to reveal two SUVs. Black as night, headlights coming on as they enter the warehouse.

"Just relax, Jensen. Trust me; Liam is great. One of the best bosses I think I've ever had."

"You set me up. After all the shit that's happened, you've been after me too? What is this about?" Jensen says, looking for a way out. "I don't have anything. I have a terrible job, a worse apartment, a bike that is on its last leg, and almost no money,"

"Now, that last part we both know is a lie," T says with a smirk.

"Wait. What? How…" Jensen's question is cut short as the two SUVs come to a stop about eight feet from where Jensen stands, in the middle of a warehouse with no exit in sight. For three days, he's almost been kidnapped, beat up, ran off the road, and chased. And the one person he thought he could trust just stabbed him in the back.

The SUVs stop with a high-pitched squeal from the tires. Six doors open, and six people step out, all looking at Jensen. All except one. An older gentleman who looks as though he is made of money. His suit— probably from one of those businesses out front—cut to the exact dimensions of his frame. With a dash of brown still left in it, his gray hair is perfect in every way. Not a strand out of place. He stands tall as if asking to be admired by anyone and everyone around him. He aims his smile—two perfect rows of teeth—at T. T, that son of a bitch.

"Terry! Good to see you. I see you did not disappoint. You brought old Jensen here just like you said you would," the handsome stranger says now, looking at Jensen as he fixes a cuff on his sleeve. "Jensen. Jensen Atwood, right? Good to finally meet you. Terry over there has told me a lot about you."

"And he's told me nothing of you," Jensen replies.

"He hasn't? Well, isn't that awfully rude of him? I'm Liam Turner. Owner of this fine establishment and a political hopeful. I'm running for Senate of this fine state during this upcoming election. I'd ask for your vote, but I know you're from Jersey."

"You seem to know a good deal about me, so can I ask what the hell this all is about?" Jensen says with a little more anger in his tone than he anticipated. He realizes that the other five guys are armed. Each carries some type of a submachine gun underneath his suit jacket. Jensen feels every muscle in his body go taut. He's afraid to move, afraid to breathe. He realizes he doesn't think he has ever been this close to a military-style weapon like that in his life. Sure, he's shot a pistol or two with Luke at beer bottles in the woods when they were younger. But not like this.

Liam notices. "Don't worry about them, Jensen. They are for me. Can't be too careful in this city; you know what I mean?" He walks over, putting his arm around Jensen's shoulders.

As soon as Liam's arm touches Jensen's shoulders, he feels something. A jolt passing down his neck. He turns and reaches back, but there's nothing there.

"Whoa, easy there. I don't bite," Liam says, laying his arm back on Jensen's shoulders, directing him toward an office in the corner of the warehouse.

There it is again, the tingly feeling—it almost feels like when you are a kid, and you put your tongue to a nine-volt battery. But all up and down his neck. Jensen isn't sure what it is; he's never felt this before, but one thing is for sure. Something isn't right.

Liam leads Jensen into the office, followed by Terry and two of the armed guards.

CHAPTER 7

Sloan and Aiden sit a block over in their worn-out Buick, watching Jensen and T wander around the side of the building then down the alley.

"Look at the balls on this guy! He named his store Empyrean Art Gallery. Jesus Christ! Talk about hiding in plain sight. And we still couldn't find it!" Aiden laughs out loud. "We're terrible at this."

"Shut up, Aiden. Now's not the time," Sloan says, staring out the front window at T and Jensen. "I am getting so sick of this simpleton helping out Liam. He is constantly getting in the way."

"Why do you think a guy like Terry, who has no powers, is helping out a guy like Liam Turner, anyway?" questions Aiden.

"My only idea is the fact that, if Liam's plan of Transcendents taking over works the way he wants, maybe Terry thinks he will get off easy, seeing as he was with him the whole time," she guesses.

"Yea, that makes sense, I guess; he'll be Liam's first slave."

Sloan just shoots Aiden a look.

"Oh, come on. I didn't mean anything by it. You know I love you," Aiden smiles and winks. Sloan rolls her eyes and goes back to looking at the storefront.

"We have to get Jensen out of there. This same thing almost happened to me years ago. Liam had sent someone to recruit me, and if it hadn't been for Mason sending Tyler like he's sent us for Jensen, who knows where I would be?"

"So, what's your game plan?" Aiden says, taking the final sip from his water bottle then tossing it onto the floorboards.

"Well, we won't know how many people are inside till we are in there, so stealth is the key here," Sloan says, stopping for a thought. "My idea is, you do you and slide through the door and check out the ground level. I'll bounce up to the roof and hopefully find a window leading in so we have cover from the top. Depending on how many guys are in there, if any, that'll be a real-time call."

"OK, sounds good to me, boss," Aiden says, swinging open the passenger door.

Sloan follows, and the two of them take off down the sidewalk leading to the art gallery. Once out front, they take it slow, using their peripherals to see if anyone is inside the showroom.

"Not a soul in sight," Aiden says, stopping in front of the huge glass windows.

"Come on. We don't have any time to spare. We have to get Jensen out of there."

Once down the alley and next to the door Jensen and T used, Sloan looks at Aiden and nods. Sloan bends slightly at the knees, pointing her palms to the ground. A slight bluish wave suddenly emits from her palms, propelling her upward toward the roof.

"What a showoff. Look at me. I can fly up to the roof," Aiden says to himself, mocking Sloan's take-off position with his hands. He chuckles to himself as he walks toward the door. Just before he runs face first into it, his whole body goes transparent, and he slides through to the other side. The only thing giving away Aiden's position is a slight glimmer in the scenery behind him. It would almost look like a heatwave coming off asphalt on a hot summer's day if you were to look carefully. But if you didn't know he was there, you wouldn't expect a thing.

Inside, Sloan finds a beam in the ceiling to perch on and get an overhead view of the situation. No sign of Liam, Jensen, or T. There are only three guys in suits. Most likely armed up with conventional firepower or with Transcendent firepower. Either way, they must be dealt with prior to finding Jensen, who she assumes is in the only other room in this warehouse.

Sloan looks around for the patent translucent glimmer marking where Aiden is. She spots it; looks like Aiden is already on the prowl for one of the guys, who has wandered off by himself. Just then, Sloan gets an intense sensation, the same one she felt in the casino when she first saw Jensen.

"Damn, he puts off a powerful signal," she whispers to herself.

Aiden stalks his prey, waiting for him to round a six-foot-tall storage box. The man continues around the corner, and Aiden makes his move. He moves up behind him, putting his arms up next to the guard's head. The second he feels they are entirely concealed by the boxes, Aiden becomes whole once more, catching the guard in a chokehold and kicking his right knee out; the guard collapses, giving him extra leverage. Within seconds, the man is unconscious and laid gently on the ground; Aiden goes back to being invisible.

Sloan prepares for her attack, walking gingerly across the beam, which leads her right above her victim. Aiden has already moved into a position behind the third and final henchman. Sloan looks down at Aiden's glimmer, hoping he's looking up at her.

Aiden stares directly at Sloan, hoping she's thinking the same thing he is. Just then, she drops off the beam. *I guess now*, thinks Aiden as he becomes whole once more, performing the same move on this guard.

Sloan falls, landing directly behind her target, slowing her fall with the same power she used to launch herself onto the roof. She reaches around with both hands, grabbing the sides of his neck. The guard immediately reaches up to pull away the unknown assailant that has taken hold, but it's already too late.

As soon as Sloan's hands touch his neck, it is already a lost cause for the simpleton. She can feel the bones in his neck, his spine; she can feel the ligaments, the blood vessels, the blood flowing through them. She can feel his pulse rise at the shock of the attack, his adrenaline spiking. His jugular—that's what she was looking for; she focuses. Using her ability to control, to feel within her target, she concentrates on the artery, constricting it, reducing the amount of blood and oxygen allowed to enter the brain.

Within seconds, the guard loses consciousness and goes weak at the knees. Sloan lets go with her hands but catches his body with her ability. A light grayish-blue wave passes from her hands and catches the falling guard moments before he hits the ground, cushioning his impact.

Sloan releases her grip on the guard, taking the time to check his pulse. As easy as she made it seem, it's just as easy to misdirect one's ability—and instead of just squeezing an artery, you break a bone or worse.

"Man, I got to try and learn the force ability one of these days," Aiden says to Sloan as they crouch-run to the office wall, avoiding Liam and Jensen, who could easily spot them through the warehouse window.

"It's not that easy. It took Mason over a decade to master the art of dual-wielding powers," Sloan whispers as they get into position under the window.

She holds up her finger to her lips and peers inside the office, seeing Liam on one side of a desk, Jensen on the other (flanked by two guards), and Terry leaning against the door.

"Jensen's in there," Sloan whispers down to Aiden.

* * *

Liam takes his place behind his desk, making a motion for Jensen to take a seat in one of the two chairs positioned in front of him.

"I appreciate it, Mr. Turner, but I think I'll stand. I really just want to know why I was brought here against my will," Jensen says, aiming a sharp look at T. Terry doesn't even flinch; he just goes back to picking something from underneath his nail.

"As you wish, Jensen. And please call me Liam. I only go by Mr. Turner when I'm in front of the political crowds." Liam smiles and takes a seat at his desk. He starts pulling drawer after drawer open, looking for something. "Well, I'm glad you're here. I've been looking for you for a while now. And I know you're the one I've been looking for because I can feel it. Holy shit, can I feel it! Your Transcendent aura is something else, let me tell you. The last person I knew who felt like this was a good friend of mine, way back when."

"My what?" Jensen blurts.

"Your Transcendent aura—or T-Aura for short. Because, let's be honest, saying that word is kind of obnoxious. It's something that's in our genetic code. You see, it started way back during the 100-year war; it all started because of the black plague. They say Joan of..." Liam is cutoff by Jensen.

"Yea, yea. I've heard it all before from your little two-faced goon over there." Jensen throws a thumb behind him toward Terry. "He told me all about the powers and the war and people hiding out afterward, not wanting to use their powers. Blah, blah. You actually expect me to believe this fairy tale?"

Liam smiles at Jensen and then finds what he's looking for. "You don't need to believe me right now, because here in a few minutes, you will." He pulls out a pack of cigarettes and a lighter, setting them on the desk. Anyway, before I make you a believer. Since you have already heard this *fairy tale*," he says, using his fingers as air quotes. "The aura we both put off is something I believe we all have—the ones with the genes anyway—so we can find one another easier. To help us find our people, where we belong, a mate with our same genetic code. So, we don't breed with the likes of, say, Terry's kind over there." T looks up from his nails and rolls his eyes. "Jensen," Liam says, gesturing towards Jensen. "You can't honestly tell me you have never felt a weird feeling on the back of your neck or something, someone pulling your attention in a crowd of people. You see someone and just know there is something different, something special, about that one?"

"What? Like a sixth sense type of thing?" Jensen asks. "No, I don't think I have." The sound of irritation rises in his voice. "I think you better get to a point here fast, or I'm getting the hell out of here."

Liam picks up the pack of cigarettes and the lighter, stands up, and walks around to the other side of the desk. He leans against it about five feet from Jensen, flipping the lighter in between his fingers. "You know, when I was a kid here in this great city, I was a little fella. A runt, some would say. I remember the first time I had an *incident*." He draws on the last word. "Remember like it was yesterday; I was getting bullied, picked on, beat up. The kid had me in a corner, just going to town on my ribs. All I wanted was for him to stop. Then deep down, I felt it. I was a young kid still learning about my body; I didn't know what it was. But it kept building and building." Liam uses his hands to emphasize it. "It was like a pulsing feeling, deep in my lunges. At first, it was uncomfortable. I wanted it out, so I let it out. There was a pulse; it almost felt like your ears popping when you open a window while driving. I opened my eyes, and that bully had been pushed away from me, a good ten feet. Neither one of us knew what the hell happened. Took me years to figure it out. You ever have anything like that happen to you, Jensen?"

"Can't say that I have, Liam." Jensen can't hide his dread any longer.

"I've seen it," T says, now sitting on one of the couches. Liam looks over Jensen's shoulder while Jensen turns to half face him. "I've seen him do it twice. Once in the casino. He moved the dice to what he wanted at the craps table."

Jensen laughs. "Are you kidding me? It's a game of chance."

"I also saw him move a cue ball into his hand from like six inches away."

"Mr. Turner, I don't have a clue wh—" Jensen turns to face Liam and stops midsentence at the sight in front of him. Liam is standing there, both hands in his pockets, leaning against the desk, a cigarette in his mouth. The lighter floats an inch or two away—the lighter sparks. No flame. It sparks again, and Liam lights his cigarette with it.

He tosses the lighter aside with a mere flick of his eyes while pulling a slow drag from the newly lit stick. Liam takes the cigarette out of his mouth, using his index and middle finger, letting the smoke escape his lungs. "Now, back to what we were talking about."

"How the fu…" Jensen can't even finish his thought.

"I told you, Jensen, we are special. We…" Liam points at the two of them as he says it. "…are unique. And I brought you here to help show you your potential. There are more of us out there, quite a few actually, and for some reason, they want to stop me and others like me from coming out about who we are. They think it will cause a war or something. I think we should take what God has given us and rise to where we belong! On top of this food chain. Looking down at the people who are lesser than us." Liam pushes himself off the desk, making himself stand straight up.

A tight, tingly feeling hits Jensen's neck, just like before. He throws a hand up, rubbing it away. "This is too much; I'm getting out of here." He turns to see T sitting on the couch, flanked by the two men in suits. The look in his eyes says it all.

"Before you go, Jensen, let me help you out. I can awaken the ability you already possess but refuse to acknowledge. Most people who have the gene and have trained with it for a long time can do this, unless you're special. Like Joan of Arc, for example, which I'm sure Terry told you about. She could awaken the powers within people without any training. Show them their true strength. And that's what I plan on doing with you. That's why I brought you here."

Jensen is frozen; he doesn't know what to do. The exit is blocked, and he is surrounded by lunatics. Everything in his body is telling him to run. The hairs on his neck are practically ripping out of his skin. But there's nowhere to go. He looks from T to Liam.

"Come here, Jensen. Let me show you something." Liam signals for him to come closer.

"Nah, I'm good where I'm at," Jensen says as confident as he can. "I actually think I'm just going to get out of here." He goes to take a step, but his feet won't move. He looks down, expecting to see something holding him, but it's just his old beat-up shoes.

"Please...I insist," Liam says, holding up his hand then closing it into a fist.

Jensen begins sliding across the hardwood floor of the office toward Liam. He waves his arms wildly, expecting to lose his balance, but he continues to slide on his heels until he is a foot away from Liam.

"There we go. That wasn't so hard now, was it?"

Jensen feels frozen. He can move everything but his feet. He doesn't know what to do. He frantically looks around, expecting an idea to come to him.

"Now, let's release that energy. See what you really have going for you." Liam reaches up with both hands. Jensen moves to slap them away. Liam snaps his fingers, and Jensen's whole body freezes. All he can move are his eyes. He tries with all his will, but none of his limbs respond. He's powerless as Liam continues forward, putting a hand on each temple.

"Now, let's try and find it," says Liam, looking into Jensen's eyes.

Suddenly Liam's eyes turn a very hazy shade of blue. Jensen could swear his irises are swirling like a cloud around his pupils. He can feel something inside him, something moving through him. It isn't painful, but it isn't comfortable. Jensen continues to try and move—to no avail.

"And there we go. How do you feel?" Liam says, taking a step back, leaning against his desk. Liam lets out a short laugh and points at Jensen's arm. "See, T? Look. Look at his arm. As soon as I turned it on, he was able to start fighting my hold on him. Damn, Jensen, you have some natural power within you."

He is right. Jensen can feel his right arm moving. *What the hell is going on?* Jensen thinks.

Liam pushes himself back up and gets right next to Jensen, holding up his right arm. "Now, you want to really see something?" he asks rhetorically.

Liam holds up his arm so Jensen can clearly see it, then in the blink of an eye, it's gone. Jensen wants to yell out but can't; he can still barely move his arm. He looks down and sees Liam's arm ends at the elbow. But it's different; there is a haze of some kind where the rest of his arm should be. It reminds him of a heatwave on the horizon of a hot summer day.

Liam leans forward, pushing his now-invisible arm through Jensen's chest and out the other side. He can't see the arm, but he sure can feel it move through him. Liam pulls out his arm just as fast as he pushed it through, allowing it to go back to normal. He laughs.

Liam snaps his fingers again, and Jensen falls to the floor, unable to catch his own bodyweight. He scrambles backward, crashing into the couch T has been sitting on in the middle of the room. Jensen grabs his chest, half expecting an arm to still be in it. He starts to hyperventilate.

"Now it's your turn," says Liam as he makes a pencil from his desk rise, tossing it at Jensen without so much as a twitch. The pencil bounces harmlessly off Jensen and lands on the floor by his feet. Liam continues to hurl small objects from around the room into the panic-stricken Jensen, who is still trying to wrap his mind around what is happening.

"Look, Jensen. I'm a busy man, so we are going to have to speed up your learning curve." He signals to one of the guards, who walks toward Jensen and immediately begins kicking him.

"Use your ability, Jensen. Fight back with what was given to you! Use it!" screams Liam.

Jensen tries his best to cover up his vital organs with his arms, tucking in his knees to help block. But it's helpless. It seems every single kick is getting through his feeble attempts to block.

"I grow tired of your weakness, Atwood," Liam calls out as he walks back around his desk.

Jensen doesn't know how much longer he can hold out. With every breath he takes in, the man above him kicks it right back out. He's starting to cramp—or is it a knot? It's a tightness right below where his heart is. It feels like it's getting bigger. Pulsing. *What is going on? What is happening to me?* Jensen tries to grab at the man's shoe to stop the kicking, but it opens him up for a clean shot to the sternum. He rolls to his back from the kick, freeing up his sides for punishment. The pressure inside is getting bigger, harder to hold back. It needs to get free; he needs to free it.

He screams, a little from the pain—but mainly from the release, whatever it was. The kicking has stopped. Jensen opens his eyes to see the chairs in front of Liam's desk overturned. Picture frames blown off the walls. The man who was kicking him lies on the ground against the adjacent wall. He looks back toward Liam.

Liam stands behind his desk, leaning forward, staring at Jensen, smiling. The most sinister smile Jensen has ever seen.

CHAPTER 8

Aiden and Sloan continue to look in at Liam and Jensen talking back and forth. Jensen doesn't look happy about the situation, and his body language is showing it. *Wonder what Liam is planning?* Sloan thinks.

From outside of the office they watch in horror as Liam controls every aspect of Jensen. Where he stands, what he moves, or in this case, what he can't move. Jensen seems only in control of his thoughts, but even that might change if Aiden and Sloan don't act quickly.

Liam reaches for Jensen's head, putting a hand on either side of it. They watch as Jensen's body trembles and goes rigid as if a bolt of lightning just entered it.

"What the hell is he doing?" Aiden asks, staring in horror.

"I...I think...I think he's...turning on his abilities, like opening the door to the gene. I've heard of this from Mason and Tyler. I thought it was just a rumor. Highly trained Transcendents can sometimes wield power to enhance or activate someone's ability. Look. Look at his eyes! There is no way we can allow Jensen to leave this place at Liam's side."

"Well, let's get in there then," Aiden says, reaching for the doorknob.

"No!" Sloan hisses through her teeth, "Let's just wait it out. I want to make sure he is who everyone thinks he is before we go opening ourselves up for attack." Sloan brings a hand up and presses it to the wall, squinting her eyes as if trying to concentrate.

"Look," Aiden says, getting Sloan's attention and pointing through the window.

Sloan peeks through and sees one of the men kicking Jensen with all his force. "Come on, fight back. If you are who everyone thinks you are, fight back," she whispers to herself.

The glass in the windowpane rattles; it is followed by a thump. They both look at each other and then back through the window to see the guy that was attacking Jensen lying on the ground. They look at each other one more time, and in unison, they say, "Definitely a Transcendent."

* * *

The guy on the ground scrambles to his feet, anger rising, and steps toward Jensen to continue the onslaught. Liam moves his index finger on his left hand, stopping the six-foot guy dead in his tracks. He looks at Liam, who just shakes his head.

"Give him a minute," Liam says to the guard.

Jensen pushes against the wall, using it to help him up to his feet. Still bent at the waist from the pain, holding his stomach, he looks at the guard with a hatred he has never felt for anyone. He glances over at Liam, who is tossing a baseball in one hand. Next to his other hand, resting on his desk is a pistol. A large caliber with a bright silver finish, like something you would expect from a typical movie villain.

"Well, now that we know you are who I think you are, we can get to the good stuff." He continues to toss the baseball from hand to hand. "You ready?" he says, taking a moment and pointing at Jensen.

"For what?" asks Jensen as Liam tosses the baseball underhanded to him; Jensen instinctively catches it.

"No. Not with your hands. Use your gift. Use your mind. Instincts. Reach down deep and feel it within, the same feeling you just used to defend yourself."

"Look, I don't know what the hell just happened, and I sure as hell don't know how to control whatever it is you are talking about."

"Well, you better figure it out in the next two minutes. I'm a very busy person. With the race for the Senate and running this business, I only have…" He looks down, moving his cuff out of the way, revealing a gold Rolex. "…five minutes left to waste on you. So, here is what we are going to do. This here stapler is your last chance before we move on to more drastic measures." He holds it up, red in color; light shines off the metal that contains the staples, briefly blinding Jensen. "Ready? No hands now." He tosses it at Jensen. Jensen casually moves out of the way, allowing it to bounce off the wood floor and slide into the wall. "All right, looks like tough love then." Liam picks up the pistol and pulls the hammer back; it makes the iconic clicking noise everyone knows. "You are going to stop this bullet with your mind or your body. At this point, I don't care which one you choose."

Panic sets in; adrenaline is now coursing through Jensen's veins. His body is trembling; his knees feel weak. Sweat builds upon his brow as he looks for a way out, a place to take cover. The last place he looks is at T, who's just sitting there, legs crossed, arm draped across the back of the couch like it's just another Saturday at work.

* * *

"This is fucking insane! We have to get in there!" Aiden goes for the door again and feels his body go tight like he's hit a wall. He turns to Sloan, who is holding two fingers out toward him. "You're using your force on me? Are you kidding?"

"Give it a second. Please, I want to see what he does. Look, if he dies, he's no longer our problem. If he stops the bullet, we grab him and get the hell out of here; it's a win-win."

"There is something wrong with you; you're a monster. I hope you know what you're doing," Aiden says, settling back in against the wall, preparing for the gunshot.

"So do I," she says, still with her hand on the wall. *I can feel something. Something I have never felt before, not even with Mason. And it's powerful.*

* * *

As if in slow motion, Jensen watches as Liam's finger moves on the trigger ever so slightly. The hammer falls, striking the firing pin, hitting the primer, igniting the powder, and propelling the projectile out the barrel.

How did I end up here? Jensen's life doesn't flash before his eyes. *Was that just a rumor?* If it did flash before his eyes, would he be disappointed? Would he be satisfied? He's never loved, he's never had a career, and—hell—he's never even owned a car. *What kind of life have I led?* The last flash before his eyes is the flash from the muzzle of the gun sending him to the afterlife.

Acting on instinct, Jensen puts his hands out in front of him. Not because he thinks it will stop the bullet that will end his life but just from pure primal instinct for survival.

The flash is long gone. The sound of the explosion has now dissipated into the walls of the office. All that's left is a ringing in their ears. *Wait. What?* Jensen opens his eyes, and the first thing he sees is Liam looking at him, then to the ground, then back to him. Smiling from ear to ear like a proud father who just taught his son how to ride a bicycle.

Jensen looks down and sees something next to his foot; he bends to pick it up. It's a bullet, a bullet that is completely caved in as if it hit a brick wall.

"What the....?" Jensen's voice trails off.

"You did it!" Liam exclaims. "I knew you could do it. Sometimes it just takes a little bit of fear to get that adrenaline going."

"You son of a bitch! You shot me!"

"Shot *at* you technically. I didn't shoot you," Liam counters.

"How...How..." Jensen tries to get the questions out.

"Because we are special. We are demigods created by one of the worst plagues in history. We are the next evolution of the species. We were made to thrive, to survive, to be kings. No, gods!" Liam yells.

"This is crazy."

An explosion ruptures the air, sending wood splinters everywhere from behind Jensen, who falls from the concussive force, using the couch for cover. T, who was a few feet from the door, is taken out as collateral damage. The girl with the beautiful blue eyes enters through the flying debris caused by the explosion, followed by the pockmarked blond man. *What now?* Jensen looks over at Liam, who lifts and throws his desk against the wall without touching it. The caramel-skinned girl waves a hand to her left, and the guy who was kicking Jensen is sent crashing into the wall, crumbling next to the desk on the floor.

The blond man turns invisible, just like Liam did with his arm, but with his whole body. It looks like a shimmer floating through the air toward the other guard, who is still standing. The blond man comes back into view, throwing a punch that lands on the guard's chin, but he barely flinches. The guard swings at the blond. Seconds before his fist lands, the blond man disappears, and the punch swings wide. *Or near. I can't tell.*

The blue-eyed girl is now pushing against what looks like an imaginary wall. As is Liam. They both look like two mimes locked in battle on a street corner, trying to make a buck. Just then Jensen sees it. There's a cloud forming between them, almost separating them from one another. It's a light blue, almost grayish color. Like two clouds colliding and rolling away from each other. *They both have the same ability*, thinks Jensen, who is still cowering behind the overturned couch.

"I can't do this forever, Aiden! Move your ass!" the girl yells over her shoulder.

The blond guy, who has been ducking and dodging every punch the guard throws at him and returning with his own counter, pops into view.

"Fine! Always nagging!" he shouts back, disappearing one more time then appearing behind the unsuspecting guard. The blond grabs the nearest blunt object, an overturned lamp, and smashes it into the back of the remaining guard's skull, ending the battle.

Aiden runs toward Jensen, grabbing him under the arm. He leans in. "Come with me if you want to live."

"Terminator? Are you being serious right now?" Jensen snaps.

"Just come on," he says back, pulling him from his hiding spot. "Time to go, Sloan! make your move!"

"About time!" Sloan shouts back as she plays a paranormal game of tug-o-war with Liam. She leans back, pulling from deep inside for a final push. She pushes forward with everything she has, releasing a bright blue wave from her palms toward Liam.

Liam, not prepared, loses his balance from the unsuspecting attack, falling backward over his chair, which is lying on its side from the initial explosion.

With this opening, Sloan turns and runs out the door she blew off its hinges, stepping over T, who lays unconscious under the rubble.

Aiden, still holding onto Jensen, forces him to run, gets to the Buick, and pushes him into the backseat. He looks up and sees Sloan rounding the corner from the alleyway. He jumps in, starting the getaway car in a single fluid motion. The Buick is in drive and starting to roll as Sloan slides into the passenger seat. She turns, looking back at Jensen, the high-value target they've been after for weeks now. Looking over Jensen's shoulder as they speed off down the road, she sees him, Liam, standing in the middle of the street. She can feel his anger from here; this isn't over, not by a long shot.

CHAPTER 9

"**W**ho the hell are you guys? Why have you been following me? What or who is Liam?" Jensen begins as the Buick breaks traction around a corner to create as much distance as possible. Jensen continues asking Sloan and Aiden questions, but neither one of them is paying him any attention. "How did I…? How did you two…?" Jensen can't even finish his sentences, let alone finish any thoughts. It just seems too farfetched, too much like a dream. He looks down as the wind rushes past the open window; he grabs and pulls a few hairs from his arm. "Ow! Well, I'm not dreaming, I suppose."

"Is anyone following?" Sloan asks Aiden as she continues to scan for tails.

"No, I don't think so. I don't think there was anyone left standing to chase us anyway. Except for Liam," Aiden answers back.

"He was strong. There's no way any of us can take him down."

"Excuse me," Jensen asks from the backseat.

"Shut up. Give us a second," Sloan snaps at Jensen, not even looking at him. "All right, slow down—no need to get pulled over. We somehow made it out alive. Let's just find a place to lay low before we head back to AC," she says, pulling out her phone to start a search for a cheap motel close to the highway, in case they need a quick escape.

Meanwhile, Jensen still sits in shock, afraid to say another word after what he just saw these two do.

"All right, stay on this road for four blocks, make a right, and the motel will be right next to the on-ramp, in case we need it," Sloan orders Aiden, who just nods.

They slow down for a stop sign and Jensen makes his move. He swings the rear door open and steps out to escape. Just before his foot hits the asphalt, he feels a tug from behind, pulling him back into the car. He looks up to see Sloan, whose palm is facing toward him. She appears to be the one holding him down. She makes a twitch with her free hand, and the door slams shut.

"All right, Jensen, I know this is all real crazy, and nothing makes sense. Trust me, I was in the same position you are just a few years ago. Give us thirty minutes, let us get to a safe place to lay low, and we will explain everything we can. We are not the bad guys here. Liam is," she says, trying to calm him down.

"That's what a bad guy would say," Aiden says, smirking at Jensen through the rearview mirror.

"What he said," says Jensen.

Sloan rolls her eyes. "Can I let you go without you trying to escape again?"

"I don't really have much choice now, do I?"

"Well, you do; you just don't know how to yet," Aiden says as Sloan smacks him in the head.

The Buick slows and enters the parking lot of a motel. "Highway Motel," the old worn-out sign reads above the front office. Jensen looks around. It reminds him of every stereotypical cheap motel he has ever seen. Two floors, old yellow faded paint, rusted railings traveling around the edge, with a pool located in the middle. A sign for no lifeguard on duty no longer hangs on the gate; it just lies on the ground next to it. *I'm sure it's safe to swim in.*

Aiden pulls up out front and runs inside. Sloan and Jensen sit inside the Buick in the most awkward, uncomfortable silence Jensen thinks he has ever experienced. He keeps finding himself wanting to ask questions. To say something to her. But if there were ever a wrong time to talk, this is that time. Jensen knows one thing for sure—that feeling that Liam kept talking about. About knowing people like him are near. It's been happening the whole drive. But not like at the art gallery. No, this is different. With Liam, it was a scratchy, stinging feeling. With them, it's more like goosebumps—or like a cold chill hitting your neck on a breezy fall day. At the gallery, all he wanted to do was get out of there. Now he feels safe, almost secure, protected.

Aiden returns, holding keys. He drives around, looking for their room number. Number 8. He pulls in next to it, and they all get out simultaneously, each looking at the entrance of the motel, expecting multiple black SUVs to come blasting in. But nothing happens.

Aiden unlocks the door, and they head in. Aiden gives Jensen a look as if he forgot something and heads outside, while Sloan finds a contact in her phone and walks into the bathroom to talk.

The room is as basic as you could get. Two queen-sized beds with busy patterns, the kind that hide stains. Headboards that are attached to the wall. Two night-stands, a bible in each drawer. A single chair next to a circular table against the only window in the room. The only thing remotely new is the thirty-two-inch TV that is screwed to the dresser to deter stealing.

Aiden returns, holding a bag and pulling out a small bottle of whiskey.

"If you don't need a drink after that, I don't think we can be friends," he says, grabbing two clear plastic cups off the dresser in between the cheap coffee maker and the TV.

"Friends, huh?" Jensen questions. "I can't figure out if you kidnapped me or saved me back there."

"Definitely saved. Well, and maybe a little bit of kidnapping. But you're not a kid, so is it really *kid*-napping?" Aiden says with a smirk as he pours the whiskey out.

Jensen smiles back and takes the drink from Aiden, who sits on the opposite bed.

"So...what the hell?" Jensen finally asks.

"So, it's kind of hard to explain without sounding completely insane," Aiden answers before taking a sip.

"I just had a guy keep me from moving with nothing but his mind, then I stopped a bullet with what? My hand? And then you two blow the door off its hinges. Then you! I can't tell if you were really fast or invisible." As Jensen says it, Aiden disappears.

"Invisible. Well, it's not invisible technically. It was explained to me that people like me can separate our atoms, which causes us to look invisible. But really, we are just breaking ourselves down and then reassembling. That's how we can go through doors and such."

"Go through doors? Like travel through solid objects?" Jensen asks.

"Yea. And people who are skilled Translucents—that's what people with my power are called, FYI—can manipulate individual body parts instead of just their whole body, like myself," Aiden says, allowing one arm to become invisible.

"That Liam guy did that. Did it to just his arm, then the bastard stuck it through me," Jensen explains.

"No shit. Liam is a dual wielder?" Aiden says, making a mental note. "Should have known. I'm sure Sloan already does. But anyway, so I'm guessing you're a Force Transcendent?"

"A what? Man, I have no idea what you're saying to me," says Jensen.

"Don't worry about it too much. When you meet Mason, he'll be able to explain things better than I can," Aiden says, finishing off his drink while standing up to get another.

* * *

"Yes, sir. Yes, we got him, but it got a little messy. Liam was there. We took out that T guy, along with five simpletons that were with them," Sloan says into her phone. "I understand. We will be on the road as soon as we all get some sleep. And you were right. There is something about the Jensen guy. He seems to have a natural ability, an ability I haven't seen before. I had to hold him down while we escaped, and it took a lot to keep him from moving. And he just had his powers *unlocked.*" Sloan stops to let the person on the other end talk. "Sounds good; we will be at Soteria in the morning. If I had to guess, it'd be around ten-ish."

* * *

Sloan comes out of the bathroom, putting her phone into her back pocket, and looks up to see Jensen waving his hand from side to side and around a floating cup held by a hand with no arm.

"Never take anything seriously, do you," Sloan scolds.

Aiden pops back into view, and Jensen lets out a short laugh.

"This is wild," Jensen says, sliding across the bed to lean against the headboard.

"All right, I guess I owe you a little explanation," Sloan says, taking a seat next to Aiden and grabbing his drink from his hand.

"That would be nice," Jensen says, taking a sip from his own cup.

"I'm going to give you the short and sweet. Mason will probably go into a deeper dive tomorrow when you meet him," Sloan says. "Actually, what all did Liam tell you?"

Jensen goes into the details of what Terry had told him on the drive to New York about the Transcendents' history. Then he follows it up with what Liam told him about becoming a senator and Transcendents taking their rightful place at the top of the food chain.

"That sounds about right for Liam," Sloan says, looking in the glass of whiskey. "Liam and Mason used to work together. As Transcendents, that is. They were both in a group created by Mason's uncle, who was also a Transcendent. He wanted people like him to be able to be themselves without causing a public out-cry. It allowed us to work on who we were, enjoy our gifts without creating fear from the public. Every now and then, we would have a Transcendent go rogue, but Mason and his uncle were always able to stop them and bring them back. But Liam was a different story. He was powerful, naturally powerful, and when he set off on his own, there was no stopping him. So, our group turned into an underground fight club, prepar-ing for when Liam and his Empyreans decided enough was enough. And that day has finally come, we think."

"So, how long has this been going on? With Liam, I mean?" says Jensen.

"Since about 1990," Sloan answers. "Liam has been slowly making a name for himself, preparing for the right time to open up about our kind."

"I can't believe you all have been able to keep this a secret for so long," Jensen says.

"There have been a few close calls all over the world. We and the Empyreans have groups everywhere. It's a constant fight of one group trying to do bad things while another group like us tries to stop and hide the truth from coming out," Sloan says.

"And for some reason, both sides want you. Aren't you a special boy?" Aiden says, his childish smirk curling across his face. Sloan doesn't even acknowledge him.

"We have a nice drive tomorrow, and if you have any questions, feel free to ask. I know it's a lot to take in. We have all had to go through it at some point. And any tough questions to answer, we will just leave for Mason when you meet him," says Sloan.

"I do have one question. Who the hell is Mason?" asks Jensen.

CHAPTER 10

Liam stands in the middle of the street and watches as the one person who could change the tide of this war is ripped from his grasp due to incompetence.

"I should never have trusted Non-Transcendents to do anything," he says as he turns toward the front door of the Empyrean Art Gallery. He swings the giant glass door open wide and strides into the store as he reaches into his pocket, pulling out his phone. He stops in the middle of the gallery to make scrolling his contact list easier. Riley. The only person he should have ever trusted with this task. Not Terry. And not the five untalented goons who lay unconscious throughout his warehouse. Riley—she is his most trusted and experienced Transcendent. She has been with him almost since the beginning. He found her. Brought her up, taught her. Kept her from joining Mason and his other plebs.

He brings the phone up and starts punching at the screen with his thumbs. *Get your ass here now! Bring your best and contact our boys in Atlantic City. Find Mason Knight and his followers.* He presses the send button and then continues into the back to deal with his incompetent help.

As he enters the warehouse and looks around, he can see the two people lying in the middle of the floor.

"Where is that third one?" he asks himself.

He holds a hand out in front of him as if testing the temperature of the room. "There he is." He closes his fist and turns, heading back toward his office with his hand still closed into a fist. Behind him trail the three bodies of the unconscious guards who failed him. Failed to alert them of the presence of the others. Other Transcendents probably would have felt them coming.

He steps over the door, which is still lying on top of the comatose body of Terry. He stops and turns to look at T, who is starting to come to.

"Pathetic," he exclaims, flicking his finger with his free hand toward the overturned door. Sending it into one of the two couches in the room. The other guards who Sloan and Aiden fought are now awake but not fully lucid yet. He looks at them and points a finger toward the door. "Find them, now."

They wrestle each other to escape the presence of their boss. Stepping over the three guards who are being pulled through the open doorway by what looks like an invisible rope.

His phone chimes from his pocket. He pulls it out, checking the message that just came in. It's a response from Riley. *K,* is all it says. He stashes the phone back where it came from and turns his attention back to his three failures.

He reaches down as if grabbing an imaginary object from the ground. He slowly pulls up, and the three individuals slowly rise to their feet as his hand moves upward. All three look confused about where they even are.

"So, what the hell happened out there?" Liam asks in the calmest voice he can muster.

The three guys all exchanged looks with one another and then stare back at Liam. Each wants someone else to answer.

The guy to Liam's left takes a breath and answers him. "I think they got the jump on us."

Liam closes his eyes, takes a deep breath in frustration. "No kidding. Your guns are still in your holsters for Christ's sakes. I can't even take you seriously right now." And with that, he moves his left hand at the guard as if swatting a fly away from a plate of food. The man jerks backward off his feet and flies through the window.

"Who's next? Anyone else have an explanation as to what happened out there? How the person I've been after for months slipped through my fingers? Anyone?" Liam looks at the two guys in front of him; both are shaking nervously, trying not to make eye contact with him.

The man on Liam's right goes to make a comment but, at the last moment, decides against it. But it's too late; Liam saw his lip move.

"No, go right ahead; say whatever you were just thinking."

"I don't have an excuse, sir. We messed up; I messed up," he says quickly. "Please, all I ask is forgiveness. I have a wife and a kid. Please, sir," he stutters through his nervous shaking.

"That's right. You do have a wife and kid, don't you? Well then, I'll take it easy on you. Hold your hands out for me."

The man hesitates to follow Liam's instructions.

"Now," Liam says in a low growl through his teeth.

The man does as he's told. Arms out and bent at the elbow, hands flat, palms to the ground. His fingers shaking as if he's just done the polar swim.

Liam reaches out and grabs the man's forearms. He gets close to his face. "Be thankful, for I could have killed you," Liam whispers while squeezing down, the knuckles on his hands turning white. The pain is instant in the man's face. He's not sure what's going on, but one thing is for sure. He wants it to stop.

Liam continues to squeeze, a smile beginning at the edge of his lips. There's a slight cracking noise. It echoes through the quiet office, bouncing off the hardwood floors. Another cracking noise, grinding, like two rocks rubbing together. The man's face twists in pain, his legs tremble, and his body attempts to collapse, but Liam won't let him. The man looks down at his hands. They are starting to turn purple. His thumb is bent in the opposite direction, his pinky is broken at the first knuckle, and the tip is pointing straight up. Tears flowing freely from his eyes as Liam slowly breaks every bone in his hands. Crack after crack. Finally, the man's hands go limp at the wrist, each finger bent in an unnatural way. His knees give out, unwilling to hold the man's weight any longer. Liam releases him.

Letting him crumble to the floor in agony. The man pushes with his feet to create as much distance as possible between Liam and himself.

The third failure stands nervously. Liam steps to his left, aligning himself right in front of him. His body continues to shake, and he refuses to make eye contact. Liam looks down to see the front of the man's pants soaked with urine. It pools around his shoes.

"My God, man. Get ahold of yourself," Liam says as he looks over to see Terry finally pulling himself off the floor. "I'll get to you, Terry. Now be a good lad and wait your turn," he brings his focus back to the individual in front of him.

"Pl...lease...sir," he begs, struggling to talk through his fear.

"Now, now. I can't let this go unpunished. And I sure as hell can't allow this type of weakness to spread throughout the Empyreans. What kind of leader would I be?" Liam gestures toward the man's pants. "We Empyreans are supposed to be godlike, the next evolution of man. And here you are soiling yourself. That to me, is weakness, and I wouldn't be doing my part if I allowed such weakness to continue to travel through the ranks. Even if you are just a basic commoner," Liam explains as his right arm slowly becomes transparent above the elbow.

In one swift movement, as if he's been practicing for this exact scenario, Liam brings his transparent arm up and pushes it through the chest of the final guard who failed him. The man never saw it coming, but he sees what happens next. And he feels it. Once his arm is through to the other side, Liam allows his arm to transition back to normal.

The man stands there in shock, staring down at his boss's arm, elbow deep in his chest cavity. He can't see it, but he knows. He can feel Liam's arm protruding out of his back. He struggles to talk; he struggles to even think. To comprehend what is happening to him. He can feel the arm inside his chest, where it doesn't belong. He reaches up, grabbing the part of Liam's forearm that is against his sternum and gives it a slight pull. He can feel his blood pooling up in his mouth, separating his lips ever so slightly to allow it to fall from the corners of his mouth to the floor.

How has he ended up like this? How is this the end? His family shall never know what happened to him; Liam will make sure of that. He will just fade into the background and be a distant memory of the few he kept close.

As the last bit of life escapes his lips, his pupils dilate, letting Liam know this simpleton is no longer his problem. His arm goes transparent once more, allowing the man's body to fall freely to the ground, with a perfect circle passing through his chest. The man with the shattered hands looks on in horror. T squirms where he sits, looking up at Liam, who is now just pointing at him. His right sleeve is covered in blood from elbow to wrist. His hand clean, balled into a fist, with the index finger extended.

"You're next, Terry."

CHAPTER 11

Aiden opens the door to the cheap hotel room, sunlight filling the darkness. Sloan and Jensen stir where they sleep. One in each of the old worn-out queen beds. Their eyelids flutter and open at the light and the smell of fresh coffee. Aiden awoke earlier and snuck out to prep the car for their trip home to Atlantic City and for the morning coffees that he places on the nightstand between the two beds.

Jensen sits up, dropping his feet over the edge. Aiden slides one of the aroma-filled coffee cups to his side of the nightstand.

"Not sure how you like it, so cream and sugar are on the table, if you want it," Aiden says, turning toward Sloan with her cup.

They pack up the room in silence; the whole time Jensen stifles his myriad of questions. Questions that were not answered last night. But he gets the feeling Sloan isn't in the mood or even a morning person. He keeps to himself, helping pack what he can; after they double-check the room for anything left behind, they pile into the Buick for the trip home.

The next thirty minutes bring another awkward ride for Jensen. His eyes shift from Aiden to Sloan and back again. No one talks; he swears nobody even breathes.

Jensen thinks as they make the turn onto the Garden State Parkway, heading back to Atlantic City. *Now what? Where are they taking me? How is any of this real? And am I really one of these Transcendents? How could I have never known about this if it's been happening my whole life? Holy shit! Is this how I've always won at craps? By just merely flipping the dice to what I've wanted all these years? I'm not lucky at all. I'm a magician! Or I'm a...what did Liam call us? A demigod. Wow, that makes me sound completely conceited. Hi, I'm a demigod. Yeah, that makes me sound like I have my own head up my ass. All right. The hell with this. I must know the plan here. I mean, I'm one of them now, right?*

"So, what exactly are we doing here? Where are we going, and what is the plan?" Jensen asks, breaking the rhythmic beating of the tires against the asphalt.

His question is met with silence, the wind whistling past a gap somewhere in the car. Aiden is driving again, pretending not to hear, but Jensen can see his eyes in the rearview mirror bounce from Sloan over in the passenger seatback to Jensen. Jensen stares back at Aiden in the mirror then over to the back of Sloan's head. Sloan glares out the side window, paying no mind to Jensen.

"Sloan. Sloan? Hey, what are we doing?" Jensen says again, raising his voice, hoping to snap her out of it.

Sloan finally acknowledges Jensen. "We are going back to Atlantic City," she says as she goes back to looking out the window.

"OK, look, I feel I deserve some explanation for what is going on or what exactly the plan is. I didn't ask for any of this, and I've been kind of forced into this situation. I get that I have some type of power and that I'm apart of some magical gene pool that has survived the black plague and whatnot. But what is the route forward? Where do we go from here?" he says, leaning forward in between Aiden and Sloan.

"We are taking you to see Mason. He is very eager to meet you. He has felt your presence in Atlantic City for quite some time now. He is the reason we were there. Mason will know what to do with this whole situation," Sloan says, not even turning to look at Jensen.

"I see," Jensen responds, pausing, hoping for a little more.

"At this point, Liam has most likely called down to his people in Atlantic City, and I wouldn't be surprised if they are already looking for you," Says Aiden without taking his eyes off the road.

"How many people does Liam have working for him?" asks Jensen.

There's a moment of silence between the two before Aiden finally realizes Sloan isn't going to answer. "The best way to think about it is he probably has a group of twelve to fifteen easy in almost every major city down the eastern coast."

"He has what?" Jensen blurts, shocked.

"The main cities we know he has focused on are New York, Atlantic City, DC, Philadelphia, and Atlanta. The other groups, for the most part, are just like Liam's in New York. A bunch of people, all Transcendents, with one main dude as the leader, just like Liam. That leader has been preparing himself, just like Liam has been, to enter the government in some way. Whether that's in a local government as mayor, in Congress, or even higher. But they will be entering the political game in some fashion," Aiden continues.

"That's crazy. How would entering the government give them any type of advantage?" asks Jensen as he leans far enough forward to rest his elbows on the two front seats.

"Because then he can push laws to the government about how Transcendents aren't bad. Just an evolution in humanity. Just another stepping stone for mankind," Sloan says, coming out of her trance. "Once he has enough people in the government supporting the idea of letting us just be us, he will begin his push to make everyone within the government a Transcendent or a Transcendent sympathizer. After a few years, Transcendents will have the majority, and anyone who opposes them will simply be pushed out. Either figuratively or literally, by force. Not to mention everyone out there who doesn't know they carry the gene will then find out."

"I don't get it. Why is that bad?" Jensen asks, confused.

"Because it'll be the classic good guy versus bad guy scenario. Heroes versus villains. The world isn't ready for it. It wasn't ready before, and it isn't now.

Yes, there is the chance that nothing happens and the world accepts change. But when have you known this world to accept change so freely? Hell, this country alone had a war for fewer taxes, a war to end slavery. Fought back against women's rights to vote. Fought back when prohibition became a thing. People do not like change. And this will be no different. I expect it will be worldwide. Here's a good example. Think of the countries that still don't even allow women to drive or even show their faces. Now imagine a third of those repressed women finding out they have powers. Powers that could literally topple buildings if used correctly."

Jensen sits back in his seat at the thought of it all. "I never thought of it that way."

"Yea, neither did I, man. It's crazy to think about," Aiden says.

"So, if Liam has these groups he's working with everywhere, who's out there trying to stop them? Are they all called Empyreans?" Jensen asks. He sees Aiden crack a smile in the mirror.

"No, just Liam's people in New York and Atlantic City," Aiden says, then he asks a question of his own directed at Sloan. "That's a good question, though. What are the other groups called?"

"You two are idiots. Anyway, there are groups just like the Knights in Atlantic City all over that work to slow down their progress because—let's be honest—there is no stopping them at this point," says Sloan.

"Who the hell are the Knights?" asks Jensen.

Aiden groans. "I wish you would stop calling us the Knights," Aiden throws Jensen a frustrated look. "It's what she calls us. You will see why," he says, answering Jensen's question while shaking his head.

"As I was saying," Sloan continues, "these other groups, the good ones, stay in constant communication, letting each other know what they've heard or what they have done to slow the progress of each city's version of the Empyreans. When one group needs help with a problem, someone provides a helping hand and vice versa."

"This really is just like a little crime-fighting family, isn't it?" Jensen says with a smile. "So, do you guys wear costumes when you go out and fight crime—you know—to hide your identifies?" Jensen sees Aiden smirk, and he looks over at Sloan. They both see her face and can tell she's getting annoyed.

"What do you want to wear? A cape or something," Sloan says.

"No capes!" Aiden and Jensen both say in tandem, letting out a short laugh.

"You two, I swear. Can you go any faster, Aiden? I need to get away from the two of you."

"Are you always so serious?" Jensen asks Sloan, who ignores the question.

The conversation dies away as the Buick continues down the highway. The rhythmic thumping of the tires takes over when the words fall short. Aiden takes the exit leading to where Jensen will meet Mason. The one who might finally answer his questions without dancing around them—like Sloan and Aiden have in a tango of words.

The Buick pulls off the highway and heads toward the industrial side of Atlantic City. Old factories that haven't been worked in years, warehouses that only store dust and mice. They pass row after row, building after building. *This can't be where they have their hideout, can it?* Jensen thinks as they continue to drive. A few more turns and Aiden eases the Buick to a stop.

Aiden and Sloan immediately get out, leaving Jensen sitting inside the vehicle by himself. He stares out the window to the broken-down shell of a building. *This is it, huh?* He can't believe this is where the group of people who are meant to stop someone like Liam and the Empyreans hideout. Bricks are missing from the walls; the metal roof is rusted and full of holes—piles of trash and debris litter the sidewalks leading around the warehouse. Every door and window seems to be boarded up and marked with faded condemned signs. Graffiti covers every square inch from the bottom to the top.

Jensen opens his door and slides out to meet Aiden and Sloan next to a boarded-up door. Some old police caution tape flaps in the breeze.

"This is where the infamous Knights live and protect the city from evildoers. The heroes of Atlantic City," he says while gesturing at the building.

Sloan takes a few steps and gets within inches of Jensen; she is so close, he can smell the brand of deodorant she uses. He gazes into her bright eyes in wonder, lost in the blue of her irises wrapped around her pupils. She immediately snaps him out of his trance.

"You need to start taking this more seriously. This isn't a damn game. What you have been brought into, whether you like it or not, is serious. People have and will continue to die until something changes," she finishes, pushing Jensen enough to throw him off balance.

She storms off and heads down a side street. Jensen, not knowing how to react, just stands there. He feels a slight squeeze on his arm and looks to see Aiden grabbing his elbow and leaning in to whisper in his ear.

"Easy, man. I'll explain it later. Just ease up a little on the jokes when it has to do with the *Knights*," he says, doing finger quotes with his free hand.

Jensen just gives him a nod, and they run after Sloan, following her around the corner. They come around the corner to see Sloan with her hand up against the wall. Jensen looks up and down the wall and sees every door, every window still boarded up. Graffiti is everywhere, but for some reason, Jensen can tell the place Sloan is touching is special. She lifts her hand, revealing a different type of graffiti—a symbol he has never seen before.

"This symbol is a symbol for people like us. To let us know that, no matter where we are, what city we are in, that this place is a haven. Mason trusts you; otherwise, you wouldn't be here yet. I still have my doubts, but that's not my call," Sloan explains, a note of distaste flickering beneath her voice.

Aiden steps up and says, "It's a Norse symbol. It's called the Troll Cross, worn by the Scandinavian people for protection."

The symbol is a solid circle that crosses over itself at the bottom and then twists into itself on both sides, creating two smaller circles. It appears to have been painted with one fluid motion. For some reason that Jensen doesn't quite understand, it gives him peace of mind. Almost like he's finally found his home after wandering for twenty-four years.

Jensen places a hand against the symbol. "One question." Jensen pauses, and the other two just look at him. "How the hell do we get in here?"

Sloan finally smiles, the first time Jensen has seen her smile. "I don't know how you're getting in, but this is how I get in." She bends slightly at the knees, points the palms of her hands toward the ground. Makes a slight motion like she is pushing off something. And with a subtle burst of blueish gray appearing out of her hands, she propels herself up and out of sight, onto the rusted roof.

Jensen's mind races with questions; he continues to stare after her, even after she is long gone. His thoughts finally become his own again, and he brings his view back down to Aiden. Aiden, chuckling to himself, says, "You'll get there; don't worry. But until then, I guess I can help you out."

Aiden walks up to the Troll Cross and puts his hand to the brick. The wall wavers, and just like that, it's gone. Just as Aiden and Liam did with their bodies.

Aiden motions for Jensen to walk through. "Age before beauty, as they say."

"First off, I'm pretty sure we are the same age. Second, is it even safe?"

"Well, if you would like to try your hand at the roof entrance, be my guest," he says. "Now, get in there." Pointing toward the opening.

"You better not close this on me," Jensen says as he hesitantly walks through the doorway leading into the Transcendent sanctuary.

Jensen gets through the other side and can't believe what he sees. It's like a giant clubhouse from the 80s. Graffiti covers the walls top to bottom, just like on the outside, but these images have more personality to them. Like they mean something to someone from past or present. A dozen people are scattered around the building, doing various activities. Some watch TV while relaxing on a couch as if it's an extension of their living room. A corner of the building seems to be dedicated to working out, with a full gym at the ready. Each side of the building has a staircase leading up to an office, four in total, one in each corner. Jensen imagines those offices used to belong to the foremen of whatever company used to work out of here. Underneath one office is half a dozen arcade and pinball machines from the 90s. Catwalks run along the ceiling from office to office, providing an overhead view.

And in the back is what looks to be a firing range, but not a typical type of range. This one is different. There is a single person using it. He holds his hands out like guns, index and middle finger pointing out as if they are the barrels—like kids do when they play cops and robbers. Except his are apparently real, kind of. Blue projectiles fire from the tips of his fingers, connecting with the dummy targets at the end of the range.

Jensen can't believe his eyes. *What other powers are there? Telekinesis, the ability to turn invisible, and apparently the ability to turn your hands into weapons.*

Jensen has stopped walking and is now just standing in front of where Aiden created the door. Aiden walks into him but goes translucent at the last minute, allowing him to pass right through Jensen. Jensen jumps, realizing what has just happened.

"Come on, man. You can't just walk through people like that. Not cool," he yells after Aiden, who continues to walk.

"Don't be mad because I've been inside you! It just brings us closer," he shouts over his shoulder, laughing as he goes.

Sloan falls from one of the catwalks, feet from where Jensen stands. Just before impact, using the same technique she used to get on the roof, she cushions her landing with ease. A blueish gray material flowing out of her hands and rippling across the floor like an aircraft's downwash.

"So, can you fly, or is it just a boost type of thing?"

"No, I can't fly around. Not yet anyway," she says, turning to walk away, leaving Jensen standing there.

Jensen continues to stare at everything around him. Completely overwhelmed and overstimulated by the sights and sounds, he doesn't notice everyone looking at him. He looks from one wall to the other, imagining what it's like to be a part of something such as this. To have powers that ninety-nine percent of the world doesn't even know about. To be that one percent.

He finally snaps out of his trance and notices the dozens of eyes on him, watching his every move. The hairs on his neck stand up. His sixth sense is a little late this time, but better late than never. He sees Aiden and Sloan watching from their new position on one of the couches. The one who turned his fingers into guns leans against a wall, looking in his direction.

That's when Jensen sees him. A rather old man, at least compared to the rest of this group of misfits. He seems to be in his late fifties or early sixties. A black guy with thinning, gray, curly hair on his head. He's wearing a V-neck short-sleeve shirt revealing the tattoos on both arms—bright white tattoos running the length of both arms, from his wrist to his shoulders. The rest of him looks worn and beaten. His face is wrinkled and rough, like leather on an old couch. He looks as though he has lived a long, rough life.

The man slowly descends the stairs from one of the four offices. Everyone waits in silence, watching in anticipation as he makes his way to the floor and heads in Jensen's direction.

As the man reaches him, putting out his right hand, he says, "Jensen Atwood, I assume? It's a pleasure to finally meet you. I've felt your presence within Atlantic City for quite some time now. I am Mason Knight."

"Knight? Oh, like the Knights? That's how everyone here got the name?" Jensen says, without thinking much of it.

The whole room lets out a groan, and several of the group glance in Sloan's direction.

"I told you to stop calling us that!" Aiden says, trying to make the situation more awkward for her.

Mason pays no attention, keeping his eyes on Jensen. The man who turned his hands into pistols walks up beside Mason. "Jensen, this is Tyler. Consider him my right-hand man. He is one of my most trusted and talented students."

"Just call me Ty. It's good to finally meet you," Tyler says, shaking Jensen's hand.

"Seems like everyone knows everything about me, and I know nothing about any of you, other than you like to be called Transcendents, you're at war with a group called Empyreans, and Sloan is the only one who calls you the Knights." Jensen glances in Sloan's direction; she doesn't appear amused.

"We will get to everything in due time, Jensen. Right now, let's start off slow. This whole thing is a lot to take in. You went from being a normal person to almost being killed by Liam in less than twenty-four hours," Mason says as Jensen just nods in agreement. "So, what do you think of Soteria, Jensen?" Mason gestures around the building with his hands.

"Soteria? Is that what you call this place?" Jensen asks.

Aiden has moved from the couch without Jensen even noticing, leaning into his ear to answer the question. "Soteria is the Greek goddess known for safety and salvation."

"Oh." Jensen chuckles for no particular reason other than feeling out of place. "That is actually pretty clever." He nods awkwardly, waiting for the tension to cease.

"Let us walk and talk, Jensen. Try and ease this weird tension looming around. I heard about your meeting with Liam Turner. What do you think about what happened? I want to hear from your perspective," Mason says as he turns Jensen away from the prying eyes to try and get a little one on one.

"I really don't know what to think. It was one of the wildest experiences of my life. He was able to hold me in place without touching me," Jensen starts.

"He's a well-versed Force Transcendent, among other things. But continue."

"He also said he *unlocked* something inside me. I felt something change when he did it, but I don't know what exactly. It felt as though something had been locked inside me and was finally able to get out," he says. Mason just nods.

"Did you have any senses go off? A tingling feeling? Goosebumps? Even pain?" asks Mason.

"Yes," Jensen says excitedly. It's like Mason is reading his mind. "It was a sharp pain in between my shoulder blades, like a hot knife was being pushed into my back."

"That's our natural ability to sense other Transcendents. It's like a sixth sense allowing us to detect one another and to feel danger coming. The most skilled Transcendents can see danger coming from any direction." Mason pauses before continuing. "I am not going to lie, Jensen," they stop walking. "It is very rare for someone as new to this as you to be able to have those feelings. And for them to be as strong as you say. The feeling was painful instead of pleasant because your body felt that it was in danger when you were in the presence of Liam. That is a very rare trait so early on. Very curious." They continue their walk.

"I've only had the feeling once or twice where it didn't hurt, and that was when Sloan and Aiden pulled me from Liam's office." Mason nods as they continue.

"Your natural ability is definitely something I hope you are willing to explore. I have a good feeling about you. Ever since I felt your presence, I knew you were different," says Mason.

"He totally force pushed a guy!" Aiden blurts from behind them.

They both stop; only Jensen looks back at Aiden.

"So, you're a Force Transcendent. Most people are," says Mason, continuing forward with Jensen following suit.

"What does that mean?" asks Jensen.

Mason answers, "There are three known types of Transcendents. There's force, energy, and translucent."

"Can you be more than one?" asks Jensen.

"You can, but it takes years, if not decades, of practice," he answers back.

"I guess that explains how Liam was force and a translucent." Jensen says.

"Force, as I'm sure you have gathered, is the ability to move stuff with your mind." Mason pulls a beer can off a side table, catching it, then moving it through the air to the nearest trash can. "This is the most common power in our circle, as I said, but it's more than just moving stuff around. You can use the ability to protect others or yourself. Like when you pushed that guy off you. You can also use it to create a shield around yourself or a group of people."

"So that's how she deflected those bullets!" Jensen says, looking back in Sloan's direction.

Mason looks over his shoulder and follows Jensen's gaze. "Correct. The number of things you can do with this power, along with the other two, is limited to your imagination. I've been doing this for over thirty years, and I still find new abilities I can do. That is one of the greatest advantages about this place, Soteria. We learn, practice, and teach one another."

"So that means I'll be able to fly myself to the roof at some point?" Jensen mentions with a little too much excitement.

Mason's face cracks, divulging a smile, "It does. Another power I'm sure you saw when you walked in was Tyler's. The energy ability. This is a unique power. It allows you to essentially create whatever your mind can produce using the energy that surrounds us all. Tyler's favorite is the ability to fire projectiles. Some like to create swords and shields. I myself prefer a spear. An energy wielder could even create a chair if they wanted."

Across the room, a person does just that and sits on a chair made from energy. Jensen can't believe what is going on; it feels as though he is in a very lucid dream.

"Also, it is said a very skilled Energy Transcendent could create a bomb from his energy if he's able to concentrate the energy. I personally have yet to see such power, but as I said, there is so much to still learn about who and what we are. Most of the knowledge of our powers died away with the 100-year war and the Transcendents who decided to keep their powers a secret, out of the public eye."

Jensen says nothing. He just continues to listen, taking everything in that is going on around him.

"And finally," Mason states, coming to a stop next to the training area that Tyler was originally in, "there's the Translucent, like Aiden here. The rarest ability. Much is still unknown about it. Translucent is essentially the stealth of our world. The ability to break down atoms or molecules of the body and become nearly invisible to the naked eye. Turning themselves transparent, they can also make objects see-through or passable, as I'm sure you saw coming in here. Hopefully, though, with Aiden and Zoe, our most skilled Translucents here, we will be able to unlock the mysteries of the Translucent ability and take our fight to the next level."

"This is some wild stuff, Mason. So, what exactly do you want me to do?" Jensen asks.

"I want you to train, practice with my best. Refine your skills. I'm sure you're aware of Liam Turner and what he is going after. We cannot allow that to happen. Not just for our safety, but for the safety of the rest of the world. Revealing our powers to the public will more than likely lead to mass hysteria and conflict from all sides. There will be no winners if Liam gets what he wants. Liam and I were once colleagues. We were brought up and trained as young Transcendents learning how to control our powers. Liam was different, though. He was one of the naturals, such as yourself. One of the powerful ones. And once he realized what he was, what he could do, he started recruiting his own people for a different cause. One of his oldest soldiers is named Riley, and she is as brutal as they come. Do not hesitate to cut the head off this snake if the opportunity presents itself, Jensen. If you hesitate with her, you will not win. Remember, you give off the same energy that Liam gave off when he was your age. Do not squander it."

CHAPTER 12

"I want to see what you have. See what you have to offer," Mason says, moving his arm through the air as if throwing a frisbee, creating a light blue wave and knocking over a target dummy at the end of the range. "Feel the energy from within. With the force ability, it's all about the buildup. With time, you will learn the different pressures you need for different applications. The bigger the buildup within yourself, the bigger the force will be when you project it."

"That's kind of what it felt like when I pushed Liam's guard off me. It felt as though I had taken a deep breath and was unable to exhale."

"Yes, that's it. Once you can feel it and control it, you will be able to use it to your advantage," Mason continues.

Mason stands back and allows Jensen to try a few attempts at the dummies. Jensen feels out of place, especially with everyone watching. But he can't make anything move or even wobble. He just stands there with his hand out, feeling like a fool.

"Is there a technique that I need to be practicing, or a stance?" he asks.

Sloan comes up from behind him to offer a few tips. "You understand how it's supposed to feel, so that's a start, but everyone is different on how they initially build the energy. Once you figure that out, it will be much easier. Sometimes, it's a specific thought of someone or something. A feeling, a dream, or just the thought of doing it. Just be careful because the first few times you figure it out, the release is going to be erratic, unpredictable, and most likely dangerous for anyone near you."

"Oh, that's comforting. Thanks," he says, giving her a smile without receiving one back. "I still can't believe all of this is real. I went from being a nobody to potentially moving objects with my mind, like that." He finishes the sentence with a snap of his fingers. A blue spark appears from his thumb and launches a small amount of energy into the wall next to Aiden, who looks just as shocked as the rest of them.

"Very interesting," Mason says, looking from the side of the training area, where he's been watching, toward Sloan and Jensen. "Very interesting," he repeats.

"Wait, what do you mean? Is that a bad interesting or a good one?" Jensen calls out to Mason as he begins to walk up the stairs toward his office. "What's that mean?" Jensen says, shifting his eyes to Sloan.

Sloan can't hide the look of shock on her face and stares silently at Jensen. It's the first time she has looked directly into his eyes without an expression filled with anger and disdain. Maybe now, she's noticed the gold flakes within his auburn colored eyes. "You might be a natural dual wielder, like Liam."

"Like I have two powers? I can barely control one. I don't need two."

"Look, we will just concentrate on the force ability for now. I don't need you overwhelmed this early on in your training. You'll end up blowing the walls off this place. Just practice what I've said and try different thoughts and feelings to build up the pressure. Once you figure out what your trigger is, the rest will be easier." She walks away, leaving Jensen to practice his newfound power.

Jensen continues to look and feel like a duck out of water, attempting to figure out what gives him the ability. Aiden walks up behind Jensen, pulling a chair with him. There is something about Aiden and Jensen. From the time they met, there has been a link between them, a connection. Something neither one of them can quite explain, even if they wanted to.

"You'll get it. Don't worry. It usually takes people weeks, sometimes months, to figure it all out," he says, taking a seat in the chair. "Most of the people here learned about their powers early on, which of course, made it much easier for them," Aiden says.

"When did you know about your power?"

"I've only been training with it for the last four years or so, but my brother and I remember the first time I phased out. I was like five years old. And I phased right through the locked front door, into the yard. My mom still blames herself for leaving the door open."

"Phased out?" Jensen asks.

"Sorry, I'm a bit of a nerd. In the X-Men comics, there's a superhero who does essentially what I do, and she calls it phasing. I just kind of picked up the phrase and ran with it," explains Aiden.

"What about your clothes? Can you do it to any fabric, or do you need a special material?"

"At first, you can't affect your clothes. It takes a while, but eventually it's second nature, and the clothes just come along for the ride. Being a Translucent is different. No one knows much, other than the rumors we have all heard. The only thing known about Translucents is that no one can touch them except another Translucent who is also phased out."

"I don't know if that will ever come in handy, but I'll keep that in mind." Jensen laughs, continuing to practice with nothing to show for it.

"There are rumors that some Translucents can make others, such as Non-Translucents, invisible with them. Like I could phase you out with me. There is no one here who has proven that rumor, but that hasn't stopped us from trying," Aiden says with a chuckle.

Just then, a test dummy bursts into the air, emitting a bluish-gray trail behind it as it screams across the warehouse, landing next to the group on the couch watching TV, who barely even acknowledge the disturbance.

"Well, that was it. Now you just have to learn what caused it and then how to control it," Aiden says, laughing. "Another rumor floating in the Translucent circle is that Liam is able to phase into people and kill them from the inside."

Jensen stops practicing and just looks at Aiden, expecting a punch line. "That sounds like fiction. There's no way that can be true."

"You just flung a dummy across the room without touching it."

Jensen smiles. "Valid point."

Jensen has had his fill of attempts to create havoc and knows that he still has a day job even though he is a hero in training. He walks around with Aiden, saying his goodbyes to the few people he was able to meet in the short amount of time in Soteria. He looks up the stairs to Mason's office and sees Mason and Tyler standing just outside his door, discussing something. Not wanting to interrupt, he throws up a wave in their direction, getting one back in return. Jensen goes out of his way to say goodbye to Sloan, who pretends to not acknowledge him; as he walks away, he swears he can feel her eyes on him. Staring, judging, trying to figure him out.

"Don't mind her, man. She has had a rough go at it in the community. A few years back, when she was just learning, her brother went after the Empyreans and was killed for it. Since then, she's seemed to have lost her sense of humor and no longer jokes around or allows anyone to get too close. So, if she ever gives you the cold shoulder, try not to take it too personally."

"Thanks for the advice, and thanks for trying to help me out back there," Jensen says, pulling out his phone to order an Uber. Jensen continues to walk and stops at the wall he entered through. "Question. How am I supposed to get out of here?"

"I got you, but this is the last time. Next time you're going to have to figure out how to shoot yourself onto that roof." Aiden puts his hand up to the wall, making a passage for Jensen to travel through one last time.

* * *

Mason and Tyler watch from at the top of the steps outside Mason's office as Jensen finishes his training.

"What do you think of him?" Tyler asks, tilting his head in Jensen's direction.

"I think he has a lot of potentials," Mason says, still watching Jensen. "However, he still has so far to go at this point. Honestly, I am just glad we found him when we did. If Liam had succeeded in pulling him to his side of this war, we would have never stood a chance against his powers and Liam's combined."

The two continue to observe the training ground in silence until they feel the metal staircase shift from a new weight. Both look down the rusted stairs to see Sloan making her way up, a concerned look evident on her face.

"Hey, Sloan. What do you think of Jensen?" Tyler repeats the question to Sloan as she reaches the top.

"I think I would like to talk to Mason," Sloan says.

Tyler gives Mason a searching look. Mason smiles and nods as if permitting Tyler to leave. Tyler gives Sloan a hug and a quick peck on the cheek before saying, "Be gentle," and continuing past her down the steps.

"Do I even have to ask?" Mason questions as he turns his attention back to the Knights beneath him on the ground floor.

"Do you think this is such a good idea?" Sloan asks squarely. "His powers are questionable at best, and who even knows where his loyalty lies." Sloan lets out a sigh showing her frustration with the whole situation as she leans against Mason's office door.

"What makes you question his loyalty? What has he done to make you think he would turn against us?" Mason asks in return.

Sloan goes on to say something, her lips parting ever so slightly, but decides against it and remains silent.

Mason continues, catching her response. "He even said it himself: he felt he was in danger while in the presence of Liam. His natural and untrained abilities signaled to him he was in danger and needed to flee. If he had felt any other way, do you think he would have come with you and Aiden willingly?"

"I mean," Sloan starts to stumbles over her words. "Liam was acting crazy, ordering his goons to attack Jensen and even shoot at him. Any sane person would have looked for the quickest and easiest way out. I just don't know if it was the smartest idea bringing him here and revealing our secrets so quickly to a newcomer."

"Well, we were all newcomers at some point, and we all had to take that leap of faith. Sometimes you get bad apples; that's just life. Not everyone will be pure of heart and on the right side."

"And what if you are wrong about him?" Sloan asks defiantly.

"Then, that is something I will have to deal with and live with for the rest of my life. But I would stake everything I have ever owned and loved on my instinct. He will be the deciding factor in this war; he may be the single reason we all make it out of this alive. Liam is planning something, something big, and that scares me."

Sloan sees the worry wrinkle across his wizened brow and says quietly. "I just don't want what happened to Chris to happen again."

On hearing this, Mason's tone immediately becomes firm. "Sloan, what happened to Chris wasn't your fault. You need to stop blaming yourself for something that was completely out of your control. What have I always told you?" Mason asks.

Sloan sighs. "That if it's something we can't change, there is no point in worrying about it."

"Exactly. Only worry about what *you* can affect and change; everything else will work out how it's meant to."

"You and your damn philosophy," Sloan says with a small smile.

Mason smiles at her remark and continues. "I know you miss Chris. I miss him too. You two are the closest I will ever get to having children. Not a day goes by where I don't wonder what if, what if he had just listened to me and left Liam and the Empyreans alone that day," Mason pauses. "What do you think he would say about Jensen?"

Sloan takes a long moment to think about it. "He honestly would tell me the same thing you have. He was always more level-headed when it came to letting in new people, always more welcoming."

"You were too before he died."

"Disappeared," Sloan corrects him. "We never found proof he isn't still alive."

Mason ignores the statement and continues. "The day he left, you changed. You used to love teaching new members how to focus their powers and abilities. You *need* to go back to your old self, to come back to me. Not just for Tyler or me, but for yourself. All this rage is only going to hurt *you* in the long run. You were angry before, too, just like this. When I found you and Chris on the streets living on scraps, did you ever wonder how I found you?" Sloan doesn't reply, and Mason continues. "Same way I found Jensen. So, give him a chance; if not for yourself, do it for me and the love we have found in these weird times that we live in. For the family we have built over these last six years or so. For the bonds that we have formed. For me. Promise me," Mason says as he raises her head with both hands.

Sloan nods in agreement before moving forward to hug Mason. "I just fear this may all be for nothing," she says into his shoulder. "How we could go through all of this. Practicing, preparing, building our forces for nothing. What if Liam just runs right through us and nothing stops him?"

"Then, as I said before, we only worry about what we can change. If that is what it is to be, then we do our best, and in the end, we can say that at least we tried. But just promise me one thing."

Sloan looks up from his shoulder.

"No matter what, you'll keep fighting. You're the only thing that matters to me in this world.

And no matter what happens to me, you promise me you will keep fighting and that you will do everything in your power to stop the Empyreans from ruining everything that you and Chris helped build."

Sloan nods again as she buries her head into Mason's shoulder, a trail of tear smearing across his shirt.

* * *

As the wall seals behind Jensen, the Uber appears down the street. Jensen activates the app's color function, turning his phone screen a bright orange, letting the driver know he is his customer.

"You Jensen?" the driver says, pulling up.

"Yea. Mike?" Jensen asks as the driver nods back.

He climbs in and sits back, reliving the day that he just had. What started off as a typical day turned into one of the most interesting days of his life. Jensen wants to continue practicing but remembers what Sloan said about the uncontrollable power. He just might blow the doors off this Prius, so he restrains himself and watches quietly as he heads home.

The Uber pulls up in front of his apartment, letting him out. After thanking Mike, he wanders toward his apartment, letting his mind contemplate what his life might turn into now that he is a part of this super-power-wielding family. What the next few years of his life might hold for him. And about Sloan. Those eyes. There's something about her.

He reaches into his front pocket, removing his keys to unlock his door. The door opens freely, swinging inward as he tries inserting the key into the lock. He stands in the doorway, the moonlight shining at his back, casting a shadow across his apartment. Looking down, he notices splinters of wood scattered across the floor. Following the trail of destruction, he spots the damage in the door frame where someone obviously forced their way inside.

Jensen pulls out his cell phone, activating the flashlight, pushing the door fully open with his foot. Looking in, he can already see his apartment is trashed. What little furniture he possesses has been pushed around or thrown on its side. Every drawer in the kitchen pulled out and emptied, his refrigerator left open with its contents scattered across the floor. *They drank some of my beer, those savages,* he thinks. It doesn't take Jensen long to walk through his four-bedroom apartment, ensuring no one is there. His couch was turned over, and the cushions ripped open as if someone was looking for something hidden within it. The bedroom is much of the same thing. The mattress pushed off the box spring and shoved up against the wall. He still doesn't know what in the world anyone could be looking for at his place. He doesn't have much, and the money he has been saving up to leave Atlantic City is in the bank, where any sane person would put it.

He leaves his wrecked place and heads down the stairs and into the bar below.

"Cooper!" Jensen yells over the crowd.

Cooper sees him and gives him a friendly wave, and he turns and starts pouring a drink. He walks toward where Jensen is waiting, sliding a rum and coke into his hand.

"Eh, thanks, Coop, but that's really not what I needed," he says, taking a sip of the freshly poured drink, not wanting to be rude. "Hey, did you notice anyone going up into my apartment today?" he asks, swallowing a mouthful of a lot of rum and a little bit of coke.

"I didn't see them go up, but I imagine they did. Two fellows came in a few hours ago asking for you. Said they were coworkers from New York and had a job they needed to talk to you about. Told them I hadn't seen you, but they could try upstairs. Why? Did they find you?"

"No, they didn't find me yet; they just left a message for me up there," Jensen said, looking around the bar then toward the door. "What did these two guys look like?

"Two white guys, medium build, probably about your height," Cooper tells him.

"So, they looked like every other white guy in New Jersey?" Jensen says with a hint of sarcasm.

"Sorry, man. You know how many people I see a day. They all start to blend together after a while. They definitely didn't seem like locals though," Cooper continues. "Ringing any bells?"

"No, not really, but it's all right, Coop. I appreciate it."

Jensen leaves the bar, looking up and down the street as he stands outside the entrance. No suspicious cars, not even a car on the street. He turns and heads back up to his newly remodeled apartment.

"What could they possibly have been looking for?" he asks himself.

Jensen wanders around the small apartment, racking his brain over what it could be, but he eventually gives up. Looking at his watch, he thinks, *At this point, it doesn't really matter. I have to get some sleep for work tomorrow, so I can at least be somewhat useful.* Jensen closes the door as best as possible since it will no longer latch on its own anymore. He pushes a dresser from his bedroom up against the door and then adds his couch for a little more *security* and heads to his bedroom.

He lays his head down and attempts to get a good night's rest.

CHAPTER 13

Morning comes fast for someone who tossed and turned all night, flinching at every sound and bump. As his phone vibrates against his nightstand and the alarm slowly gets louder and louder, he sits up and swings his legs over the edge of his bed to the floor.

As he brushes his teeth and fixes his bed-head hair-style, all he can think about is how he wants to go back to Soteria and practice his new gift. To hang out with Aiden, get more tips from Sloan, and get to know more people who are just like him. To find out what it's like to be a Transcendent.

He reluctantly gets dressed and grabs his bag with his work polo in it. He lets out a grunt as he pushes his couch and dresser out of the way, thinking to himself, *I wish I could just force it out of the way, but with my luck, I would throw my dresser through my wall and into the dumpster behind the bar.*

Jensen climbs onto his motorcycle, starting it up as he gets his helmet set. He pulls the clutch and pushes down on the shifter, sending it into first gear. As he rides to work, he knows deep down this will be the longest workday of his life. His mind races with thoughts of Empyreans. Thoughts about Mason and his followers. About the slow war that rages on between the two groups under the nose of so many civilians. If they only knew the truth. Would they accept it like Liam thinks, or would they fight against it?

As usual, Jensen arrives at work right on time, no need to be too early for this type of work. Just before opening the front door, he pulls out his phone and sends a quick message to Aiden asking if he will be at Soteria later today to help him practice. He pushes send on his screen and swings the door open while pressing a button on the side of his phone, causing his screen to go black. Inside the showroom stand his three coworkers, Nate, Zach, and Claire.

"Morning, Jensen," Nate says as he enters.

"What's up, Nate?" he responds as he continues into the break room.

Jensen puts his helmet in his locker and changes into his work polo. As he heads back out into the showroom, Nate immediately starts his daily routine of antagonizing him.

"Do anything useful this weekend, Jensen, or did you just gamble everything away?" Nate asks.

Jensen fights the urge to force-slam him into the wall and end the constant barrage of annoying questions. "Nope, just gambled. And so you know, I rarely ever lose. As a matter of fact, on average, I make roughly one to two thousand dollars every weekend," he says back with no answer from Nate. Jensen doesn't look up from his computer but can feel the looks from the other two.

Jensen was right about one thing. This turns out to be the longest day of his life. One customer, one stupid question, and one pink phone cover after another. The only thing that keeps him going is the message from Aiden two hours into his shift about how he can't wait to see how he gets into Soteria later. Jensen just smiles to himself after reading it while also wondering the same question.

Halfway through his day, Jensen is in the back, heating up a Hot Pocket for lunch that he had found in the freezer. *Who knows how long this has been in there?* He thinks as he pops it into the microwave.

"Hey, Jensen. You have two customers in here," Zach says from the doorway leading into the breakroom.

"Are you kidding? I'm on my break. Can't you help them?" Jensen responds, annoyed.

"I would, but they asked for you by name. You must have sold them a dud or something," says Zach.

"All right. I'm coming." Leaving the Hot Pocket in the microwave, Jensen pushes the door from the break-room open and heads into the salesroom. He looked around the room for someone he would recognize but doesn't see anyone—just two men about his height and about his age. One with a close buzz cut like you would see on someone in the military and the other with long hair coming down just over his ears, with a slight outward curl. The hair on Jensen's neck shoots straight up, so fast, it would leave his skin without follicles. The pinching feeling between his shoulder blades that he got with Liam has returned. It isn't as prominent, but it is there. Jensen immediately knows something is wrong. These guys are Transcendents, and they are not part of Mason Knight's group. They do not belong to Soteria.

Jensen tries to act normal. "Hey, good to see you. How can I help you out today?" he says, walking toward them with an outreached hand, looking for a hand to shake.

The man with the long hair takes his hand and shakes it while also pulling him in close so only Jensen can hear him. "Don't make a scene; you're coming with us."

"Sorry, guys. I'm going to have to decline. I have essential work to do today. What if some Jersey girl loses her pink phone case?" Jensen says back to the guy.

As he finishes the sentence, the guy with the buzz-cut grabs him, forcing him into the wall.

Nate sees the commotion and comes out from behind the sales desk. "Hey, you can't just come in here and start pushing people around."

The one holding Jensen looks at Nate, holds his hand out in his direction in the shape of a C, and a grayish-blue pulse fires from his palm. Nate is hit by the Transcendent's attack, and he flies over the sales desk and onto the floor, taking the computer monitors with him. Zach immediately runs over to see if his boss is OK while Claire lets out a blood-curdling scream and hightails it into the breakroom.

"It wasn't a request," says the man with the buzzcut.

The man holding onto Jensen pushes him up against the wall in between the front door and window.

"We aren't here to play any games with you," the man with the long hair says from behind his friend.

Jensen is at a loss for words. Obviously, these two are Transcendents, and they most likely are part of Liam's Empyrean army. He looks down and notices his feet are no longer touching the ground. This guy is either extremely powerful or is using his obvious force ability. Jensen reaches up, grabbing at the man's grip, trying his best to loosen it.

The man with the buzzcut steps in close to Jensen, so close he can smell the brand of toothpaste he used that morning.

"Look, I don't know who you two are, but I'm sure you have the wrong person," Jensen says. "Unless you are looking for a sweet new cover for your phone or a screen protector, I don't think I can help you." Jensen smiles. There's no point in trying to hide who he is now, even if it does get him killed. They obviously know who he is.

The man with the long hair steps forward, and a glimmer of blue light catches Jensen's eye. From nothing, the man creates a dagger within his hand. It looks like a dagger a pirate would use, except it's made from a blue transparent material. The blade curls inward from the hilt, stopping about six inches up. *That is incredible*, Jensen thinks. It glimmers from the florescent lights in the ceiling as it moves through the air.

The man with the dagger steps in fast, bringing the weapon up to Jensen's neck. The blade grazes him, and Jensen feels it cut into his skin, burning as it goes. He can smell the burnt flesh, and he feels the blood trickle down his neck and into the collar of his shirt.

"Easy there, Goldilocks," Jensen says to the man. He reaches up, grabbing the wrist attached to the dagger with one hand while trying to hold off Buzzcut with the other. These two are powerful, and Jensen is outmatched, but he isn't going to let them win without a fight.

"Mr. Turner is not happy with you. He had to kill three of his minions because of your little stunt. We're here to make sure you go quietly," says Goldilocks.

Buzzcut chimes in, "Or don't. That's fine with me. I like a challenge."

Jensen doesn't see a way out of this. *This is starting to become a trend.* He continues to fight off the dagger from piercing his neck. He knows they need him alive, or they would have already killed him. They wouldn't have waited around just to toy with him. Or would they. His mind races for a plan, a way to fight them off and to escape. To get them away from his coworkers, to keep them from getting hurt.

He starts to feel it. Jensen's eyes grow wide as he now knows what it is. But he doesn't know what to do with it or how to control it. It's that same feeling he got when that guard was kicking him. The pressure building in his gut. He can feel it, growing bigger, getting stronger. His hands begin to tremble and sweat. He's nervous; he doesn't know what to do. He can't release this anywhere; his coworkers are still here.

He looks around for Nate and Zach. He can't see them; he hopes they are still behind the sales desk.

The pressure is so strong now, the feeling is so intense, he feels like he might vomit. He has to get rid of it; he has to let it out, he tells himself. *But how? Where?* With the only instinct he has, he grips the wrist with the knife tighter, reaches up with the other, and grabs Buzzcut's shoulder, seizing a handful of fabric. Not knowing what to do next, he relaxes his arms while keeping the rest of his body tight and rigid. He thinks vaguely that the energy force will follow the path of least resistance. *Out of my hands,* he thinks. He hopes. He prays.

The release of the built-up energy is the best feeling he's ever had, like a weight lifted off his chest. He feels as though he is underwater, holding his breath, and the release of the pent-up energy is him coming up for air.

The pulse is instant; he feels himself get forced back, and he loses his grip on Buzzcut and Goldilocks. The sound of glass shattering and the sickening crack of cement and wood fills the air.

CHAPTER 14

Jensen awakes in the middle of the street, covered in rubble from the store walls that exploded outward. Dust fills the air, his ears are ringing, but he can still hear the faint sound of car alarms echoing in the background. He looks down at his shaking hands; he can't get them to stop. The adrenaline pumps through his veins. He can feel it; it fuels his gift.

He tries to stand, but his legs feel weak; he wobbles and falls to his knees. Sitting back, he looks around, seeing for the first time that he sits in the middle of the busy road, surrounded by cars and their wide-eyed passengers. Onlookers from across the street and from stores around them look on at the destruction.

He looks toward the store; the whole front half is missing and lies with him in the street. The Verizon logo barely hangs on above where the door used to be; all it says now is "-izon." The debris from the store riddles the block in one hundred feet in all directions. *I can't believe the amount of power that just came out of me*, he thinks as he gets his feet underneath him.

He stumbles over the rubble back into the store, seeing Buzz and Goldie lying beneath parts of the storefront, covered with now destroyed cell phones. Jensen gets to the sales counter and looks behind it, and sees Nate and Zach. They are OK—confused and covered in the remains of the sales counter, but OK. He gets to the door leading into the back and pushes it open to see Claire cowering in the corner, tears falling from her cheeks. *Poor girl.*

"I have to get out of here before these two wake up," he says, leaving the store through the massive exit he created moments ago. As he passes, the two Transcendents start to stir under the debris.

Jensen runs to his bike, which was blown over in the explosion, forcing it back onto its wheels and inserting his key to start it. The ringing in his ears has subsided, and the sound of sirens is as clear as day. *I have maybe a minute to get out of here*, he thinks, giving Buzz and Goldie one last look over his shoulder. He shifts his bike into gear and tears out of the parking lot, spitting dust and rocks into the air.

The last thing he sees as he straightens his motorcycle is his two attackers climbing over the store's rubble to their car.

"How the hell are we still alive after that explosion? How did they recover so quickly?" Jensen asks himself while making a mental note to ask someone later about it.

Jensen speeds west away from the main strip of Atlantic City toward who knows where. At this point, he has no plan. His plan was to escape, which he did an outstanding job at. But now what?

"Where am I going to go?" he asks himself out loud while racking his brain. He knows he isn't strong enough for this fight. That much is obvious. *Backup.* He needs to call for backup, but he must stop and pull over to do that. He can't go to Soteria; that's in the complete opposite direction, and he doesn't exactly want to lead them back to Mason's hideout. The last thing he needs to do is give up his new sanctuary to the man they are trying to stop.

"Luke!" he yells, slamming on his brakes to make an immediate turn. His motorcycle skips across the ground, the back tire completely leaving the asphalt. Causing Jensen to do a stoppie on his front wheel all the way into the intersection. The bike comes to a stop, and the rear wheel lands with a bone-jarring thud. Cars behind him lock up their tires, and horns blare as they drive around him while making his unannounced right-hand turn.

At this point, he just needs to buy some time, and if he trusts anyone in this city to help him, it's Luke. He will have some type of weapon lying around, especially in his garage.

Turn after turn, Jensen takes every back road he can think of, in case Buzz and Goldie saw him make that first turn. Road after road, alley after alley. Finally, he sees the street Luke's garage is on.

He comes to the street, slowing down just enough to make the turn, dragging his footpeg as he goes. There's his garage up on the left. Jensen slows down just enough to safely hop off while it's still in motion. He lands on his feet, catching himself and running toward where he hopes Luke will be. The bike continues without its driver for ten feet before wobbling and falling to one side.

The bike makes an ungodly noise as it slides down the street, probably waking the dead. Luke runs out of the open garage door to investigate the noise, wrench still in hand.

He sees Jensen running up to him. "What the hell are you doing, Jensen?"

"Luke, you've got to help me," he says as he gets to Luke. "Don't say anything. Just listen. I have supernatural powers. I'll prove it in a second. These guys are trying to kill me, and they also have powers. I have nowhere to go, and I need help, and some time so I can call the good guys," he half yells while trying to catch his breath. Luke studies him for a moment before following his commands without question.

"You sound like a lunatic, but if even a third of that is true, let's get off the street." They turn and head into the garage.

Jensen ducks behind one of the cars Luke has been working on, pulling out his cell phone. No answer. He calls again.

"What!" Aiden says, annoyed, "I'm at work."

Jensen tells Aiden the quick down and dirty of what happened. He looks up and sees Luke pulling two pistols from one of his workbenches, handing Jensen one.

"All right, I'm calling in the cavalry. You stay put and stay hidden. No need for unnecessary bloodshed," Aiden says, and then he hangs up.

Jensen puts his phone back into his pocket as Luke slides down the side of the vehicle next to him.

"All right, what is going on?" Luke asks.

Jensen tells him everything in more detail. About how Terry lied and stabbed him in the back. About Liam and the Empyreans. How Liam unlocked something within him, how Sloan and Aiden were the good guys the whole time, and about their powers. Jensen tells him about Soteria and the rest of the groups along the east coast trying to stop people like Liam.

Luke doesn't move; he doesn't smile or laugh. He sits there, almost in shock but still confused.

"Let me try and show you. Hopefully, it works since my adrenaline is pumping; that seems to be a trigger or something." Jensen puts a hand out toward a wrench lying on the floor. Luke looks at the wrench, then back at Jensen. Back at the wrench. The wrench slides a few inches; Luke's eyes widen. The wrench lifts off the ground as if it has a jet engine attached to it, missing Jensen by inches and slamming into the wall behind him.

"I'm still learning, obviously," Jensen says sheepishly.

"What the…Oh my God…That…That was awesome," Luke says, astonished.

The sound of a car stopping pulls their attention outside. They both lookout, trying to stay behind the car for concealment. The doors open, and out steps none other than Buzz and Goldilocks.

"It's them, the two that attacked me in the store."

"How the hell did they find you?" asks Luke as he slides over one of the pistols.

"I forgot to mention that. Apparently, we Transcendents give off a vibe or a sense that others can pick up on. They are obviously much better at this than I am," Jensen says, watching his attackers.

CHAPTER 15

Back at Empyrean Art Gallery, Liam Turner sits behind his desk with a disgusted look on his face. His office in shambles, the body of the man he killed already cleaned up, and before him kneeling on a see-through tarp spread out on the floor, is Terry. Terry sits there on his knees, whimpering softly as Riley stands behind him. Riley, Liam's right-hand man—or woman, in this case. The one Liam found and trained from a young age.

Riley is a short, petite woman, but anyone who knows her knows you shouldn't judge her based on that. She is a deadly Transcendent assassin. Trained for years with energy, a force to be reckoned with. She stands behind T a solid five feet, four inches, her signature dual-energy whips flowing out of both hands and wrapping around T's neck. She keeps them taught to not give him an inch of wiggle room. Liam looks at his protégé and smiles at her, looking her up and down. She is not only a dangerous animal when released into the wild but a beautiful woman behind her tattoos, which travel from the knuckles on her hands, trailing up to her neck and all the way down her body. Shoulder length jet black hair shaved on all sides. If only Liam were a little younger, he thinks quietly.

Behind her stand her go-to men. Ezra and Luis. Ezra is a formidable Force Transcendent. He stands somewhere around six foot, two inches, 230 pounds of pure solid muscle, with a skin tone as dark as night helping to accent the definition of his arms. His hair cut is short and tight to the sides of his head, fading downward into his neck.

Luis is a Translucent Transcendent, new to the battlefield of their hidden world but a quick learner. Riley found him in Mexico hustling a group of tourists as a street magician. She knows how to spot talent with the best of them. His skin is tan and dried-out like leather from being in the sun day in and day out, without even a thought of sunblock. His hairstyle is the complete opposite of Ezra's; it's long, and it curls as it travels down to the meaty part of his back in between his shoulder blades. His broad frame holds plenty of muscle, as well as a gut, showing he doesn't put much thought into what he eats or drinks.

"Damn it, Terry, you failed me. You should have told me how strong Jensen was. His natural talent is amazing, out of this world even. I think he might even be stronger than Mason or myself after a little training," Liam says, staring at T. "You have been following and tracking him for weeks now. You should have known better. This is your job, for goodness sake."

"Yes, sir. I'm...I'm sorry," T stutters out.

"I know you're sorry, Terry; that much is obvious. You should have called for backup immediately when you realized his strength, especially when you knew Mason Knight's peons were also after him. By the time you told me, it was a little too late, now wasn't it?" Liam says as T just nods. "What the hell am I going to do with you? I mean, now I must kill probably the strongest Transcendent to walk this planet in the last hundred years. Why? Because you couldn't make a simple phone call."

Just then, Ezra's phone rings; he looks down, sees who it is, looks at Riley, and gives her a nod as he steps away to answer it.

"How could I have possibly known how strong he was before today, sir? It's not like I can feel his presence. I'm not a Transcendent for Christ's sake," Terry says back, with a little too much hostility for Riley.

Riley pulls the whips around T's neck tighter, causing him to choke on his last few words. Riley's anger causes the whip to heat up, burning T's skin. The smell of burnt flesh fills the room, causing Luis to pull his shirt collar over his nose.

"Man, that smells terrible," says Luis, voice muffled beneath his shirt.

Ezra pushes on his phone's screen, ending the call. "That was Vince. He and Wes found Jensen. He was at his job. They tried to take him quietly, but he put up a fight. Somehow, he blew the whole front end of the store into the street and escaped."

"God damn. I told you he was powerful, and the scary thing is he doesn't know how to control it yet," Liam says, looking at Riley, who just nods back.

"He said they followed him to a street but lost him. They can still feel his aura, say it's real strong right now. They have it narrowed down between two stores, where his motorcycle is. They want to know what their orders are. Capture or kill?" says Ezra.

"Damnit, tell them to kill him and any witnesses. I can't have this screwing up everything I worked so hard for. If he isn't going to be on our side, I want him gone before he has time to hone his skills," Liam says.

Ezra steps back and types Liam's response into his phone and sends it to Vince before stepping back up to stand beside Riley.

"Now, what to do with you," Liam says, looking down at T.

"Please, sir. I'll make it up to you. I promise I'll do everything I can to fix this," T says through the tears rolling down his cheeks. The tears contact the whip wrapped around his neck and evaporate into steam.

"What do you think we should do?" Liam says, shifting his gaze up to Riley.

Riley stares back for a second. "Fast or slow?"

"I liked him; he was super helpful at times. Make it fast," Liam says, sitting down in his chair, shifting his attention to something in the newspaper.

T's eyes swell up with tears as he realizes this is it. He pulls in a breath to make a last-ditch appeal for mercy. But it's too late. Riley has begun removing the slack out of the whips. Her hands move in opposite directions, stopping ever so slightly once they run out of slack. T instinctually reaches up to his neck. The whips have already done their jobs before his hands make it. The whips go through him like a warm knife through butter and now drape lazily at Riley's sides.

T's arms fall to his sides, and his head rolls forward off his shoulders, hitting the floor with a thud and rolling into the base of Liam's desk. His body falls to the side into a pile of useless limbs. T's head stares lifelessly, eyes wide open at the person who ended it all. Riley stares back with a smile.

CHAPTER 16

Jensen and Luke watch as Buzz and Goldilocks walk around, seeming to almost home in on Jensen's location.

"I don't know why Mr. Turner thinks you're so damn special, but I'm growing tired of chasing you around this shit city," Goldilocks yells into the open street.

Buzz pulls his phone from his pocket, bringing it closer to his face to read.

"Come on, kid. We know where Knight's hideout is already. So, you're not exactly saving yourself or anyone at this point. The longer this takes, the more pissed off I'm going to be. I bet when everyone arrives at Knight's place, it's going to be one hell of a party."

"Hey, Wes!" Buzz yells at the one Jensen has been calling Goldilocks. "Just got word from Ezra; it's a no-capture type mission," he says with a grin.

"Good to hear. You hear that, Atwood? Get your ass out here and make it a challenge at least," Wes yells. "Hey, Vince, you got anything? I think I got something coming from this garage," he yells back to Buzz.

"What are we going to do?" Luke says, looking over at Jensen.

"I don't know. I wish I had more training. Hell, I wish everyone would hurry up and get here. But if what they say is true, they might already have their hands full. We might be on our own. Sorry about dragging you into this," Jensen says, looking back over his shoulder.

"Yea, it's got to be right here," Vince says to Wes. "Oh yea, right here." He points toward the garage where Luke and Jensen are hiding. He opens his hand, palm facing toward the car, closing it into a fist and pulling his fist down and back behind him.

The car Luke and Jensen are hiding behind begins to shake. It rattles and shifts in its spot, and it slowly starts to slide its way out of the garage; the tires squeal across the smooth cement floor. Luke pushes away from the car toward one of his workbenches, looking back at the car as if it's been possessed. Jensen remains where he's at; the car continues to move out of the garage and toward the street, picking up speed as it goes. The vehicle is soon moving with speed, and Jensen and Luke are in full view of Vince and Wes.

The car passes right between Vince and Wes, neither paying it any attention as it slams into the building's wall across the street. The back tires coming slightly off the ground before coming to rest against the curb.

"There you are! I've been looking everywhere for you. Everyone has been worried sick," Vince says with a sneer.

Jensen and Luke both stand up simultaneously. Luke keeps his back leaning against the workbench with the pistol still in his hand. Jensen steps slightly forward, completely forgetting he also is armed with the other weapon given to him by Luke.

"What do you think you're going to do with that?" Wes says, pointing at the weapon in Jensen's hand.

Jensen lifts the gun to look at it, and it's ripped from his hands, landing next to the car that once acted as a barricade. "Look, guys. It's over; you found me, OK? I don't want anyone to get hurt. Leave my cousin alone, and I'll just come along quietly."

"Oh, the time for coming along quietly is long gone, boy. It's now moved on to the killing phase. And like Wes said earlier, we don't want to miss the big meetup at Mason's place. I hear it's going to be a blast," Vince says, stepping forward.

Luke, being the older brother figure he always has been, always looking out for Jensen, steps forward, pointing his pistol at Vince and Wes. "All right, that's it; get the hell out of here before I end this right now!"

Vince and Wes look from Luke to each other and begin to laugh hysterically.

"Are you kidding me?" Vince says back toward Luke. "Did you not just see that car get ripped out of this building and thrown across the street?" he says, tossing his thumb over his shoulder.

Wes looks over at Vince. "Would you mind?"

"No, not at all. I'll just be back here as a backup. How does that sound?" Vince says.

Wes looks back toward Luke. He holds his hand by his side, turning it so his palm faces forward. Luke watches in amazement as a blueish gray swirl begins to mix within his palm. It slowly gets brighter, then it starts building and growing toward the ground.

"What...the...fuc..." Luke says, letting the pistol waver and drop slightly while he is distracted.

The blue energy continues to build upon itself until finally, it forms a mace the length of Wes's leg. Even though it's made from energy, it still has a long handle that resembles wood or has wood textures. At the end of the handle, a spiked metal sphere juts out, just smaller than a bowling ball. Wes lifts it up into the air as if it weighs nothing at all, and it lands softly in the palm of his other hand.

"My favorite type of weapon. Very crude in design, but damn, it's efficient," Wes says, stepping forward toward Luke.

"Stop! I'm not kidding! You better back up, you freak," Luke yells through the apparent fear in his voice.

"Or what?" Wes says, continuing to walk forward.

Luke fires the pistol twice. The sound echoes off the walls of the garage. Jensen reaches up, covering his ears, trying to recover from the ringing that now invades them. The cloud of burned gunpowder clears in between Luke and Wes. Wes remains standing. He looks down and sees no blood, and feels no pain. He looks back at Vince, who is holding his hand out.

"Sorry, man. I had to step in. Can't let you get hurt; the boss would kill me," Vince says to Wes.

Luke looks confused as he tries to figure out what just happened. Then he sees it. The two bullets he just fired are just feet from Wes. They remain floating in the air at chest height, still spinning from the rifling of the barrel.

"This is incredible," Luke says, allowing the arm holding the pistol to fall limply to his side.

Vince smiles. "It sure is, kid." He bends his hand at the wrist and then brings his hand up as if swatting a fly. In the blink of an eye, a light blue wave flows through the air, contacting the bullets, changing their trajectory—the bullets hurdle toward Luke, spinning end over end. One hits him in the chest and enters his lung, while the other pierces his neck on the left side of his Adam's apple.

Luke is pushed back from the force and collapses on the floor. His hands immediately go up to his neck. Jensen watches helplessly as blood flows through the gaps in his fingers and out his mouth, pooling over the floor. Luke looks up at Jensen with fear and tears in his eyes. Within seconds, Luke is lifeless. The only family Jensen has known for years, dead.

Jensen stares in horror as Luke's lifeless body looks up at him. The blood no longer flows from his wounds, but the puddles continue to expand across the floor toward a drain in the floor. *These damn powers*, he thinks. *These powers have been nothing but a burden. A curse.* What he thought would be a new chapter in his life, a fresh start, a blessing, has led to nothing but the misery and the loss of the only family he had.

Looks like his luck has finally run out. No more winnings. No more one-night stands. This is it. He is sure he has the power to stop these two but knows he doesn't possess the skill yet to use it. But one thing he does know is that he now has a reason to live. He is going to make it out of here alive or die trying. Luke will not have been killed in vain just so he can be killed without a fight.

He looks down at his empty hands, staring at the hand that once held a pistol that obviously would have been worthless against these two. One a Force, the other an Energy Transcendent. He brings both hands up, staring into his palms. *Now is the time. If I can fight and use my abilities, now is my last chance*, he thinks, closing his hands into fists, feeling his anger start to build. He allows himself one last glance toward Luke, letting a single tear flow down his cheek before giving his undivided attention to Wes. Wes is smiling, strolling toward him, dragging his mace across the asphalt and sending blue sparks into the air. The mace gouges a groove as it goes.

"Thanks for giving up so easily and making my job a quick one, Jensen," Wes says as he inches closer.

"I'm not even close to done with you, Goldilocks," Jensen says to Wes.

Wes brings his mace up, resting it on his shoulder and gripping it with both hands. Wes takes a step before swinging like a baseball player, aiming for the side of Jensen's head.

Jensen can't explain what he is seeing, but everything seems to slow down. He can feel the air moving around the blue mace made of energy, can feel the force it is generating. Jensen moves narrowly avoiding the mace, surely turning his lights out, ducking underneath the swing. Wes, not expecting it, loses his balance as the swing continues to follow through. Jensen's arm is already cocked back, ready for the attack. He steps forward, bringing his fist up with him.

Jensen's fist comes up fast; he can feel it getting faster and faster, heading straight for Wes's chin. He can't remember the last time he ever punched anyone, but it probably didn't feel like this. His arm feels like it is traveling faster than the speed of sound, not that he would know what that is like.

His fist connects with the left side of Wes's face. The force of the punch makes Wes stumble backward, releasing his grip on the mace; as it falls, it dissipates into the air just before hitting the ground.

"Oh, nice throw, Jensen. I prefer a good fight anyway," says Wes as he recovers from the punch. He takes two steps forward, regaining the distance he lost with the punch, bringing his hand over his head in a swinging motion as if the mace is still there. As his hand gets to the apex of the swing, the mace materializes in his hand and continues toward Jensen.

Jensen moves quickly to his left as if he's been training for this his whole life, allowing the weapon to swing wide and smash into the ground, cracking the cement floor of the garage. He falls to one knee, bringing both hands into his chest. Jensen has no idea why he's doing this, but it feels right, feels normal. There it is, buildup in his chest, the pressure forming. He pushes up and forward with his legs, at the same time extending his arms. The palms of his hands feel hot then cool as a bright blue wave erupts from his hands, hitting Wes in the chest. The force of the blast propels

Wes off his feet, past Vince, and onto his back in the street. Jensen's feet leave the ground as he is launched into the wall behind him from the blast, sliding to the ground.

Jensen thinks as he pushes himself to his feet, *Newton's third law at its finest, equal, and opposite reaction.* The only thing driving him now is the fear of death. He puts one foot to the wall, pushing off and using his hands like he saw Sloan do to get on the roof of Soteria. It works, and he leaves the ground, body sailing straight into Vince.

Pushing Vince to the ground and coming to a stop in the street. He stands up straight and looks at his hands, stunned at what he was able to do. Looking back toward the garage, he sees Vince getting back to his feet and Wes joining him at his side.

"Cute trick, Jensen. Now let's see if you have what it really takes," Vince says, dusting himself off.

Vince pulls his hands back then thrusts them forward at Jensen. A vast wave of blue comes crashing toward him. Jensen follows suit and mirrors what Vince did, creating his own force wave, just a duller lighter blue. The forces meet in the middle with a crash, causing loose rocks and debris on the road to jump into the air.

Jensen and Vince are now in the same back-and-forth, tug-of-war style battle that he saw Sloan and Liam in at the art gallery. The sound the shields make against each other sounds like rocks being slammed. *There's no way no one can hear this and not call the cops,* Jensen thinks. The waves continue to move back and forth. Jensen gains ground then loses it, allowing Vince to gain ground. Each time stepping forward, then sliding backward. Jensen can tell that Vince is better trained but that he himself has more kinetic energy built up within him, if he can figure out how to properly use it.

Vince has pushed Jensen so far back now that he has his back foot up against the wrecked car that once stood in Luke's garage. Jensen isn't giving up, not yet, not ever. This is for Luke; whether he dies or not, he's going out fighting. He pushes off against the car bumper, trying to use it for extra leverage; he gains a little ground just before he sees Wes. Wes has flanked him. Jensen sees the mace coming at him from his right; he releases one hand from its force wave duties and creates a shield protecting himself from the mace. The mace bounces off, inches from his face, and he flinches.

"You can't hold out much longer, boy. I don't care how natural of a Transcendent you are," Vince yells over the sound of the force waves, and the mace bounces off the shield.

He's right. I'm not prepared for this. I'm not trained for this; I am merely surviving off instincts and dumb luck, Jensen thinks.

"I have to do something, and I have to do it soon," Jensen says out loud. Trying to think of something, anything at this point, to give him an advantage.

Jensen continues to battle Vince and Wes off, dedicating one hand to each of them protecting himself from their attacks. He can feel his body cramping, feel his energy slowly draining from his untrained body.

Over the sound of the crashing mace and the cracking of the waves, he hears something. Something out of place. He looks over his shoulder, through his sweat-soaked hair hanging down in front of his eyes. A car has pulled up; an innocent bystander has stopped and gotten out to investigate what all the commotion is.

"No! Get out of here!" Jensen yells over his shoulder, trying to be louder than the sound of the battle going on around him.

The innocent man either can't hear Jensen or isn't interested in what he is saying.

"Hey!" yells the man. "What is going on here? How are you guys doing this?"

"Fuck off!" Vince yells back.

Vince takes one hand from the battle and waves it toward the bystander leaning over his open car door. The vehicle shifts its weight on its suspension then launches into the air, doing a barrel roll as it leaves the ground. Jensen sees the vehicle rollover its unsuspecting owner as it comes to rest on top of him.

"Another innocent person dead because of this curse. These damn powers!" Jensen says out loud. He feels the anger within him boil to the top, overflowing with hatred. Jensen digs deep, pushing with what energy he has left toward Vince. His right foot pushing off the car with so much force, the bumper collapses. The power generated from inside Jensen and pushed out toward Vince is too much for him to block. Vince, distracted by the innocent man, doesn't see the attack coming, and he is thrown off his feet into a parked car next to Luke's garage. With car alarms in the background, Jensen turns his focus to Wes while Vince is trying to recover.

Jensen now uses both hands to generate a shield, protecting himself from Wes, who is now wielding two maces—weighing nothing, Jensen assumes. Jensen waits for Wes to attack again with a big swing. After a few attacks, he sees his opportunity. Wes takes a step back and winds up for a haymaker of a swing. Just before it bounces off Jensen's shield, he releases, allowing Wes's mace to travel freely, throwing him off. The momentum of Wes's attack causes him to spin on one foot, giving up his back to Jensen.

Jensen takes full advantage, launching himself forward like he did before, catching Wes in the back with his shoulder. Driving him to the ground, causing the maces to disappear as quickly as they appeared. Jensen climbs up his back and is now mounted on top of Wes with a knee on either side of his hip. The perfect position for a ground-and-pound maneuver, just like in MMA fighting.

Wes immediately covers his head to protect himself. Jensen redirects his punches to Wes's ribs, punch after punch landing, right then left, one after the other. Finally, Wes moves his arms to stop the onslaught against his ribcage, leaving his head open for what Jensen hopes is the final blow.

Jensen clasps his hands together, bringing them over his head for a classic hammer fist attack. As he brings them back, he can feel the energy build-up, as if his arms are the rubber bands in a slingshot. He thinks about the poor man killed by his own car, about

Luke, about what he has been put through in the last five days. This is not what he wanted, ever. The anger builds; the kinetic energy behind his hand above his head gets stronger. He releases. The swing comes down with incredible strength and speed.

Jensen feels a push from behind that causes him to miss his target, Wes's head. His hands hit the asphalt and shatter the road like it's made of drywall. His fists go two inches into the warm asphalt. Pieces fly up, hitting Jensen in the face and raining down onto his back.

Wes pushes him off when he feels the opening present itself. Jensen rolls free, sitting up, and looking at his hands. He's shocked at what he sees and feels surprised at the amount of power he just had. No pain, no blood. Barely even a scratch on his skin.

"What the hell?" he mutters to himself.

Jensen and Wes both scramble to their feet simultaneously, Wes backpedaling to take his place at Vince's side. Jensen tries to catch his breath, realizing he is winded and quickly running out of stamina. *If I survive this, I need to run more. My cardio is shit*, he thinks to himself with a smile.

"Something funny, Jensen? I wouldn't be laughing; I can tell you are almost done. Look at you. Pathetic," Vince says.

Jensen continues to smile. "What's pathetic is that you've been training and practicing for years. I just found out about these abilities three days ago. And yet here I still stand."

The humor washes off Vince's face. He is no longer amused at this battle, and now it's time to end it.

"You're right. This is it. I'm over this, and I want to be there when they kill Mason. So, let us finish this right here, right now."

Jensen says nothing; he just prepares himself for the second wave from these two goons. Jensen takes a stance like he's seen fighters like Bruce Lee do in the movies. He's almost positive that he looks ridiculous, but at this point, does it really matter?

Vince and Wes start forward toward Jensen. After three steps, they both slow, looking past him. Jensen looks back and sees Tyler running up the street. Jensen, relieved, allows the tension in his shoulders to disappear and relax.

Tyler slows and takes a step like a pitcher on a baseball mound, extending his arm in front of him. An energy blast is propelled from his fist, missing Jensen by feet and slamming into Vince's force shield. Vince is well-trained and a powerful enemy against someone like Jensen, but against Tyler, he might as well be a student. The energy behind the blast is too much for Vince to handle, and he is launched backward, taking Wes with him as he goes down.

Wes is less shaken by the blast since Vince took the brunt of it. He is back to his feet in no time. Mace rematerializing, he runs straight toward Ty. Tyler picks up the pace, running at Wes. Jensen stares from one to the other—Wes with anger in his eyes, Tyler calm and collected, almost as if he is picking the perfect time to strike. They get within feet of each other. Wes swings wildly while Ty dances around the attack so quickly, no one knows what happened except Tyler.

Wes continues for a few steps before slowing to a stop. He turns and looks at Tyler, who is now focused on Vince. Jensen's eyes drift down to Tyler's hands, which are holding two bright blue daggers, each about a foot long. Steam rises off them as they vaporize the blood they collected from Wes.

Jensen looks back at Wes, who is now looking down at his wounds. His shirt is torn under his right armpit and on his left side above his hip. At first, there is nothing but a torn shirt, then within seconds, blood drenches the fabric. Wes drops his mace, and Jensen watches as it disappears after a single bounce against the road. Wes falls to his knees, pressing his wounds in an unsuccessful attempt to stop the bleeding.

Vince stares helplessly as Wes falls limply to the blood-soaked ground. Vince turns away from Tyler and Jensen, taking off in a dead sprint. He makes it twenty yards before he falls to the ground as if he was tripped. He attempts to get up, but something is holding him in place.

Sloan falls from the roof of the building the car had crashed into, slowing her descent with her hands. One hand outstretched in the direction of Vince, keeping him still.

"Nice moves," she says to Tyler as she walks over. "Can't believe you're still alive," she says to Jensen.

"Not all of us are," Jensen says back, looking at the overturned car then into the garage at Luke's body. Sloan and Tyler both acknowledge what happened before they arrived without saying a word.

Sloan gives a tug at an imaginary rope, pulling Vince across the road until he is lying at the feet of Tyler, Sloan, and Jensen. Six pairs of eyes stare down at Vince as he wiggles helplessly against Sloan's power.

Jensen thinks, *How powerful is Sloan if she can hold this guy down while having a normal conversation—or am I just that underpowered? Does everyone with this ability keep getting stronger, or do we max out at some point? What about the innocent guy in the car? How can we cover this up and keep the public from knowing about this? How did I not get hurt when I hit that road like that? What about Liam?* So many questions, but now is not the time. He makes a mental note about needing to ask Sloan, Aiden, or Tyler about all of this later, but there are more important things at hand right now. Like protecting Soteria.

"So, what the hell are we going to do about this guy? We need to get out of here, but we can't just let him go," Sloan says.

"I say we take him to Mason. Maybe he can get something out of him," responds Tyler.

"Are you kidding? This piece of scum isn't going to turn on Liam. I say we kill him now and be done with it." Sloan says with a little too much anger.

A phone rings and Tyler pulls one from his pocket. "Well, we can't let him go, and we can't stay here waiting for the cops to finally make it over." He answers the call.

Sloan and Jensen look awkwardly at each other and then down at Vince. Meanwhile, Ty is in the background, excitement building up in his voice. Something is obviously going on. He hangs up and rejoins the group around Vince.

"Soteria is under attack right now, and they are fighting for their lives. We don't have time to deal with this guy. Make it quick and let's get out of here," Tyler says to Sloan.

A devilish smile creeps onto Sloan's face for the smallest amount of time, but Jensen catches it. Sloan makes a quick, jerking movement with her hands. Vince's head follows the movement and his neck snaps. His body goes limp with his head twisted in an unnatural way, his eyes looking up toward the sky. Jensen, caught off guard by Sloan's actions, is horrified but doesn't have the time to think about it.

He is pulled away as Sloan starts to walk. She pulls him in close, using her ability, and whispers to him so Tyler can't hear her.

"You better be worth all of this trouble, and you better figure out how to fight in the next ten minutes. People are dying, my people, my family! And this is all because of you, so you better make this worth it." She pushes him away without touching him and marches to the car.

Jensen runs behind them toward their car. "I hope I'm worth it too," he says to no one under his breath as a final tear falls to the ground for his cousin Luke.

CHAPTER 17

At full sprint, they arrived at the Buick that followed him to New York, carrying Sloan and Aiden. The same vehicle that he was shoved into just a few days ago to escape the grasp of Liam Turner. The escape that most likely changed the tide of the war that looms over them, a shadow of death. It has only been a few days, but to Jensen, it feels like a lifetime since that long awkward drive home from New York to meet Mason Knight. To be given entry to a place called Soteria, a place they now race back to, to try to save. A constant, vicious cycle.

No one talks. No one breathes. Jensen wonders if they are thinking the same thing he is. *If only Liam had never found me. Maybe none of this would be happening. If only I wasn't cursed with this ability, this power.*

Tyler is at the wheel of the Buick, pushing it as hard and as fast it is willing to go. Swerving in between cars, going through parking lots to skip red lights. Doing everything he can not to stop, every second counts right now.

Sloan's phone rings and she struggles to get it out of her back pocket. "Aiden!" she exclaims into it. "Slow down. What?"

Tyler locks up the rear wheels and fishtails around a corner to the street leading straight toward Soteria. The smell of burnt rubber lingers in the air. A dust cloud rises from what they can only assume is their home, their sanctuary.

Sloan stares straight ahead, listening to Aiden on the other end of the phone. Her heart racing so fast, Jensen can see the pulse in her neck. She pulls the phone from her ear, looking down at the screen as the call time stops and fades to black.

"It's bad...really bad...Aiden says we have already lost one or two people. The Empyreans surprised them; there was no stopping them." She pauses. "There are at least a dozen well-trained Empyrean soldiers. The only thing that is in our favor is that there are just as many Knights as there are Empyreans right now. We have to get there, and I mean right now."

"Still calling us Knights, I see," Tyler says, trying to lighten the mood slightly as they crest a small hill in the road. Soteria looms ahead.

The dust cloud is larger than he expected; debris from the building riddles the road. Multiple cars are stopped in the middle of the street. Some belonging to civilians, some probably belonging to the enemy. Abandoned during the surprise attack. Groups are starting to form around Soteria, with onlookers trying to figure out what is going on.

They pull up to their home, sliding to a stop with all three jumping out before the Buick's suspension even settles. The sounds of screaming, small explosions, and a cracking noise Jensen can't quite place echo up and down the block. Sloan wastes no time and pays no mind to any civilian who can see her; she flattens her palms parallel with the ground and propels herself onto the roof, running for the window she always used for entry.

Tyler and Jensen run as fast as they can to an alley, away from prying eyes.

Jensen looks at Tyler askance. "How does an Energy Transcendent get in?"

"Remember, we can make or create anything we want from the energy around us," Tyler says with a smile as he takes three steps and ascends a staircase made from nothing. Only three stairs appear at a time as he climbs toward the roof. The one he's on, the one he just stepped off, and the next one. With every step up, a stair disappears back into nothing. He continues racing upward until he vanishes over the roof, where he saw Sloan land.

"This is insane. I'm not ready for this. I shouldn't be here." Jensen looks around, and the thought of running away passes through his mind. "I can't. I have to help. They brought me into this world because they saw something in me. I can't just run now." He gives one last look over his shoulder as another small explosion goes off, followed by the sound of a rock cracking against another. *Wonder how long we have until the cops get here?* he questions as he flattens his palms parallel against the ground, just like Sloan did.

He is starting to get the hang of the energy buildup Sloan was talking about. He has begun to realize that, for him, it's merely letting his mind relax freely. He feels the buildup; it starts deep in his chest. He commands it out; he feels it flow out of his chest, into his arms, and down into his hands and out his palms. His feet leave the ground, the force launching him into the air. His hair is pushed back against his head, away from his face.

Afraid he will miss the roof entirely, he adjusts his hands so his palms are at an angle to the ground, now pushing him not only up but also over the metal roof. He lands with a hard thud, tucking his knees and rolling to a stop. He comes to rest on his stomach, lifting his head to see an open window he can only assume is the way in.

Jensen reaches the window, putting one leg in then ducking his head under. His foot hits the catwalk, and he pauses at what he sees in front of him. Soteria, the place he just left twenty-four hours ago, is the center point of an all-out supernatural war. One of the offices in a corner is destroyed, resting on the ground floor. Small holes riddle the brick wall, from where a powerful Transcendent has blown out a brick or two into the street. Parts of the catwalk hang from the ceiling to the floor; fires burn in random places. He spots two bodies lying within the battle, one completely missing an arm, the other with a hole the size of a baseball through his stomach. He can only assume they are dead, but Jensen is unsure of which side they belong to.

Jensen spots Aiden in the distance, covered with soot, his clothes torn, fighting a Force Transcendent. The speed at which Aiden can transition from solid form to translucent is incredible. Every time the

Empyrean soldier moves to strike either with his fist or with his ability, Aiden moves, disappears, reappears, and counterattacks in his own way.

A blast from an unknown Energy Transcendent hits the ceiling feet from where Jensen stands, blasting dust and debris toward him. *I've got to move! I'm a sitting duck,* he thinks.

Jensen pulls his other leg in from outside and slides down one of the catwalks, barely hanging onto the ceiling. He hits Soteria's ground floor with a thud, using the momentum to lurch to his feet. The sounds of war around him are now much louder. He can barely hear himself, but before he even has time to think of his next move, he's hit by a sharp jolt of pain. His head screams in agony, and his knees give way. Catching his fall by grabbing a broken table next to him, he pivots to face his assailant.

When he turns, he's met by nothing. Not a soul to be seen, a shimmer against the rubble. A fist appears, hitting him across the chin and pushing him back, causing him to see stars. *A Translucent. How do you fight something you can't see? I never got to ask Aiden or Sloan how to use my powers against different Transcendents,* he thinks, trying to come up with a way to fight back.

He follows the shimmer now that he knows where to look. He swings, knowing deep down it won't hit anything. The swing passes through where the enemy is, and a foot appears in front of his stomach, knocking the air from his lungs. Falling to one knee, he swings wildly, missing—another punch from the Empyrean. Jensen falls to his back and sees the shimmer closing the distance, getting taller as it nears. Two hands appear from nothing and wrap around his neck.

Jensen fights, throwing his hands wildly, hoping to connect with someone, something. The hands tighten around his throat. There's no more oxygen coming in, no more air going out. What he has in his lungs may be the final breath his body ever takes. He grabs the enemy's hands with his, trying to pry them off. The strength of this person is strong and deep. He is unable to get his fingers underneath to pull them away. *This is it*, is the only thing that goes through his mind. A Transcendent for less than a week and then snuffed out like a pawn on a chessboard.

His grip tightens on the unknown wrists. Something strange is happening; Jensen can see the hands—not with his eyes, but he can mentally see the hands. The bones, the ligaments. Every knuckle, every blood vessel, even the nerves. It's like looking at a poster you would see in a doctor's office.

His vision is starting to dim; his field of view is beginning to narrow. *Do something, dammit!* His mind screams. He closes his eyes, focusing on just the thumb. Without the thumb, you can't grip anything. The thumb becomes his target; it's the only thing he can see now. He thinks, *Pull back...pull back...pull... release...release!*

He watches in horror from inside his mind as the thumb bends at the first knuckle, making an L shape. It makes the sound of a twig snapping as you step on it. The snap is followed by a bloodcurdling scream. A woman? The grip on his neck loosens, and a rush of air enters his lungs, filling his blood cells back up with the oxygen they so desperately need. His vision returns, and he opens his eyes.

The shimmer of his killer remains but is less trans-lucent; the enemy is coming into view. It reminds him of television static. This time he focuses on the oppo-site hand, the pinky. It takes less time now; the pinky fights against his ability then snaps upward, right at the second knuckle. Another scream drowns out the battle around them. The shimmer shifts again, showing what looks like a shadow on top of him.

The other thumb! he thinks. He does it even faster this time, more aggressively than the last. He sees the thumb; he grabs it with his force. The thumb cracks, but it doesn't bend this time; this time, the bones shat-ter and collapse. The figure above him howls in pain, releasing her grasp of his throat, pulling her hands to her face. He sees the thumb he just mangled and the skin where the thumb was hanging limply down by the wrist. His attacker has lost the ability to stay invisible and appears whole. It's a woman, a girl, maybe twenty years old, no older than twenty-two. Beautiful in every sense of the word. Flawless features, long blond hair, green eyes, green eyes full of pain and anger. Anger toward him.

She fumbles with a knife tucked into her belt. Jensen reacts at the fear of death, putting his hands together and releasing a push of force from his palms. The girl launches into the air, dropping the knife onto the floor. She lands on a piece of the wall that has col-lapsed inward.

Jensen's getting the hang of his power; he pushes off the floor, springing back to his feet. He runs over to continue the fight that she started. As he reaches her, he catches her last breath then spots the rebar protruding from her chest. Her body is covered with dust, debris, and blood. The mixture of the blood and dirt creates a mud-like substance around the wound.

I killed her, he thinks. *I took someone's life. Someone's daughter, sister, lover, maybe wife. How many more will I have to kill?* He knows he can't dwell on what he did to survive right now. Others are in danger; he turns to see Aiden battling two Transcendents, the one from before and an Energy Transcendent.

Jensen runs toward them, cutting the distance for his attack in half. He steps as if throwing a baseball and pushes with both hands. Launching a bright blue wave through the air toward Aiden and his attackers. The force push is wild but accurate, hitting the other Force Transcendent and hurling him through a nearby office window. The blast pushes both Aiden and the Energy Specialist away from each other and to the ground.

Aiden and the Empyrean scramble to their feet, continuing their battle with one less enemy for Aiden to worry about. The Energy Transcendent materializes a sword from nothing and swings the two-handed blade at Aiden. He vanishes less than a second before it would've ended his life. Jensen watches in amazement as Aiden's shimmer passes through the enemy, reappearing on his backside. Aiden grabs a loose brick from the ground, spinning and smashing it against the Energy Specialist's head in one fluid motion.

Aiden looks up to see Jensen standing in the middle of the battlefield. Both are covered in blood and dirt. Aiden gives Jensen a cartoonish smile and a thumbs up before running off to find his next target.

Jensen laughs to himself, turning in time to see two fellow Knights fall lifelessly at the feet of a female Empyrean. Two energy whips flow from her hands and move as if she was born with them. Tattoos seem to cover her entire body, all the way up to her steampunk-styled haircut.

One Knight falls to her knees as the whip-wielding Empyrean holds her neck; blood oozes freely from a laceration across her chest. The other lays already dead, a whip still wrapped around his neck. The tattooed girl stands victoriously over her slain enemies as Liam walks up behind her, smiling and placing a hand on her shoulder, gazing out upon the war he has created.

Aiden disappears into a group of people, battling, leaving Jensen alone in the middle of the room and staring at the whip-carrying Empyrean. He feels something from his left; he dodges away from instinct, allowing an arrow made from energy to pass by his head and embed itself into the ground before dissipating into the air.

Jensen turns to see the Energy Empyrean loading another arrow into a crossbow. Jensen lets the power build-up in his chest, releasing it at his attacker, throwing him end over end into a crowd. Another sixth sense hits Jensen, but instead of moving or dodging away, he pushes his hands out to his sides, creating a light blue shield around himself. An energy blast from some-where to his right impacts the shield with a loud crack. An enemy Force Transcendent appears in front of him, releasing a dark blue wave of energy into his shield and causing him to slide across the floor while keeping his shield engaged.

He looks left to see Mason holding an energy spear that reminds him of the spear that Leonidas wielded in the movie *300*. Mason blocks a sword attack from his right, simultaneously force pushing two Empyrean soldiers away, one into a wall and the other across the floor into a TV.

"This is insane!" Jensen exclaims, trying to get his bearing in the midst of the battle. He hasn't seen Tyler or Sloan since their arrival. And who knows where Aiden is? He continues his search while still block-ing a constant attack against his shield. He catches a glimpse of Mason as he throws an Empyrean, then pulls another straight into his spear. The bright blue tip of the spear protrudes from the backside of the enemy soldier. Mason allows the spear to disappear, letting the dead soldier fall freely to the ground before the spear returns to his grip.

"Tyler! Tyler!" Mason yells, his voice booming over the sounds of the battle.

Tyler appears to Jensen's right, wielding the same two daggers he used to kill Wes earlier.

"Sir?" he yells back.

"Get everyone out of here! Soteria is lost! Retreat and save yourselves!" Mason shouts, still blocking incoming attacks.

Jensen looks at Ty, who hesitates. He knows he must follow Mason's command. He knows this place is a loss, and if they stay any longer, they will surely be killed. Ty looks at Jensen. "Open up," he says, pointing at the shield.

Jensen releases the shield long enough for Tyler to step inside the safety it provides.

"I can't believe this. It's all over. Where is Sloan? Have you seen her?" Tyler asks.

"No, I've been looking," he says, scanning the battlefield around them. "They're on the catwalk!" Jensen exclaims, spotting her fighting her own Force Transcendent.

"Sloan!" Tyler yells, getting her attention among the chaos. She looks up but says nothing. "Exit! We need an exit!"

Without a word, Sloan releases the biggest blast Jensen has ever seen from a force wielder and knocks two Empyreans away from her. Making her way to one of the walls that Jensen knows leads to the street where they came from. With one hand, she creates a shield barrier to protect herself from an attack, putting the other against the wall. A blue light begins to appear underneath her hand. Jensen can feel the floor rumble beneath his feet. The wall begins to shake and tremble from her touch. With a thunderous crack, Soteria fills with a cloud of dust, blinding everyone in the building.

"Now is our chance! Move!" Tyler yells at Jensen, grabbing him by the collar and pulling him to where Sloan is.

The dust cloud has settled, and Sloan stands at the top of a pile of rubble from the destroyed wall; an opening big enough for a pickup to drive through looms behind her. She continues to defend the escape as the Knights flee through the hole in order to survive the battle. Jensen and Tyler join on her flanks to help.

Sloan grabs Jensen by the collar, pulling him in close. "Follow my lead!" she yells over the noise. She grabs one of his hands and begins creating a shield. The barrier grows in size and strength.

Thinking he understands what she is doing, Jensen begins feeding his energy into the shield as well to make it even stronger than it was. The force shield is a deep dark blue, and it is now covering the whole exit, including Tyler.

Tyler stands at the edge of the shield, waiting for any other Knights to make their way to them for the retreat. Every time one gets close, Jensen and Sloan release just enough of the shield for them to pass through and make their escape. Then they promptly return the shield back to full strength. Tyler tells each escapee, before they head out, that they will contact them when the time is right so they can escape to the safe haven.

The three of them scan the warehouse for any more survivors. They see Mason in the middle, still pushing away enemies and blocking the onslaught of attacks. He's slowly making his way to them. He finally creates an opening for himself and takes off running. Sloan and Jensen release a small portion of the shield, just enough for Mason to get through. Tyler sticks his hand out to help him.

"Come on, Mason! We got to get the hell out of here!" Tyler says, reaching out. Mason reaches back in return.

Mason grabs Tyler's hand, a smile of relief on his face. As he looks up at Sloan, the smile washes away, replaced with a look of fear. He begins to pull away from Tyler's grasp.

"Hold on, Mason!" Tyler screams, trying to hold on with both hands.

It's no use. Tyler feels like he's pulling against the whole world. His grip slips from Mason's, and Tyler falls back, landing in the rubble. All three look at Mason in time to see him mouth the only word he can think to say. *Run.*

Mason spins on his heels and is pulled across the warehouse floor with his feet dragging behind him. His body hangs by invisible strings in a sign of defeat. He comes to a stop a foot from Liam, Riley standing behind him leaning against her henchman, Ezra.

"How is he so strong?" Jensen asks.

"The same way we made the shield strong," Sloan says, defeat in her voice.

That's when Jensen sees it—multiple Empyreans are linked together, arm in arm, hand in hand. The last ones in the chain grabbing Liam's shoulders. As if putting all their combined power into Liam for him to use as he sees fit.

"Mr. Knight, it's so good to see you again. It's been too long," Liam says to Mason, who is dangling helplessly a few inches above the ground.

"Just get it over with," Mason says with what little energy he has left.

177

"Aw, come now, we used to be such good friends. What happened to us?"

"You became a murderous, selfish traitor," Mason says without hesitation.

Riley steps forward, slapping Mason. "Watch your tongue, old man."

Liam looks up at Jensen, Sloan, and Tyler, who stand helplessly behind the shield. "You have nowhere to go. If you leave, I will find you one way or another. I would say join me, but we all know that will never happen. So how about you come back over here and die with honor?" Liam pauses, and no one moves, "So be it. You will die as cowards then," Liam turns his attention back to Mason.

Sloan releases her grip on Jensen's hand; the shield goes with it, and she starts to head toward Liam. Jensen grabs her by the arm to stop her. An influx of emotions surges into Jensen's body. It's full of pain, sadness. *What is this?* he thinks, then he realizes. Just like he could feel the bones of the girl he killed, he can feel Sloan. Everything within her, her thoughts, her emotions. He has never felt such sadness, self-doubt, pain. So much pain.

"You can't! It's suicide! We must go. We must!" Jensen shouts, pulling her back to him. She spins into his arms. Her eyes meet his. Her eyes swelling up with tears, ready to burst. She knows it's true, though she doesn't want it to be. That he can feel.

"He's right; we need to get out of here," Tyler agrees, pushing up the pile of debris toward the exit. He looks outside to see crowds of people staring at them. "Shit." Sirens wail in the background.

The three of them look back toward Mason to get one last look. Liam is staring back, waiting, his right arm translucent.

"I'm going to miss you, old friend," Liam says, pushing the invisible arm into Mason's chest, as he once did to Jensen not too long ago.

Jensen, Sloan, and Tyler watch in horror as Mason's body struggles against the will of Liam's power. His body twitches, and he tries to escape the pain.

"What is he doing to him?" Sloan asks through the tears that can no longer be contained.

Mason shakes, convulses; his head and his body begin to swell. Liam smiles with his hand still inside him. Mason appears to fight before letting out a scream of agony. Blood starts to trickle from his ears and nose. His eyes bulge from their sockets.

"Oh my God...he's releasing his force from within him," says Jensen.

Sloan cries out in pain along with Mason. Jensen and Tyler fight to pull her back and out of the only exit they have. They pull to keep her from seeing what is happening, but she continues to fight back, forcing herself to watch.

Mason's body convulses as he hangs in the air. Blood flows freely from his ears and nose; it begins to come from his mouth, muffling his screams as it runs over his chin. His eyes finally concede to the pressure behind them and fall from their sockets, blood rushing past them, streaking down his cheeks to the floor.

Sloan collapses to her knees.

"Pick her up now!" Tyler screams. "You take the Buick; she will know where to go," he shouts as he heads out the exit, running to an adjacent alley across the street.

Jensen uses his ability to lift Sloan on to his shoulder and turns to exit. Sliding down the pile of rubble to the street, people looking at the disaster behind them. Jensen reaches the car and pushes Sloan into the passenger seat. He launches himself over the hood and pulls open the driver's side door. With the keys still in the ignition, he starts it up, forcing it into gear, and takes off down one of the side streets.

Jensen races for nowhere. Sloan is lost in her own mind, and he is lost in a world he thought he knew but is now a stranger to. As he drives away from the place he assumed would be his home in a car that saved him from a place that would've been his hell, he tries to process the death of Mason Knight and the fall of Soteria.

CHAPTER 18

He races through backroads, unsure of where to go. Red and blue lights bounce off the walls from adjacent buildings and in the distance. Sirens wail, echoing through the quiet part of the warehouse district and into the open driver's window of the Buick. Jensen concentrates on his speed, making sure he uses his blinkers when making a turn or even switching lanes. The last thing he needs to do is get pulled over leaving the area that is sure to make the news. Soteria was destroyed by the power of the Transcendents. Bodies scatter the floor, including some that Jensen only knew in passing, given he was only there for one day. The only one he knew personally was Mason. Mason died protecting everyone he could, including himself. This was all because of him.

"Sloan. I don't know where to go. You have to help me out here," he says, talking softly. Afraid to say anything. Glancing at Sloan from the corner of his eye.

The streetlights illuminate her face for seconds at a time as they drive down unknown streets. He sees her convulse, sucking back the tears. Curled up in the fetal position in the seat next to him. Jensen is lost.

"Sloan, please. I need you more than ever right now." Jensen tries again to bring her back to the situation at hand.

"Sloan! Please! Snap out of it," he says, grabbing her by the shoulder, pulling her away from the window, streaked with her tears.

She turns, and Jensen sees the anger within her. She swings her left hand back toward him, and Jensen barely blocks it inches before it hits him. He slides to his left, trying to build even the slightest bit of space between them. She continues the onslaught of slaps and punches. Jensen does his best to block what he can while keeping the Buick in its respected lane.

The hairs on his neck stand tall, and he feels the goosebumps signaling that friendly Transcendents are near. At the same time, he feels the pinch between his shoulders. *She wouldn't*, he thinks. *She is!* Jensen slams on the brakes while turning the steering wheel to the side of the road. The Buick bucks at the sudden stop.

With barely any time to react, Jensen creates a small force between Sloan and himself. Sloan lets out a scream that would rival a banshee, pushing her right hand forward. A blue streak slams into Jensen's last-minute shield, bouncing in every direction. Jensen is forced against the driver's side door; he sees the roof of the car buckle outward toward the sky, and the windshield cracks down the middle all the way to the dash.

The attack from Sloan lasts only a second. She lets her head fall into her lap, gasping for air.

"It's your fault," she says at almost a whisper.

Jensen sits in silence, knowing what she means, and he agrees but doesn't tell her.

She sits up, facing Jensen with pure hate in her eyes. Jensen prepares to defend himself again.

"It's your fault! They all died because of you, for you! You better be fucking worth it. Their blood is on your hands. Mason's blood is on your hands."

"I know…" He can't finish the sentence.

She continues at almost a whisper. "You better find a way to make it worth it. You better be the second coming of Jesus Christ, or so help me."

"I hope so too. I didn't ask for any of this. If I could go back and let that bullet hit me to prevent all of this, I would," he says, his eyes filling up with tears of his own. "But we have to get out of here. We need somewhere to hide, to lie low. And I am a stranger in my own city. I need you."

Silence fills the air, "Steelman Bay." It comes out in a hiss.

"I'm sorry. Did you say Steelman Bay? Like the island?" he asks.

She raises her head from her hands. "Yes, head toward Longport Somers Point Boulevard and drive toward Steelman Bay. We have a hideout on the land there between Steelman and Great Egg Harbor Bay."

Jensen turns the wheel and begins to drive; the sound of sirens faded into the city's background. They drive in silence for what seemed like hours. As they begin to pass the line of casinos littering the boardwalk, Jensen can't help himself. He's been biting his lip this whole time, but he has to say it.

"You don't have to say anything. Actually, I don't expect you to. But I have to say it. For everything that it's worth, even if you regret it for the rest of your life, thank you for coming to rescue me at Luke's place. If you hadn't shown up, they would've surely killed me, and if it takes me till the day I die, I will repay you somehow, some way."

Silence fills the car once more; Jensen keeps his eyes on what's in front of him. Sloan brings her head up and turns toward him. *No pinching feeling; that's a good sign*, he thinks as he turns to look at her. She stares at him, wiping a lonely tear from her cheek, but she says nothing, turning her head back to watch the city pass by.

"Can I ask you something?" he asks hesitantly.

She shifts in her seat and looks at him.

"During my fight at Luke's, I somehow smashed the asphalt in the road with a punch and barely scratched my hand. Is that normal?"

Sloan looks at him, Jensen turning to see her. The moonlight and the glow from the casinos bouncing off her cheeks, her eyes wide like a baby doe. In all that has happened, she is still beautiful, Jensen thinks.

"Have you learned nothing? Were you born this stupid?"

And so much for that, Jensen thinks.

"You are superhuman," Sloan continues. "Once your gene is activated, your body becomes more efficient, more indestructible. You have been like this your whole life, just to a lesser degree. Have you ever broken a bone?"

Jensen thinks back as far as his brain will allow. "No, not that I remember."

"And I bet you have always healed quicker than all your friends growing up. Like bruises, stitches, even papercuts seem to just heal overnight, don't they?"

He has never really noticed or thought about it till now, but she is right. A bruise barely lasted a day, even when he took that lacrosse ball right to his eye. The blackeye was only there for two or three days.

"We have the ability to heal incredibly fast. In fact, say you were to break a bone—I think the only time I have ever seen a Transcendent break a bone was during battle with another Force Transcendent—afterward, if you or someone you knew was a highly skilled Transcendent, they would be able to set the bone. Within three days, if it was done correctly, it would be healed."

She continues to talk about how she can't believe no one has told him, can't believe he hasn't figured it out yet. Jensen feels he should be insulted because he's only known about these powers for about five days at this point. But, right now, he is just glad she is talking and not trying to kill him anymore.

"That's why Liam wanted you on his team so bad. Because you are obviously so naturally powerful. You are different than anyone I have ever seen. Even Mason said it." She chokes a little saying his name. "There is something about you, Jensen. You are just like Liam in many ways; maybe even more powerful, but only time will tell."

Sloan takes a breath, and Jensen continues to drive, contemplating everything that has happened. Since his awakening in New York, he realizes that thanks to Liam Turner, he has felt stronger, healthier, like a new man altogether. Like he could almost take on the world, almost.

"I don't know if you noticed, but did you see how many people it took to hold Mason?"

Jensen nods, recalling the Empyreans using their powers together.

"That's because of the strength Mason held from his years of training. In this world, it isn't about your muscle mass; it's about your knowledge of what you can do. How far you can push your body, your mind. That's why Liam fears you. I saw you fight against him in his office. He flipped that switch, and you began moving. Not much—but you moved. Against a Transcendent who was naturally strong in the beginning and has been training for years, decades." Sloan is now completely facing toward Jensen as he drives. "You were able to fight against him. I know that scared him. You may be the only person who can stop him."

"I have noticed my strength, my abilities increasing. I still have no idea how to control them, really. Like when I helped Aiden out during the battle, I knocked over the guy I was aiming at, along with Aiden and one other," he says, seeing a small smile creep up her cheek. "And I have noticed now that I can tell the difference between friends and enemies. I was able to see attacks coming before they hit me, and even when you attacked me earlier, I could sense you were good but could also tell you meant me harm. Which is how I blocked it."

This piques Sloan's interest, and Jensen notices.

"What? What did I say?" he asks.

"Nothing. Never mind...Actually, remind me later. I want to try some stuff after we get to a safe place. Our turn is coming up," Sloan says. "Up here on the left; slow down."

"Where? All I see are trees."

"There. Turn here. Now!"

Jensen does as directed and turns the car toward what looks to be just a group of bushes. Sloan waves a hand, and the bushes separate in the middle, attached to a gate. Jensen slows down enough to drive over the curb and continues past the fence. As they pass through the gate, Sloan waves her hand out the window, and Jensen watches as the gate closes in the rearview mirror.

They travel along a dirt path that doesn't show any sign of ending. The trail curves slowly right, then comes back to the left, ending at a giant warehouse or barn-style structure in the middle of nowhere.

"What is this place?" Jensen asks, staring up at the warehouse in front of him.

The Buick's brakes squeal as it comes to rest.

"This is a place Mason put together after Liam became a turncoat as a last-ditch effort. Just in case all hell broke loose—kind of like what happened today. So, Liam shouldn't know about this place. It's completely off the grid."

Jensen stares out at the worn-down building in front of him and wonders if this is what his life will consist of now—always on the run.

Jensen steps out of the car and scans the area around them. The trees stand tall, just tall enough to conceal the warehouse from view. He has lived here his whole life, and the thought never crossed his mind that there would be a building this far back in this swampy area.

Sloan steps out shortly after he does, walking around to the front of the Buick.

"All right, there should be solar panels on the roof of this place," Sloan mentions as she looks up at the roof. "According to Mason, there should be generators out back as a backup for the panels. I'll fly up to the roof and check those while you go around back to check the generators. Make sure they have gas and oil. And then see if you can get them to start."

Jensen nods without saying anything and turns to head alongside the warehouse. He hears the swoosh of air behind him as Sloan propels herself upward onto the roof.

The grass is overgrown; weeds have started to take over. There's no telling how long this place has gone without proper maintenance. As he gets to the side of the building, he pushes a bush away from the wall, trying to create some space for himself.

His shin hits something solid hidden from view by the bush, "Son of a…" he hisses under his breath. He pulls at the bush; it moves freely, and Jensen notices it has been removed from the ground. As he tosses the brush aside, he spots an old sedan hidden from view.

He places a hand on the hood, rubbing his shin at the same time. *Still warm.*

"Hopefully, it's one of us," Jensen whispers to himself.

He continues his movement alongside the building and past the hidden car. The darkness takes over, the trees above blocking the only source of light provided by the moon. At this point, Jensen is walking blind.

He reaches into his pocket and pulls out his cell phone. He activates the camera flash, using it as a flashlight to find his way through more brush, past another tree, and through an open area of knee-high grass. Jensen spots a door to his right, stepping forward to get a closer look. He spots a familiar symbol, the Troll Cross. The sign of a safe haven, just as Sloan showed him on the wall of Soteria. Hopefully, this place proves to be a little bit safer.

Jensen finally reaches the corner of the warehouse and peers around to what he assumes is the backside of the shelter. He sees a small shed a few meters away from the building, with an exhaust pipe extending from its top and a thick electrical cable leading into the warehouse.

"That better be it. I don't see much else here."

Jensen swings open the door to the shed, spotting the generator. He follows the directions on the inside of the maintenance door, and after a few failed attempts, the generator roars to life, spitting a thick black cloud of smoke into the night air.

Jensen heads back the way he came, up the side, through the brush, and past the car. He rounds the corner and spots Sloan sitting on the hood of the Buick.

"Took you long enough. I think the solar panels will still work. The connections seemed intact, but let's leave that generator running for a little bit to make sure the batteries can hold a charge," she says as Jensen approaches.

"Sounds good to me. Where are the batteries stored at?"

"No idea. Inside somewhere, I would imagine. Let's try and find it," she says, approaching the giant barn doors.

Jensen looks up at the front of the building. The doors leading in are at least twelve feet tall and appear to be on a roller system. There's no telling how well they work or when the last time they were lubed was. He grabs one of the two handles to open the giant steel doors and puts all his weight into it. The sound of metal on metal fills the night air, but the doors don't move an inch. Looking back, he sees Sloan just staring at him.

"I'll take care of the doors since you still don't know how to control yourself. Back up, will you?" says Sloan as she hops down off the Buick's hood.

She brings both hands up, palms facing out, then pushes against two imaginary walls in front of her. The door on the right slides opens with ease under her power. The other door grinds metal on metal, fighting against itself and echoing across the swampy forest.

The doors open enough for them to walk through, allowing enough moonlight in to illuminate the warehouse. Against the back wall sits Tyler. His arms resting atop his knees and his head lolling on top. He looks up like a beaten man. His clothes are still covered in blood and dirt from the battle. Some of the blood is his; some of it is not. The moonlight dances across his face, showing dried trails of tears from the corners of his eyes to his chin.

Tyler sees Sloan and immediately jumps to his feet, running full speed. They run into each other's arms and embrace, long and hard. Jensen feels jealously fill his body, wishing it was him, wishing she would hold and squeeze him like that. Then he realizes that it's not the embrace of lovers but that of siblings. Brotherly love—a protector and protectee.

They pull away from each other.

"Have you heard from anyone else?" Sloan asks.

"A few. Eric, Eli, and Zoe have been the only ones who have reached out," Ty continues. "Zoe says she heard from Hannah, but that has been it on my end."

"We haven't heard from anyone; we barely made it away ourselves," says Sloan.

"What about Aiden?" Jensen asks.

No one speaks.

"He had to have made it out, right?" Jensen says into the silence. "There was no one left when we made our escape."

"I also didn't see him exit through the hole," Tyler answers.

"Don't worry. He'll show up; he's like a blister. Always showing up when all the work is done, as my grandfather used to say," Sloan says with a forced smile.

"So, what the hell is this place? It can't be just this empty warehouse, right?" Jensen asks.

"Think of it as a fallout shelter," says Tyler. "All this up here is just a front; everything is underneath. Now that you got the generator going, the lights should be working, along with the water pump, so we will be able to clean up at least."

Sloan moves her hand upward, causing a stack of rotting pallets to move. The pallets are merely a disguise for a door; as the stack of pallets move as one, they pivot on a hinge, revealing the secret hatch to the bunker.

Tyler leads the way, seemingly demonstrating he has been here a time or two. Jensen follows, with Sloan taking up the rear and closing the hatch behind her. The stairwell is steep and narrow, only the soft red glow of the emergency lights illuminating the way.

As all three travel the three stories down into the bunker created by Mason Knight for a purpose just like this one, Jensen can't help but think, *Will this be our tomb? Is this where our final stand will be?* They all reach the bottom, and as if in sync, retrieve their phones, activating the flashlight function. Jensen holds his, showing a hallway that appears to never end. Sloan illuminates the only room visible to her left. It appears to be a gymnasium of some kind. Tyler hunts for something then finds it. Light switches.

The whole underground structure lights up at once. The endless hallway now ending as it curves to the left hundreds of feet away. Halfway down the hallway on the right, there appears to be a full-size kitchen. The gymnasium that Sloan peered into is even bigger than Jensen imagined. It's a football field in length and half as wide. The ceiling appears to stretch up the three stories they descended. It contains targets, like the one Tyler was using at Soteria, along with other training devices

Jensen has never seen before; he can only assume they are to help hone one's skills. In the far-off corner is a weight room that appears to still need assembly, with most of the parts and pieces still in their boxes.

"All right. As you can see, to the left is the training room," Tyler says, pointing, then shifting his attention down the hall. "Down there to the right is the kitchen, and around the bend at the end are the bedrooms and the bathroom."

"Wait, *the* bathroom?" Sloan exclaims, emphasizing the word *the*.

Tyler lets out a slight chuckle. "Mason designed it so that it was as efficient as possible. There are ten bedrooms in total around that corner. The hallway splits, making five rooms on each side of the bathroom, which is in the middle for all the rooms to share. Mason was way ahead of his time apparently and designed a coed, gender-neutral bathroom shower area. Or he was a pervert. We shall never know." Tyler and Jensen smile, but Sloan does not look amused.

"Lovely," says Sloan.

"Let's all get cleaned up and then figure out where we go from here. We are going to need supplies to start off with, and we need to make sure the solar panels are actually working; otherwise, we are going to go through a lot of gas."

The three of them walk down the hallway, passing the kitchen, then turning the corner around the edge of the training area. Halfway down, the hallway bends to the left and splits in two. Tyler continues to follow the hallway to the left while Jensen and Sloan go right.

Jensen stops at the first door he comes to; Sloan travels a little farther, stopping at the third door on the left.

Jensen stops with his hand on the handle, and without looking up, he says, "Sloan, you don't have to say anything back, but I am forever in your debt."

She closes her door without a word. Jensen turns the handle and enters his future.

CHAPTER 19

Jensen tosses and turns all night in the windowless room that he will call his home for the foreseeable future. Every sound echoes through the walls, the plumbing, and the floor. Everything seems to be made of steel. The wall is made from a thick gauge steel, maybe a twelve gauge, not that he knows the difference between twenty gauge to twelve gauge. But when he knocks on it with his knuckles, it feels solid, like it could withstand a significant blast. A blast from a Transcendent, for example. Eyes adjusted to the darkness, he rolls left.

Across from him is another twin-sized mattress sitting atop a steel bedframe. At the end of each bed is a metal table built into the wall and a metal stool built into the ground. It isn't just a bunker; it's like a prison. It looks like a room from a prison documentary he watched once; the only thing missing is the metal toilet with the sink attached to it. Of course, once more people show up looking for salvation—and half a dozen men are showering in the communal shower at the same time—his mind may change.

In a distant room, he can hear a door open and close through the walls—feet walking down the hallway.

"I'm going to have to get something to absorb some of this sound if I'm going to stay here. Like a rug, at least." He throws his legs over the edge of the bed, placing his feet on the cold cement floor.

"Maybe even one of those pictures that show you the outside world to keep people from feeling claustrophobic."

Jensen heads into the hallway and makes his way toward the exit. *Going to need the basics. I can't even brush my teeth this morning,* he thinks. He turns the corner leading to the stairs and spots Tyler and Sloan in the kitchen.

"Found some coffee at least," Tyler says, grabbing another mug from the cabinet.

He pours the cup and hands it to Jensen.

"Anybody else get any sleep last night?" Jensen asks.

They both shake their heads while taking a sip of the still-steaming coffee.

"I felt like I could hear everything that happened in here all night," Sloan says, placing both hands on her mug, trying to warm them up.

"We'll get furniture and stuff to make this place feel more like home once we get settled. Who knows how long we will be here?" Tyler says. "Let's head upstairs and get some fresh air and a plan."

They make their way to the stairs and head up the three flights. Tyler is the first to the hatch, pushing it out of the way and pausing for a second as if there is a threat.

"Good morning. Glad to see you made it safely," he says as he exits.

Sloan is next, followed by Jensen. Jensen sees three individuals staring back, two men and one woman sitting on top of the hood of another old, beat-up car. He recognizes the faces but isn't sure if he's ever met them personally.

Tyler steps forward, shaking one of the guy's hands. "Good to see you, Eric."

Sloan hugs the girl. "Hey, Hannah."

"Eli," Tyler says, throwing a wave at the other guy still sitting on the car.

"How long have you three been sitting out here?" Tyler asks nobody in particular.

"Just a few hours," says Eric. "We didn't want to risk waking you after what has happened. Might've got killed by accident. Itchy trigger fingers and all."

Tyler just nods. "Jensen, not sure if you had time to meet these three before all hell broke loose. That's Eric, Eli, and Hannah." He points to each as he says their names.

Jensen goes down the line, shaking their hands.

"I recognize the faces, but it's good to meet all of you formally," he says.

Eric is the same height as Jensen, brown hair kept clean on the sides with some length at the top. Typical millennial haircut. Tattoos running the length of both forearms. It looks like some obscure art, along with a set of thin-framed glasses hanging from his shirt collar

Eli is a shorter black male, probably around five, six or five, seven. But what he lacks in height, he makes up for in size. His biceps look to be about the size of Jensen's whole leg.

Hannah looks to be about 120 pounds soaking wet, with dirty blond hair and freckles running a race across her face from cheek to cheek. She was definitely not prepared for the fight that ensued. She is leaning against the car now with a dirty torn silk blouse and a skirt that stops midway down her thighs. She is carrying a pair of white strappy high heels, looking more tan than white from a layer of dirt.

Anyone who can fight wearing that is OK in my book, Jensen thinks to himself as he gives her a once-over.

"So, how bad is it?" Sloan asks.

"It's bad. It's all over the news," Eric says, shaking his head. "Soteria has been on every major news channel. They have mentioned your place of work," he says, pointing at Jensen. "And your cousin's place. They have also continually mentioned how there have been eleven people killed in the incident. Some places are even labeling it as a terrorist attack. Some say domestic; some are blaming ISIS. It's absolutely insane."

"Shit. That means the FBI is going to be all over this in about twenty-four hours," Tyler says, shaking his head and shooting Sloan a significant look.

All six stand in silence. "So, what's our game plan then? We definitely need supplies. I couldn't even brush my teeth this morning," Jensen says, breaking the silence.

"Yea, that will be our first plan of attack. We have three cars now, which gives us extra mobility if needed, but let's not plan to go anywhere just yet," says Tyler.

"Have you three heard from anyone else?" Sloan asks.

"I think between the three of us, we've heard from about five others," Eli says. "The only one I know of that is on her way right now is Zoe. I just don't know if she has anyone with her or when she will arrive."

"What about Aiden?" says Jensen.

Silence comes over the newcomers as they all exchange looks.

"Where the hell could he be? I know he wasn't there when we left. I didn't see anybody else in Soteria when we escaped," Jensen says, looking at Sloan.

"I don't know. We were definitely the last ones out of there," she replies.

"OK. Well, keep your ears open and ask anyone else who shows up. I'll take one of the cars and go get an absurd amount of supplies and food to last us a few weeks," Tyler says. "I'll drive west from here to May's Landing. It's about a thirty-minute hike, but it's a smaller town, and I doubt any Empyreans are hanging around there." He looks at Eric. "Wanna ride with?"

"Yea, I'll go," he answers back.

"The rest of you clean up what you can. I know there isn't much, but mainly keep one person up here in case more Knights show up," Tyler smiling at Sloan as he says *Knights*.

Just then Jensen realizes his bike was a part of that whole disaster. The only thing that's going to be his saving grace is the fact that he is one of the world's best procrastinators and never registered his motorcycle. So at least, the feds won't be looking for him. Not yet, anyway.

Tyler leans out of the newest car's passenger seat as Eric starts it up. "Sloan, do us a favor and contact the Philly Boys and the DC Charter. See if they have heard anything on their end. And then see if they will be able to offer up any help when the time comes. This war is going to happen sooner rather than later, and we are going to need all hands on deck if we stand any chance."

Sloan just nods before turning away and pulling her phone from her back pocket.

A thought crosses Jensen's mind, causing him to chase after Tyler and Eric as they back away from the warehouse. Eric sees him running up and hits the brake as Tyler rolls down his window.

"This is going to sound a little strange and maybe unbelievable," Jensen says, bending down and handing Tyler his debit card. "I don't know if that was part of Mason's surveillance on me, but I've won a lot of money in the casinos. I was saving it to get the hell out of here, but I think this is a bigger cause now. Take this. My pin is 4436. It has like a hundred thousand dollars in it or something."

Tyler holds the card and shoots Eric a look. "It has how much?"

"I've been apparently using my ability for three years to win at craps. I've made a lot of money. It's all in my checking account. Pull out as much as you can from the ATM and then use it to buy the food and supplies," says Jensen. "It's not going to make up for what I've caused, but this whole thing is pretty much my fault; I have to help where I can."

Tyler looks at the card then at Jensen. "Look, man. Stop blaming yourself. This was going to happen eventually. You may have sped it up, but this is what we have been preparing years for. And don't listen to Sloan," he says with a smile. "She'll come around eventually, but thanks for the money."

They continue in reverse, turning around and disappearing around the bend.

Jensen turns back to the warehouse, or the bunker, or their new headquarters. Whatever it is, this is where it all begins. And possibly ends. Who knows what this war will bring and who will win? Who may survive, and who may perish? This is the most exciting and terrifying thing Jensen has ever been a part of, but one thing is for sure: he can't wait. He smiles to himself as he walks back.

CHAPTER 20

Tyler and Eric return after a few hours with all the supplies needed to continue the fight. Not that anyone knows when or where the next battle will happen, let alone who is leading it. Tyler was Mason's right-hand man, but nothing prepares you for what he's been thrust into. Nothing prepares you for an underground war against superhumans. Like everyone else who was a part of Mason Knight's group—now being referred to as the Knights, thanks to a very stubborn Sloan—Tyler is lost without Mason. Yes, he returned with food and much-needed supplies to help sustain life in the bunker three stories beneath the earth. But that alone isn't enough to make you a leader, let alone make people look up to you and follow you without question.

It has been a few days, and the bunker has started to fill up with displaced Knights. The count is up to thirteen, including the originals, Jensen, Sloan, and Tyler. Aiden is still missing, and no one has heard or seen anything from him.

The news has been covering what they are now calling a domestic terrorist act nonstop for the last forty-eight hours. Local police, state police, and even the FBI have all gotten involved. Forensics can't find anything that might lead to the explosion that happened at Jensen's work. His coworkers haven't seen him since and have said they think he's dead in multiple interviews. Luke's body was found, stumping police as to the cause of death. Shot with two bullets from the gun found in his possession. The destroyed warehouse that was condemned nearly ten years ago had multiple dead, including one man who, according to autopsy reports, was killed in an *unnatural way*. Eleven people were killed, and no leads. Every witness outside Soteria saw multiple people fleeing the scene before the police's arrival, but they thought they were homeless people setting off fireworks.

Jensen stands in the middle of the vast underground gymnasium, practicing his force ability. Sloan has spent the last few days pushing him, trying to help him find his full potential.

"He has some very natural abilities," Sloan says to Tyler as they stand at the doorway, watching Jensen practice launching himself into the air and then stopping his descent. "But he also has a very long way to go."

"I know. I've seen it too," replies Tyler. "I worked with him yesterday just to see if there was anything to what Mason mentioned. About him being a natural dual wielder."

Sloan nods, studying Jensen.

"He was able to create a small projectile, but it was extremely inaccurate."

"I can see that," Sloan says as Jensen fails to catch himself correctly, landing with a thud that echoes through the room.

"I want you to continue working with him and have him focus primarily on force. He may be our biggest advantage in the war with Liam."

"Will do. So what's our next move?"

"I'm not even sure yet. Mason never prepared me for something like this. I was just another kid off the streets, just like you were. I never thought we would end up fighting for our lives."

Sloan nods, then looks at Tyler. "If you ever want my opinion, let me know. Just realize everyone here is looking to you for guidance, whether you want it or not."

Tyler stares at nothing, in particular, knowing she's right. "All right, go help him out before he hurts himself."

Sloan walks off toward Jensen, leaving Tyler alone with his thoughts.

As she walks up behind Jensen, she releases a small blue wave of force toward his back. Jensen spins, blocking the attack just before it makes contact.

"It is quite fascinating how all of this comes so naturally to you," Sloan says as she nears Jensen.

"What's fascinating is the fact this is even a real thing," he says as he creates a small shield in the palm of his hand resembling a bubble. "Anything about Aiden?"

"Nothing."

Jensen looks at the ground, then back up into Sloan's eyes. "I'm starting to get worried. I don't know him as well as you do, but he doesn't seem like the type that wouldn't reach out."

"Oh, he's not, but we can't risk wandering around the streets looking for him either. We have barely gotten back on our feet as it is, but we will send out some feelers," she answers. "In the meantime, Tyler and I both agree that you have two abilities. Energy and Force. But let's focus just on force to keep from overwhelming you this early in your training."

Jensen nods in agreement.

They spend the next few hours practicing basic force-style attacks, launching themselves into the air while cushioning the landing—shields then defensive moves. And to end it all, Sloan has Jensen focus on picking up and moving small objects within the room, helping him hone his ability to aim more precisely.

"Nicely done," she says. "Let's get out of here. I think we've done enough for today. It's almost time for dinner anyway."

"I appreciate you helping me out with all of this. I know I'm probably not your favorite person here."

Sloan stops walking. "What makes you say that?"

"I don't know. How about the last seven days or so," Jensen says, an awkward laugh escaping his lips.

"I just don't open up easily to people after everything that has happened. I honestly didn't mean much by it. And how would you feel if you spent weeks following some guy around just because someone had a feeling about him?"

"Very true. And you were stuck with Aiden that whole time also. That would make anyone irritated," Jensen says as they reach the kitchen.

Sloan opens the fridge, grabbing two bottles of water and handing one to Jensen.

Jensen opens his mouth to say something but hesitates for a second. Sloan notices.

"What?"

"If you don't mind me asking. What happened that made you so closed off and distant?" Jensen asked hesitantly.

Jensen can see Sloan stop to think about her answer.

She swallows a mouthful of water. "I think it started when my brother was killed three years ago. My brother had the Transcendent gene as well. Our father left us when we were young, and our mom died of an overdose a few years later. We bounced around from foster home to foster home until he was finally old enough to be my legal guardian. He found out about his abilities when he was eighteen, and in turn, I also found out about mine." Sloan takes another sip of water. "Shortly afterward, Mason somehow found us, and essentially took us in, trained us, raised us, loved us. He became like our father at that point. We were with him four years, I think before Mason caught wind of Liam doing something shady up in New York. Something about trafficking arms or something. We never really found out. My brother, Christopher, was caught by Empyreans, and we never saw him again. That was three years ago, and I've never really forgiven myself for not stopping him from going—or at least going with him."

Jensen leans quietly against the kitchen counter, searching for a response. "I don't know what to say. I'm sorry to hear that."

"It's fine. I just try not to let anybody get close anymore because of it, so don't take it personally. I just don't ever want to feel that type of loss again. I was a mess for weeks, and it took Mason a long time to bring me back from the edge."

"No, it's fine. I totally get that. I think I've had the complete opposite life compared to yours. I have never had anyone close to me. I mean, I had Luke, but we were more best friends than family. He always knew I was going to make all the money I needed to leave this place at some point. So much for that now." He takes a breath and continues. "My parents are degenerate gamblers, and I never had any brothers or sisters."

"That's kind of ironic, isn't it? Didn't you do nothing but gamble? Every time I followed you, you were heading into a casino."

Jensen lets out a short laugh. "The difference is I usually came out on top."

"Yea, by cheating."

"Unknowingly, thank you."

Just then, Hannah comes running down the hall, nearly slipping as she makes the turn toward them. She is holding her phone and saying something. Her voice echoes off the metal walls, so it just comes in distorted.

"It's Aiden!" she says as she gets within earshot of Jensen and Sloan.

"What? Where?" they say in unison.

"He's still at Soteria. He wasn't able to escape. He was pinned in one of the rooms, and ever since, there have been cops everywhere for days."

"Where has he been hiding for two days?" Jensen asks.

"He's been translucent, apparently this whole time. He went to leave after all the cops finally left, and now there are Empyreans soldiers everywhere," she says, handing her phone to Sloan so she can read the messages.

"There's no way he can stay invisible much longer; he has to be hungry, tired, and weak. It's not like he can sleep while translucent," Sloan says, handing her phone back. "Come on."

The three of them take off running, climbing the steep staircase that leads outside. Sloan locates Tyler as soon as she exits the bunker.

"Tyler!" Sloan yells as she spots him talking to one of the newcomers named Zoe. "Hannah just got word from Aiden. He never made it out of Soteria, and he has been hiding in plain sight this whole time."

"For two days?" Zoe says, eyes widening. "I'm actually kind of impressed."

"Christ. You two," Tyler says, nodding at Jensen and Sloan. "Take Zoe here and go get him. Zoe is the most skilled Translucent we have, and I have a feeling you're going to need some stealth getting in there."

Zoe walks over to Jensen. "So you're him, huh?"

"Who?" Jensen asks, looking Zoe up and down.

Zoe is the walking definition of punk. She has short dark pink hair spiked up in no particular direction. A chain around her neck, which she more than likely bought from a pet store. She is wearing a worn-out black t-shirt with a band Jensen has never heard of and a pair of faded skinny jeans. Her boots are black and have thick soles that make him wonder if they are still considered platforms or if they are called something else now.

"The one that started this war?" Zoe says with a smile, giving Jensen a quick jab in the ribs with her elbow.

"That's what they say."

"Well, hopefully, you're as good as they say you are; we are going to need it."

The three of them turn and head for the first car they see. Sloan gets behind the wheel, and Jensen rides shotgun, while Zoe sits in the back, looking probably more excited than she should be about going back to the place where they all almost died.

The car accelerates backward, sending Jensen into the dash before he can get his seatbelt on.

"Sorry," Sloan says, giving him a sheepish look.

She spins the wheel, making the car's front end shift 180 degrees, pointing it toward the winding road leading away from their hideaway.

"So, what's the game plan?" Zoe says from the back, leaning forward and letting her elbows rest on the front seats.

No one answers as the car takes a right onto the Longport Somers Point Boulevard, heading back toward Atlantic City, with the sun on the horizon behind them.

The car stayed silent as it raced back to Atlantic City, back to where they all once called home. To where Sloan once felt safe with the person she considered a father, where she watched as he was ripped from her life in the most painful and agonizing way imaginable.

The only sound was the air as it whistled across places in the old car that weren't quite sealed anymore from years of abuse.

The tension in the car increases with its speed. Everyone can feel it, Jensen, especially. It's only been a few days since the attack on Soteria, but some things have changed. People's attitudes have changed. People's demeanors have changed; the way they train has changed. Life has changed. But since that day, Sloan has changed. Something profound and hidden away—Jensen can feel it. Ever since he stopped her from rescuing Mason, it's been like they're connected. Not physically, but emotionally, spiritually. He isn't sure if it's just him or if she can feel it too.

He glances over at Sloan as she races east toward Soteria on Ventor Avenue. The look in her eye is the most serious glare Jensen has ever seen or felt. It looks intense. It looks angry. Worried. She is terrified.

Jensen reaches over, putting his hand gently on her shoulder.

"We won't let another Knight fall, not today. We are going to get Aiden back. I promise."

Sloan glances quickly toward Jensen before adjusting her eyes back to the road; she says nothing in return.

The sun is nearly down; the sky is a dark pink and orange. It's final beams of light glare off the rearview mirror, almost blinding Sloan. She adjusts it to get it away from her eyes.

"Seriously, what's the plan?" Zoe says from the backseat, breaking the silence.

Her question is met with nothing but the growl of the engine from the car.

"Whoa, I got it. Sloan, pull into this strip mall," Zoe says. Sloan slows and does as she's told. "Give me all the cash you have in your pockets."

Sloan pulls into a parking spot and slams the shifter into park before reaching into her pockets. Jensen has already pulled his wallet from his back pocket and is fishing out all the money he has. Jensen holds up a hundred dollars in twenties and a few random ones. Sloan pulls out two twenties and a ten.

"Perfect. I have about fifty myself. Should be plenty for what I want," Zoe says, grabbing the wads of money.

"Wait, what's the plan here?" Jensen says, but Zoe slams the door without answering.

They watch as Zoe runs into an electronics store that sits between a Chinese buffet and a GNC.

A few minutes creep by without a word before Jensen interrupts the silence. "You sure you're OK? I know this has to be hard going back so soon."

"I'll be fine," she responds.

The rear door opens, and Zoe slides in, carrying a bag with a "Hobby-Town" logo on the side. She reaches in, pulling out a box that reads Blade 720 Drone.

Zoe looks up at Jensen and Sloan, who glance at each other in confusion.

"Surveillance," is all she says back.

She opens the box, pulling out a folded-up drone big enough to go in your back pocket. Zoe reaches back into the bag and pulls out a 120-volt wall plug adapter made for a car's cigarette lighter. She connects the drone's charging cable, plugs it into the adapter, then passes it up to Jensen, who plugs it into the car.

"So, what is the plan here exactly?" Sloan asks, looking back at Zoe.

"Well, Hannah said his text mentioned Empyreans around the perimeter of Soteria. As soon as I download this drone's phone app, I'll be able to do some reconnaissance of the area, and we will know what we are up against."

"Interesting," is all Jensen can think to say.

"But we don't have much sunlight left, and this drone doesn't have night vision," she says, looking at Sloan.

Sloan gets the hint, shifting the car into drive, heading out of the parking lot.

A few minutes later, she pulls the car to the curb a block away from what remains of Soteria, and Zoe hops out with the drone in tow.

"I'll be back in a few." Zoe goes transparent and disappears into an alleyway.

"How do you think Aiden has survived this whole time?" Jensen asks, peering through the windshield.

"Only because, next to Zoe, he's one of our best Translucents. But with that said, I'm sure he is on the verge of failure," Sloan says back, turning toward Jensen. "Just think how hard it was to hold up your shield against those two guys; now imagine that for three days."

Sloan drums her fingers on the steering wheel, scanning the area around them for any surprises. Jensen sits in silence beside her. He catches a movement out of the corner of his eye and turns to focus on it. He sees a cat gracefully walking across the open street under the glow of a streetlamp. Suddenly Zoe's face appears out of thin air—not her body, just her face, a foot from Jensen's.

"Jesus Christ, Zoe," Jensen whispers, jumping backward toward Sloan and putting two fingers to his neck, checking his pulse. "You almost gave me a heart attack."

Zoe lets out a chuckle as she slides through the door without needing to open it. "Sorry," she responds. "All right, I spotted three people who looked suspiciously out of place. They were just kind of standing around and walking back and forth around Soteria. I got kind of close to one, and my *Spidey Sense* went off. I'm sure he felt it too, so I got out of there. He's definitely an Empyrean."

Sloan turns to face Zoe. "You have a plan?"

"Yea, that one guy is all alone on one side. He is the only thing standing in my way. You two figure out how to draw him away, and I'll take care of the rest."

"Sounds good. Let's go," Jensen says as the three of them exit the vehicle.

Jensen and Sloan make their way down an alley toward where Zoe said the sentry would be. They stop just short of a wooden gate, and Sloan peers through a hole where a knot in the wood plank must have fallen out years ago.

"Bingo," she says, loudly enough for Jensen to hear.

Jensen moves forward, looking through the fence and spotting the target.

"This is going to sound a little crazy, Jensen, but trust me. You go get him to search for you. Your Transcendent aura is so strong, he is going to feel it way before he feels mine. When he comes looking for you, take him out, and we will be home free."

"Where will you be?"

"Right here on the other side of this fence, in case you screw it up," she says with a smile.

The smile does something to Jensen, almost calming him for some reason.

"Such a vote of confidence," he says as he pulls back the gate and slides through.

Jensen crouch-runs to the fence line, staying in the shadows. He looks over the top at the sentry, just in time to see him perk up about something. Something has grabbed his attention, and Jensen has a feeling he knows what or who it is.

The Empyrean begins walking, turning in each direction, almost as if he is trying to find where the signal is coming from. He stops and stares into the darkness, in the direction of the gate where Sloan was hiding. He steps forward, his long legs taking giant strides, covering twice the distance Jensen would be able to. As he crosses the threshold of the fence, he stops in the middle, between where Jensen is hiding and where Sloan is. A glow starts to appear within the sentry's palm, growing in length. He's created a sword about two feet in length and about four inches in width. The blue hilt presses firmly against his thumb as its curls around it.

Jensen looks back just in time to see the mirage of an invisible Zoe enter through the hole that Sloan created days ago for their escape. *Now is my chance,* Jensen thinks. His plan is simple, or so he thinks. With one hand, he will push the sentry toward the gate, simultaneously holding a force grip over his mouth to keep him from alerting any of the others. *Seems simple enough.*

Jensen puts both hands up, one in a cupping motion, prepared to cover the man's mouth, while his other hand is poised, palm out, for the push. *Now,* he thinks.

He uses his force ability to apply pressure to the sentry's mouth, keeping him from yelling. It's a weird feeling; somehow, he can still feel the man's lips on his hand, even though he is at least six feet away. The man's free hand shoots up to his mouth as he tries to figure out what is on his face. Jensen stands up, pushing with his other hand. The move is simple, but Jensen is not yet skilled enough; he creates two forces with equal pressure that counteract each other. The man stumbles forward. His back is being pushed, but his head is being pulled. He lands with one knee in the dirt, his sword digging deep into the ground, helping him regain his balance. He spins and sees Jensen standing there.

The man stands and steps forward toward Jensen, still unable to make a noise. Jensen redirects his left hand while still covering the man's mouth. Now all the force is going in the same direction. He pushes, but the man digs his heels and sword into the ground. Blue sparks bounce from the man's chest, where Jensen is directing to pressure. He can see the anger building in the man's eyes.

Sloan sees Jensen's struggle, swinging the gate open to assist. With both hands, she grabs the man; with Jensen pushing and her pulling, the man is ripped from the ground. He sails through the now-open gate, landing with a loud thud against the ground. The wind escapes his lungs through his nose, bringing snot and mucus out with it.

He tries to sit up, but Sloan, with Jensen's help, holds him in place. The man's sword lies helpless in his hand along his thigh.

A whistle from a street. They both look up and see a glimmer shifting in the air under the light of a streetlamp. The glimmer is more prominent than usual. Zoe's head and left hand are the only things that appear. She points to the haze next to her and gives a thumbs up before disappearing.

Sloan looks down at their hostage, bringing her hands up as if holding a ball in between her hands. She begins to make a squeezing motion. The man starts struggling under the pressure. A muffled scream escapes around the force on his mouth.

"Stop! What are you doing?" Jensen says in a whisper but with enough anxiety behind it to get Sloan's attention.

"We have to go; I'm taking him out."

"Are you serious? We don't have to just kill him," Jensen says. "We aren't like them; we shouldn't just go around killing people just because we can. How would that make us any different from them? Is this what Mason would have wanted you to do?"

"That's not fair, Jensen."

"This isn't fair," he says, gesturing toward the helpless man under their complete control.

A few seconds pass. "You're right. He wouldn't approve of this," Sloan says, keeping her eyes from meeting Jensen's.

Sloan brings her hand up and pinches the air with her index and thumb. The helpless sentry's eyes widen then close.

"Let's go," she says, taking off toward the car.

"What did you do?" Jensen says, releasing his grip and chasing after her.

"Cut the blood off to his brain for a second. Just like a chokehold without all the wrestling around."

"You're going to have to teach me that. We can use Aiden as a test dummy when he's feeling better."

They both laugh as they drop into the car's bucket seats. They turn, looking into the back. Aiden is lying down with his head on Zoe's lap. He looks beaten, dirty, and weak. Jensen can't even begin to imagine how he feels.

As they again drive silently down Ventor Ave, this time to their new haven, the tone in the air is different. It's brighter, happier than it was. They found their comrade, safe, and sound. Jensen smiles to himself as the wind from the open window pushes his hair around, glad that his friend is OK. He feels a sudden warmth on his hand. Looking down, he sees Sloan's hand. He looks up, his light brown eyes meeting her piercing blues. Nothing is said; nothing has to be said. Her eyes say it all. *Thank you.* Jensen closes his fingers around her hand, holding it firmly but gently, and smiles.

CHAPTER 21

He swirls his scotch around, watching it as it eddies in his glass. The melting cubes of ice bounce off the glass as the current drags them about; they make a clinking sound as they go. The TV's on in the background, a random show from a channel selected by its previous user. The lights from Atlantic City's nightlife shine brightly through the curtains in his room and dance along the walls.

A knock at the door as he puts the glass to his lips. The scotch smells of a fine wood and burns his throat as it travels down. A good burn. He stands, setting the glass down on the dark wood coffee table in front of him with a thud.

As he grabs the doorknob, he feels the goosebumps run up his neck then back down to his shoulders. Transcendents. Empyreans. At least, it better be.

"Riley, how nice to see you again. Come in," Liam says, standing to the side, letting her in.

Riley enters, followed by Luis, then Ezra. Ezra towers over Luis and has to duck slightly to keep from hitting the frame of the door. Liam looks up at the giant as he enters and smiles, glad to have such a monster on his side.

"What's the word?" asks Liam.

"We still haven't found them," Riley says as she glares at Luis, who was beginning to sit on Liam's couch before changing his mind.

"Well, I know they are still here in Atlantic City. I can feel it deep in my bones."

"I agree, sir. In fact, someone was at Mason's old hideout last night."

That piques Liam's interest; he wanders back around the coffee table, bending down to pick up his glass.

"Oh? And why do you say that?"

"One of our men was attacked there right after the sun went down," Riley says as Luis takes his spot behind her, next to Ezra.

"I'm guessing he didn't get a look at the said attacker," Liam says, taking another drink.

Riley looks down at the floor, avoiding eye contact. "No, sir. He knows it was a man and a woman, but it was too dark where he was attacked to get a good view. Said they were two powerful Force Transcendents. Well, at least one. He said one seemed kind of sloppy like he was a newbie."

"Jensen, most likely," Liam mutters.

Riley nods. "That was my guess as well."

"But why would they be going back to that place? The bodies of their dead and their beloved leader were dragged off by the police days ago."

Ezra and Luis stand off to the side, Luis looking around awkwardly as if admiring the room.

"That was very curious. Maybe there was something of value left in the building they were hoping no one found," Riley answers.

"Well, regardless, we are going to be staying here in Atlantic City for the time being. I have already called my chief operating officer for my campaign to let him know I'm down here taking a little *me time*," he says, throwing up air quotes with his fingers. "I have already booked you rooms here in the Hard Rock; just go down and claim your keys."

"Thank you, sir," Riley says, nodding.

Luis smiles, throwing an elbow into Ezra's side with a little too much excitement. Ezra ignores him while Riley again glares at his inappropriate behavior.

Liam stands and finishes the last of his drink before walking to the table near the window, where his bottle of Glenlivet sits. He pours another glass then moves one of the four chairs positioned around the table out of the way, allowing himself to stand closer to the window. The window extends the length of his suite's living room. He takes a free hand and pushes the curtain aside to look out over the water, washing up onto the beach under the lights from the casinos. The Steel Pier is just to the right of his view. The lights glaring up into the sky and back down upon the ocean. Glimmering off the waves like bits of broken glass. The infamous Steel Pier Ferris Wheel spins, taking its passengers up into the air and allowing them the same view he paid thousands of dollars for. A helicopter lands at the helipad just beyond the small roller coaster, dropping off its final tourists of the night.

"It's crazy to think that was almost never seen again," Liam says.

"What's that, sir?" Riley says curiously.

"The pier. That pier," he says, pointing with his empty hand. "The famous Steel Pier, wiped from the face of this planet years ago by a hurricane." He stops to think. "The name of the hurricane escapes me, but I remember thinking that there's no way they are going to spend money to rebuild it. Yet here it stands, better than before."

Riley stands silently, unsure of where he's going with it or even what to say.

Liam turns and looks at Riley, spotting the curious, confused look upon her face. He lets out a short, quick laugh, really just a huff of air escaping his lungs.

"I'm merely just talking out loud, Riley. Just making conversation. It's crazy, though, if you think about it. How something so insignificant as a pier had so much effort, so much money, put back into it when, in the back of everyone's mind, it could happen again at any moment." Liam takes a seat on the couch. "Just shows how the human psyche is so afraid to let go, afraid to change. Really makes me think about how, once I am elected, my fight to allow us to come out to the public will be a long road. That's all I guess I was really getting at."

Riley still says nothing, just nods as a response.

"Anyway," Liam says, reaching forward and sliding a tablet lying on the coffee table closer to himself. He motions for Riley to take a seat next to him. "We need to go on the offensive, I think. I want you to take all of our Translucents and place them around the city in these places." He has brought up a map and points to four locations on the main stretch of Atlantic City. "I want them invisible for as long as they can stand it, taking shifts if they would like, looking for Mason's little minions. I want them waiting for their sixth sense to kick in and then notifying you immediately." Liam places his index finger and thumb together on the screen, then pinching them together, he causes the map to expand by miles. "Then, I want six groups of at least two Empyreans strategically placed around. I was thinking to the south in Cape May, north to Point Pleasant, and west to Philly. We are going to trap them within Atlantic City, that is unless they have already skipped town. But I doubt they have."

"Sir, that is going to reduce our numbers drastically here, severely weakening our potential," Riley says as she takes note.

"I mean, honestly, how strong could they still be? Most of Mason's people were just homeless, leaderless teens who wanted a place to practice their circus tricks. We trap them within here," he says, using his finger to draw a circle around the islands, the bay, and Atlantic City. "And once we find them, we attack. Wiping them out and allowing me to concentrate on what's really important here. Getting elected to the Senate and getting bills passed, allowing us to become the dominant species within the US Government. Then we destroy them from the inside out." Liam's face cracks into a merciless smile.

"You think that will work?" Luis says from across the room.

Riley spins and stares at Luis. Ezra doesn't flinch, as if he's used to Luis being Luis. Liam's smile turns into a laugh.

"That's why I like you, Luis. You don't hold back. Even though that may just get you killed one of these days." Luis's smile fades away as Liam continues. "But, yes, I think it will work. We are quite powerful. If we concentrated hard enough, we could literally wipe this town off the map with a single swipe of our hands. But it's about more than that. It's not just about physical power. It's about catching them off guard. Using what they have against them. Killing them from where they will never expect it. From the inside. And once they can't stop us legally, that's where the fun really begins."

CHAPTER 22

Their weights shift forward as Sloan releases the gas pedal, her foot hovering over the brake. She waves two fingers in the air toward the concealed gate. The bushes tremble then begin to move, opening up the path to the warehouse.

Jensen looks into the back seat; Aiden is still lying on his side. His head resting on Zoe's thigh, rising and falling with each breath. Jensen's eyes flick up to Zoe's.

"He's been out since we started driving. I don't know how he lasted this long," she says.

Jensen is speechless at his friend's willpower. He smiles in response and turns back just as the warehouse appears around the bend. Hannah is sitting on one of the many cars that now line the edge of the woods. As she sees the car, she slides down to her feet; her knees seem weak as she uses her hands to hold herself upright, waiting to see the outcome of Aiden.

Sloan eases on the brake, bringing the car to a stop. Zoe's door opens immediately, and she begins pulling the half-awake, half-unconscious Aiden out. Jensen turns to help, but Hannah is already by Aiden's side.

Zoe and Hannah each throw an arm over their shoulders, pulling Aiden to his feet, helping him walk.

Sloan and Jensen sit silently in the front seat, watching as their friend is helped down the stairs into the bunker for some much-needed rest.

Jensen's mind drifts to Sloan and her touch. At that moment, the warm feeling he had drifts back through his hand and up into his arm. He glances over to Sloan and then down at his hand. It wasn't his imagination; her hand lays on top of his, cupping it gently.

"I just wanted to say thank you out loud. You know, for not letting me kill that guy. Not letting me stoop to the level of the Empyreans," she says in a hushed voice. Before Jensen can answer, she continues. "Sometimes I get caught up with everything that has happened, especially now—my brother, Mason, everyone else that died that day and before. Sometimes I just let my anger take control. You stopped me from making a huge mistake today."

Jensen gives her hand a squeeze, not wanting to ruin the moment by saying something stupid or making another movie quote she wouldn't understand.

"It wasn't that guy's fault that he was led in that direction. Hell, he probably thinks what he is doing is for the greater good, just like we do. I mean, I was almost led that way if it wasn't for Mason and Tyler." She gives his hand a slight tug, making him look at her. "You have been a rock for me these last few days with everything. I know I was kind of cold to you when we first met. I wanted to say thank you, and I'm sorry."

Jensen smiles. "Sloan, you don't have to apologize for anything that you have done. I was a stranger in your house. And there was no way for you to know if I was trustworthy or even the person you were really looking for. Besides, you never gave up on me either, did you," he says with a slight smile. "Even after T and I kept losing you, you knew there was something. You kept trying to get me away from him. Even though you two came on really strong in the casino, you tried to help me out there. You followed me to New York to try and help me and save me from Liam. Who knows what would have happened if you hadn't blown open that door and ripped me from the grasp of Liam's corruption? You saved me."

"I have a slight confession about all of that," Sloan says, a sheepish look on her face. "I didn't really try to save you in New York. When Liam pulled that gun on you, Aiden tried to go in, and I stopped him." Jensen gives her a confused look. "I figured if you died, you would no longer be a danger, and if you survived, we would rush in, which we did." She smiles. "You're welcoooome," Sloan sings.

Jensen's face holds nothing back. His smile vanishes; his jaw falls slack. He's silent for what feels like forever. "Well then, I guess I'll just go hold Aiden's hand then since he's the one who actually cares about me," he says playfully, pulling his hand away as if making a big deal of it.

That's when they hear a dull thud. Looking up, they see Tyler rapping on the hood with his knuckles.

"I need to talk with you two," he says, pointing with his other hand toward the warehouse then walking away.

Jensen and Sloan open their doors in tandem, stepping out and walking toward the warehouse.

"So your Transcendent detection ability can really tell who means you harm and who doesn't?" Sloan asks.

"Yea, it's really strange. Every time I have been around Liam or an Empyrean, it has been like a painful pinching feeling between my shoulder blades. And anytime it's been one of y'all, it's just like a tingling feeling or goosebumps. Like when I first saw you in the casino. I think that's when I first noticed it, but I had no idea what it was."

"We have plenty of rooms for you two to flirt in later. I have something important to talk about," Tyler says as Sloan's and Jensen's faces both turn red. Sloan's a little more than Jensen's.

Tyler reaches underneath a table and pulls out a paper map of the upper east coast. There is one giant red circle around New Jersey, New York, and Pennsylvania's east side. Washington DC is just on the outskirts of the circle's edge. Inside the circle are three smaller circles. Jensen and Sloan both lean forward to see what cities they are on.

"As you can see, I have circled what places I would send my guys to if I was Liam and I was looking for us. If I was him," Tyler says, pointing to each city as he says it, "I would send my people north to New Brunswick, south to Rio Grande just above Cape May, and to pretty much the whole city of Philadelphia. We have been on the run for a few days now, and Liam isn't stupid. He knows most of us are essentially homeless without Soteria."

Jensen and Sloan look at each other, then over their shoulders at the few Knights standing behind them. Their eyes come back to each other as they raise their shoulders and eyebrows as if to say, *He's not wrong.*

"He knows, or he thinks he knows, we probably don't have any money, but thanks to Jensen, that's not true."

Sloan glances at Jensen with curiosity.

"Now you weren't here for me to bump my ideas off of, so I asked the people I sent out personally what they thought and if they are willing to do it," Tyler says.

"Do what?" Sloan says, worried.

"I don't think Liam will be expecting us to have stayed in the area. I think this will catch him off guard. And I have a few sources that say he is staying in the Atlantic City area somewhere. So I sent as many Translucents as we could spare out into the city. They will be on the lookout for any of Liam's men, and they will notify me if and when they do. I know it sounds risky," he says, reading their expressions. "But I think he won't be expecting us here, so his guard may be down. And this place is pretty well secluded; I think it'll be safe for now. Also, if I'm right, and he sends his people out into these cities looking for us, it's going to greatly reduce his fighting capability if it comes down to that."

The look of worry on Jensen's and Sloan's faces lessens, but Tyler can tell Sloan has something she wants to say.

"Go ahead, Sloan," Tyler says.

"What does his fighting capability have to do with anything?"

"That's what I really wanted to talk to you two about. I wanted to get your opinions on something."

"Well, first off, have you heard from the Philly Boys or the DC Charter?" Ty asks.

"Nothing from DC, but Philly texted me back and said they have been having the same type of problem, just not as severe. If we truly need help, they can spare up to eight guys," Sloan says.

"OK, good. Any help is welcome. While we wait for our scouts to report back, we need to practice. We need to train, train, train. If we are going to have any chance of ending this cat-and-mouse game once and for all."

"What are we talking about here?" Jensen says.

"War."

"War? Like between the Empyreans and us?" Sloan asks, standing up in surprise.

"What do you think? Honestly. If we don't put a stop to this, they are just going to continue to come at us. And right now, we have the advantage. They have no idea where we are, but we know almost exactly where they are. If we can find them first and have a solid plan. I think we can end this," Tyler says with some force behind it as if he is trying to motivate his men to leave the safety of their trenches and storm a no-man's land.

Sloan looks at Jensen, then back at Tyler. "As long as we do it smartly and have a plan. I think it may work, but we have to have a solid plan, or a lot of people will never come home."

They both look at Jensen. "I mean, it's not like I have a job anymore," he responds.

CHAPTER 23

It's been ten days since Tyler, Sloan, and Jensen decided to go to war with a future senator and the Empyreans. Tyler held a meeting the day after, talking to Jensen and Sloan about the plan. Everyone agreed that if they were to stand by and wait for something to happen, they would probably suffer a prolonged death instead of taking the fight to them.

It hasn't been very long, but it was long enough for everyone to learn how to be more aggressive with their attacks. And as Mason said, one of Soteria's main purposes was for Transcendents to find out their true potential.

Even though many of their friends had died that tragic day at Soteria, one thing came out as a positive. They saw what the Empyreans could do, and if the Empyreans could do it, so could they. The training was tough. It was grueling. Ten to twelve hours a day, the Knights were in the bunker, training, practicing, finding new moves, and sharing them with one another.

Since his recovery, Aiden has also been helping scout for Liam and his Empyreans, but he has yet to find even a hint of them. Out of all the Knights, Aiden found something very unique, but it wasn't during a scout mission. Aiden and Zoe were practicing a rumor they had heard about being able to use their ability to make others disappear with them. Just as they could do with objects such as walls—but with people. They could make anyone they wanted to become stealth along with them.

While Aiden attempted to turn Zoe translucent with him, something strange happened. Something neither one of them had ever seen or heard of. This was a first for the Translucent community. They couldn't tell anyone, not yet. What if they couldn't replicate it? What if it was just a fluke? What if they had only dreamed it up? No, not yet. They couldn't tell anyone. But soon. Very soon.

Tyler was gathering all the Energy Transcendents together twice a day in the training room to practice new, more powerful techniques. They would go over the ability to fire projectiles across long distances. Working first on accuracy, then on the distance. At first, it led to the paint on the walls becoming charred with burn marks, but after nearly a week of training twice a day, Tyler was leading a squad of very accurate, very deadly Energy Transcendents.

Tyler had also figured out the explosive energy grenade that Mason had talked about a few times. He never practiced with anyone in the training room with him, though. He was still very inexperienced with it; sometimes, it was a very substantial explosion, and sometimes it was like a firecracker.

Jensen always made sure to hang out in the background during Tyler's classes. He knew he could produce energy, even though Sloan and Tyler did not want him working on it. Tyler always saw him, but what was the point in trying to send him away?

Jensen would sit in the back, attempting to make weapons appear in his hand. The best weapon he has been able to produce so far was a blade about the size of a butter knife and about as sharp as one. He never let that sway his training. He continued to push himself. Day after day. Dull knife after dull knife. Jensen even created a projectile once; even if it looked like a firefly floating through the air, it was still made of energy. *Baby steps*, he kept saying.

Where Jensen excelled was in Sloan's two-a-days. The Force Transcendent classes. They worked on creating massive shields on their own and then combining their efforts to create one shield. *Strong enough to stop a bomb*, Sloan kept preaching. They would spar against one another, pushing back as Jensen had done that day at Luke's against Vince. They would push back and forth, trying to knock the other off balance. It helped build their strength and confidence. Allowed them to see what it was like to use their powers for once.

They practiced the ability to shatter bones. They used tree branches instead of one another, of course. They would have run out of test subjects really fast. They practiced seeing the bone, *the branch*, focusing on where they wanted it to break. How they wanted it to break. Did they want a clean snap or to crush it into dust?

Then came the fun part—at least, Jensen found it fun. Flying. Not really flying exactly. More like hovering. At first, they worked on controlling themselves—the ability to hover in one spot. Then moving from point A to point B. Launching themselves into the air and catching themselves just before impact. It became a game. See who could get highest without hitting the ground. Sloan always won, but she didn't count. Jensen always enjoyed working on launching himself into the air. It was borderline flying, as far as he was concerned.

* * *

Jensen can now accurately hit a target across the training room the size of a soda can without disturbing anything around it. His accuracy has greatly improved since the Battle of Soteria, where he knocked over one of his own while attacking an Empyrean.

Jensen gathers up his lunch from the kitchen. A tuna sandwich on a paper plate surrounded by a layer of triangle-shaped tortilla chips. The tuna filling overflowing out onto the chips. A bottle of water was stuffed into his back pocket. He headed up the stairs to try and get a little sun with lunch. Being cooped up in the bunker all the time does strange things to people.

He exits the bunker and spots Aiden, apparently having the same idea as he does. Aiden sits atop the Buick's hood with his back resting against the windshield. Aiden stares into the distance, in the direction of Atlantic City, lost in thought, not seeing Jensen as he approaches.

"Great minds think alike," Jensen says as he reaches the Buick. He slides his plate onto the hood, retrieves the water bottle from his back pocket, and hops up onto the hood, sliding in next to Aiden.

"So, how's training going?" asks Aiden.

"It's not bad. I think I'm a fast learner. But right now, I kind of need to be. What about you?"

"Pretty good. Zoe and I are working on something crazy. I think I almost have it down."

Silence fills the air.

"So...are you just not going to tell me?" Jensen says through a mouthful of tuna.

"No, not yet. I want to make sure I can do it a hundred percent of the time. Don't want to look like an ass."

"In front of Hannah. You meant to say look like an ass in front of Hannah, right?" Jensen says as the corners of his lips curl into a smile.

Aiden's cheeks turn red, and the red travels around to his neck. "What are you talking about, Jensen?"

"Please, I'm not blind."

"How's Sloan?" he says, smiling back.

Jensen laughs, sucking in a chip, which causes him to cough. "I wish," he says, thumping a fist against his chest to clear his throat. "Maybe one of these days, but I think she still has her walls up."

They both sit staring off into the distance, taking bites of their lunch as the highway holds back the silence.

"It's crazy, right?" Aiden says without taking his eyes off a cloud wandering lazily in the sky.

"What is?"

"This situation. I mean, we are technically terrorists, according to the news. I heard we would be on the most-wanted list if they knew any of our names."

"That it is. And one of those so-called terrorists is running for Senate here in a few months," Jensen says

"I hope we can stop him, especially before he gets to a seat that has political power."

"I mean, that is the plan. But so far, we have found nothing."

Aiden rolls his head along the windshield and looks at Jensen. "What do you think they would do to us if they caught us?"

"Who? The Empyreans?"

"No, the government. The police or the FBI. You know, since we are terrorists," Aiden says, rolling his head to study the sky.

"I try not to think about it. Nothing good. I can tell you that. And if they found out about our abilities, it would probably be even worse. Tests. Torture. Who knows, really?" Jensen says.

Silence follows and lasts for minutes. Neither one wants to break it or think about the outcome.

"I'll tell you one thing, though," Jensen says. "What I fear the most out of any of this. It's not being arrested by the FBI or being killed by Liam. What scares me the most is, how are we supposed to fight a war with two groups of people, all with God-like powers, in a city full of thousands, without any innocent civilians getting killed? That's what keeps me up at night."

Aiden nods in agreement.

CHAPTER 24

A warehouse stands in the middle of an urban area, yet no one knows it's even there. Down a hidden staircase so steep it might as well be referred to as a ladder. Three stories down, it's naturally cold; the steel walls leading down the hallway don't help that fact. Down and to the right, a Knight stands in the kitchen, eagerly waiting at the microwave. He continually looks over his shoulder then back at the food.

"Come ooonnn," he says, dragging the last word out impatiently.

"Hey, hurry up! It's about to start!" he hears over his shoulder.

"Come on, damnit," he whispers under his breath. "I'm coming! See if they will wait."

"You know the answer to that."

Ding. The microwave sounds, and he rips open the door and pulls out the steaming bag of popcorn he's been eagerly waiting for. Holding it in between his forefinger and thumb, he races back up the hallway toward the stairs. The bag is steaming; it's burning his fingers, causing him to switch hands.

He arrives. Just before the staircase leading up into the afternoon sky of New Jersey is a door on the right. With some quick footwork, he stops on a dime and heads into the training room. The room is massive. It has to be with the type of training they do in there. The sound of a crowd cheering gets louder as he reaches the spot he left a few minutes ago.

"Just in time. You almost missed it," a man to his right says.

The Knight doesn't respond; he just smiles and folds his legs Indian style. He looks right then bounces his eyes from one corner of the training room to another, finally landing on the last corner. The Knight tastes the first piece of popcorn as he thinks, *Wonder who is going to win.*

Jensen, Sloan, Aiden, and Tyler all stand in a different corner. Jensen is standing awkwardly, trying to figure out what he just got himself into. Aiden, across from him, bounces up and down like a boxer getting ready for a fight, letting his arms swing freely at his hips. Sloan, in another corner, is pacing back and forth like a wild tiger. And in the final corner, Tyler stands, warming up by creating an energy ball in one hand then tossing it to the other.

"Everybody ready?" Tyler yells, his voice bouncing around the stadium.

"Remember, we are only here to test ourselves. Don't pull any punches but don't kill one another," Sloan says as she stops pacing.

Aiden says nothing; he just smiles menacingly. Jensen still stands awkwardly, unsure of himself.

"If you fall and any part of your back touches the ground, you are out," Sloan says loud enough for everyone to hear. "Any questions? No? Go!"

Sloan makes the first move, firing a bright blue wave toward Tyler in the adjacent corner. The wave ripples through the air. Tyler is too slow and gets trapped in the corner by the incoming wave. He brings his right forearm up to his chest, level with the ground. An energy shield resembling an old wooden Viking shield appears. It stands three feet in diameter. He crouches, allowing it to cover most of his body; only his toes are visible. The wave slams into the shield with an ear-shattering crack. Tyler holds his stance but is forced back into the wall.

He comes out swinging once the wave dissipates. The shield vanishes and is replaced with a longbow, clear blue, the bluest thing possible. Three arrows appear across the bow, already nocked and ready to be released. His finger moves out of the way, sending the arrows to their destination. The arrows arc through the air toward Sloan. Sloan pushes off the floor, launching herself into the air and out of harm's way.

Jensen still stands where he began, watching as Tyler and Sloan fight in the distance. They are now running straight at each other. Jensen looks to the corner where Aiden was. He's gone.

"Where the hell?" As he finishes his thought, Aiden appears in front of him.

"There are no friends in this, Jensen," he says.

Aiden drops down, kicking out his leg and sweeping it an inch above the ground in a semicircle. The kick catches Jensen's, ankles causing his head and feet to switch positions. Just before he slams into the ground, he holds his hands out by his waist, feeling the push release from his palms. Jensen stops inches from the ground. Inches from being eliminated.

Jensen uses one hand to push himself back onto his feet while scanning for the tell-tale sign of a Translucent. He sees the glimmer in the air, and with both hands, pushes outward, launching a wave of his own that would give Sloan's a run for its money.

The wave hits the invisible Aiden but only makes him falter slightly since most of it passed right through him.

Aiden redirects himself toward Sloan; Jensen does the same toward Tyler.

"Teammates?" Aiden yells back.

"Why not," Jensen says with a laugh.

"Cheaters," Tyler and Sloan say together.

Sloan fires wave after wave at the incoming Aiden, causing little to no damage. Aiden bounces from left to right. His haze dancing as he dodges each attack.

Tyler fires a beam of energy with both hands toward Jensen, who blocks the attack with his palms. The beams appear to dig into the shield in front of Jensen but never penetrate through. Closer and closer. Jensen is almost to Tyler, but the power pushing against his shield gets stronger with every step he takes. He spins to the left, releasing the shield, and a beam of energy passes harmlessly past him, slamming into the wall.

Aiden allows his hands to revert back to normal, giving Sloan a place to aim, but it's too late. Aiden jabs with his left, connecting with her chin, and swings low and wide with his right, catching her ribs. Sloan's lungs deflate. She drops to one knee, catching herself with her hand. A thump resounds from the crowd. A bubble of blue extends outward in all directions away from Sloan, taking Aiden with it. He never saw it coming. It passes through his body, but his hands are normal. His hands are pulled through the air by the shield pulse. His feet leave the ground, trying to follow his body, following his hands.

Aiden hits the ground with a solid *thump*, his body coming back into view. He's on his side.

"You're out," Sloan says, the words hollow, still trying to recover from the punch.

One down.

Jensen is within striking distance of Tyler. Tyler pulls the same move, spinning to his left, avoiding the telegraphed punch from Jensen. Ty brings a foot up, sinking it into Jensen's gut. Mucus is expelled from Jensen's mouth, along with all the oxygen in his lungs. He stumbles backward into the wall, which probably saves him from elimination.

Tyler gets ready for the ending blow. He brings his hands together and back along his right side like he is trying to hide something from view. A light starts to build within his palms. It grows brighter and brighter. His eyes searching for the perfect place to put the charge.

Sloan runs at full speed toward Tyler's back. She swings an arm horizontally, sending a blue boomerang shape through the air, catching Tyler behind the knees.

He loses his balance; his hands shoot up into the air as he tries to regain his balance. The ball of energy he was holding leaves his hands, launching up into the ceiling. It hits the steel beams with an explosive crack. Sparks fly in every direction, and the sound is deafening.

Tyler pivots on one knee, bringing his other knee up and digging the balls of his feet into the wood floor.

Sloan is at full speed, and there is no stopping her. Tyler takes advantage, using his size and her speed. He pushes off the floor, dropping his shoulder and catching her in the stomach. Her feet leave the ground as she folds around Tyler's torso, landing on her back as Tyler stands above her, smiling down.

"One to go," he says.

Sloan is unable to respond. Her body fails to recover from the hit, her lungs unable to draw in any more air.

Jensen brings one foot up and pushes off the wall toward Tyler. He uses his hands to give himself an extra push, and he sails through the air. Tyler spins just in time to catch Jensen. His abs flex, allowing him to keep what air he has as Jensen spears his midsection. Tyler brings his arms down, wrapping them around Jensen's waist.

Tyler releases a few short jabs into Jensen's side, trying to soften him up. They wrestle, but no one gives way. Jensen works his hands up onto Tyler's stomach, and force pushes, breaking Tyler's grip and creating distance between them.

Neither hesitates. They charge each other. Tyler brings his right arm up, and a dull mace with no spikes appears. It travels in a downward arc; Jensen steps right, holding his left arm up.   The mace glances off a thin shield, and sparks shower around them. Tyler stops and pivots, bringing the mace into a backhand swing. Jensen's left arm comes up. A blue light appears in his palm. The light grows brighter then starts to extend outward. A handle appears, then a hilt; a long, thick blade grows quickly, catching the falling mace and guiding it to the hilt, where it stops.

"What the—" Tyler says, staring at the energy sword in Jensen's hand. "When did you learn that?"

"Apparently, just now."

Tyler's eyes flick downward in time to see Jensen's palm open, emitting light.

"No, it can't...you can't..." Tyler stutters.

The blast of energy shoots out of Jensen's hand, catching Tyler in the chest. He hits the ground back first and slides across the floor into the wall, coming to a stop. The front of Tyler's shirt smolders as it burns away.

Jensen rushes over, patting the shirt to put it out.

"I'm so sorry, Tyler. I didn't mean to use that much power," Jensen says.

Tyler sits up, coughing. "It's fine. It's fine. I can't believe you can already create weapons. I'm impressed. Also, I need to go change."

The four sit outside of the warehouse on the hood of a car, rubbing the wounds they suffered. Reviewing the fight and what they could have done differently. In the distance, they hear fast footsteps pounding the stairs leading out of the bunker. Zoe appears at the entrance with a look of excitement spread across her face.

"We found him!" she yells as soon as she spots them.

"Who? Liam?" Tyler says, sliding off the hood. "Where is he?"

"The Hard Rock Casino. I'm like ninety-five percent positive," she says, coming to a stop a few feet from them. "I recognized a few of his foot soldiers coming out of the casino a few days ago while I was scouting, so I figured I'd hang around for a while. A few hours later, I saw that bitch Riley come out with her two underlings."

"But you didn't see Liam?" Aiden asks.

"No, but there's no way all those people are there without him. There's just no way."

"Well, that's not one hundred percent, but that's something," Tyler says, shooting excited glances at Sloan and Jensen.

"And if he is there, there is no way he's staying in a standard room. Guarantee that he is in one of the penthouse suites that you need a special key for," Sloan says.

"So how the hell do we get in there to prove he's there?" Jensen asks the group.

"Who? In where?" a voice says behind them.

They all turn and spot Hannah exiting the bunker, heading toward them.

"Liam. Zoe thinks he's staying at the Hard Rock Casino," Aiden answers.

"No kidding? My cousin works there. She's a concierge. I could call her if you want," Hannah says, her eyes lighting up with excitement.

"I don't know," says Tyler.

Sloan agrees. "Yea, I don't know how I feel about letting a civilian get that close to Liam on a scout mission. What if he knows it's a trap or something? He wouldn't hesitate to kill her."

"True. But this could be the only in we have," says Aiden.

"Emily?" they hear Hannah say as they turn to her. "You still work at the Hard Rock? Good. Me and my Transcendent friends need a favor."

"Are you kidding me?" Tyler hisses.

Hannah covers the microphone on her phone. "It's fine. She knows what I am and who we are. She's cool."

"Well, I guess that answers that question. So what is the game plan?" Aiden says, looking back at Tyler.

CHAPTER 25

L iam sits on the deep gray couch inside his luxury suite in the Hard Rock Hotel and Casino. Legs crossed with one arm on the armrest, and the other draped on the back of the couch. His fingers drumming away in a rhythmic beat that reminds him of a horse gallop.

It's been well over a week, and he has yet to hear even a single whisper of Mason Knight's people. He's sure there is no way they all escaped the local area around Atlantic City before getting his people out there. There's no way any of them had the money or access to enough cars. Liam even used his connections in the Atlantic City Police Department to put out a BOLO—and yet...nothing.

His eyes drift from the muted TV with a local news channel to the fake wood walls—then up to the off-white ceiling. His eyes stop as his head hits the back-rest of the couch. He stares and stares. He closes his eyes, trying to control the anger inside him; he can feel it boiling. *How have they found nothing?* He thinks. *Not even a hint of a Transcendent anywhere in the city.*

The only Transcendent they have found since he sent out his scouts was in Philadelphia. More than likely part of the Philly Boys Transcendent group. And right now, they are no threat to him. Not yet, anyway. *I'm sure they will be soon enough, especially after I wipe out Mason's followers.*

Liam leans forward, uncrossing his legs and grabbing a half-empty bottle of scotch from the coffee table with one hand and his glass with the other.

A knock at the door.

Leaving the glass behind, he stands and opens the door for Luis.

"Sir, there is a lady out here who wants to speak with you."

"About what?"

"I'm not sure, sir. She says she's the concierge for the hotel," Luis says, glancing down the hall.

Liam glances over his shoulder at the blond lady behind him. A thin petite woman stands dressed finely in a knee-length white skirt, a button-up white t-shirt, a black overcoat tailored to fit her curves. A name tag attached to one of her lapels says, "Emily." She's arranged her hair in a clean bun, showing off her innocent schoolgirl look. She looks up and smiles, holding a clipboard against her chest in one hand and a pair of thin wire-framed glasses in the other.

Liam waits for the goosebumps, the feeling that she is one of them. Wanting for it to happen but not really expecting it to. "Sure, let her in."

She enters the room, followed by Luis. Liam takes his seat on the couch, picking up his glass as he leans back.

"What can I help you with...Emily, is it?" Liam says.

"Yes, sir. Emily," she says, glancing down at her name tag. "I take it you are Mr. Liam Turner?"

"Yes, but please just call me Liam."

"Yes, sir. I just wanted to stop by on behalf of the Hard Rock Hotel and Casino to ensure you are enjoying your stay. It is our honor to have a hopeful future New York senator staying with us. Is there anything we can do to make your stay even better?"

"No, Emily. I am having a wonderful time here; I just wish it wasn't all business and a little more pleasure," he says, glancing down at her figure.

Emily tries her best to ignore the obvious flirtatious look. "Well, if you would like, Liam, we have a list of items we would be glad to help you book. You know, if you are looking to have a little more fun on your trip before you head home."

Liam looks up at the ceiling, thinking long and hard about the proposition.

"What exactly are you offering?" Liam asks, generally curious.

"Well, sir, we offer a list of different activities; some I have even been given authorization to comp for you if you so desire. Let's see here," Emily says, flipping a few pages on her clipboard and wrestling her glasses into place on the bridge of her nose. "Here's the list of activities the casino could comp you. There's the helicopter tour from the Steel Pier. We could charter a fishing boat for you and three friends. And we could offer you four tickets to the Legends in Concert tomorrow night," she flips another page. "Also, you look like a card player. If you would like, we could reserve a spot for you tonight at the high-stakes poker table. Ten thousand dollar buy-in; looks like the pot will be around one hundred and fifty thousand."

Luis lets out a long whistle.

"That is very kind of you. Please, let the casino manager know I appreciate everything."

Liam takes a minute to think about the offer, taking a sip from the scotch and allowing the aroma to fill his nostrils.

"I think I will take that spot at the poker table." He looks at Luis, who is staring at him. "And if my crew wants it..." he gestures to Luis, who is standing behind her. "...they can take the fishing charter out."

"And the concert tickets?" Emily asks.

"Sure, why not. If I don't go, I'm sure I can find someone in my entourage who's interested in it."

"OK, that sounds splendid," Emily says, jotting down everything on a notepad. "I'll send the tickets for the charter and the concert right up. And once I find out the details of the poker game tonight, I'll have someone call up to your room."

"I appreciate everything, Emily," Liam says, standing while pressing his palm against the small of her back and guiding her to the door. "Make sure you give the management my thanks, OK?"

"I will, sir."

The door closes, and Liam returns to his position on the couch. Picking up where he left off with his drink.

"I really appreciate that, sir," Luis says, a massive grin on his face.

Liam looks up with no amusement. "Out."

The smile fades, and Luis backs up toward the door, trying to make as little noise as possible as he exits.

The door closes with the familiar thud of a hotel door.

"I'm surrounded by children," Liam says, placing the cold glass covered in condensation against his forehead.

He looks out the window into the sky above Atlantic City just as one of the helicopter tours travels down the beach at five hundred feet. He finishes the final gulp of scotch and places the glass on the table.

"Well, I might as well have a little fun and enjoy myself while I'm here—before I'm forced to destroy a dozen or so people."

CHAPTER 26

A few days have passed since the reconnaissance mission that was completed by Emily. Tyler still doesn't have too much faith in her, but what other plan is there? No one has seen Liam since he sent out scouts. Zoe has been the only person to catch even a glimpse of an Empyrean.

Even though Tyler doesn't want to admit it to anyone, Emily has done a fantastic job collecting vital information about Liam, his associates, and the hotel itself. She was able to sweet talk one of the casino's maintenance personnel and got her hands on the Hard Rock Hotel schematics.

Upstairs inside the warehouse, Tyler, Sloan, Aiden, Jensen, Zoe, and Hannah all gather around a folding table.

"So what's the plan here, fellas?" Aiden asks, trying to get the meeting started.

"Go over the details again for everyone else, Hannah," Tyler says, directing everyone's attention over to her.

"So Em did a great job scouting that place out for us. Liam is staying in the Roxy Suite. His henchman,

Riley, Luis, and Ezra, are all staying in the Apollo Suites. And the rest are all staying in numerous rooms from the thirty-ninth floor to the forty-first floor," she pauses, looking over her notes. "She counted eight people, including Liam, as she went to his room."

"So we should assume he has at least twelve to fifteen people there with him," Tyler says to everyone.

Zoe speaks next. "And they often wander around the hotel or out onto the boardwalk twice a day, usually for food and to stretch their legs or to just get out of the hotel room. But still, no one has seen Liam out and about."

"Are we sure we can trust your cousin, Hannah?" Tyler asks again.

Hannah rolls her eyes, growing tired of the same question. "Yes, Ty. Em is trustworthy, trust me. She already knows what I...we...are."

"And how does she know that exactly?" Sloan questions.

"She's known since we were little. We grew up together, and she was there when I discovered my ability. She knows about Soteria and about our little *club*," she says, using air quotes. "She even knows about what really happened a few weeks back."

"And how does she know that?" Sloan says, anger clouding her expression.

"Because I told her. Duh. Trust me, she likes to live vicariously through us. She's super jealous that I was the only one between us who can do it."

"I mean, seriously, this is our only lead. Let's see where it gets us," Jensen says.

"What does she know about Liam?" Tyler asks.

"Pretty much everything," Hannah says, shrugging. "I told her he was responsible for the deaths a few weeks ago. I told her what he did to Mason and how he plans on entering the government. Trust me, she is on our side."

Everyone looks at one another with a look of agreement that this may be their only play.

"OK. Well, hopefully, these schematics are also accurate," Tyler says, pressing the home button to bring the tablet to life. He presses on the photo app, bringing up a blueprint marked at the top with Hard Rock Hotel and Casino. "Here are the rooms we know have Empyreans in them," he says, pointing at Liam's, Riley's, Luis's, and Ezra's rooms. He swipes back and forth, showing two other floor plans. "We don't know which rooms the rest of his people are in, but it shouldn't matter too much. The main problem I see is getting him out of his room. We need to get him away from the civilian population. I don't want any unnecessary casualties. Any ideas?"

The group stands in silence.

Tyler breaks the silence. "Look, any idea is better than the one we currently have now. I really don't think there is a plan that will keep people out of harm's way completely. But any plan is better than just sitting here, waiting for him to find us. It will more than likely be a much better outcome for us if we can catch him off guard."

Everyone nods, but still, no one speaks.

"I think we should try and get him on the beach, close to the ocean," Jensen says. "That way, it will help direct people away from the inevitable since there is only one way to go."

Tyler agrees, nodding. "Yea, you're right. That may be the best option from a safety standpoint, but that still doesn't answer the question of how to get him out of his room."

"What if we lure him out? What if we get him to follow one of us?" Sloan asks.

Everyone looks up at Sloan, curiosity on their faces.

"We only have to worry about the top two floors, like you said." She points at Tyler. "So what if we got into his room and made our presence known? I think he would be compelled to chase after us, instead of just sending his people."

Aiden looks at her. "So you want to somehow get past his people, get into his room, annoy him or something, and then get down to the beach? How do you plan on getting out of a room with a dozen Empyreans behind you? Jump out the window?"

"Exactly."

Silence fills the warehouse, then chaos erupts as everyone tries to talk over everyone else.

"Hey! Hey, everyone, shut up!" Tyler yells. "She obviously has a plan to go with that statement. At least, I hope so. Let her talk."

A stillness falls over everyone as they listen, directing their attention to Sloan.

"Like I was saying, all we have to worry about is getting up to his room."

"And then the trip down. I think that's important as well," Aiden jokes.

Sloan's eyes flick over to Aiden. "If I could finish, I think a well-trained Force Transcendent could make that jump. They could jump out and cushion their fall, just like we did leaving Soteria."

"OK, but the difference between the Hard Rock and Soteria is about four hundred feet," Aiden says. "Who do you plan on volunteering for this free fall of doom."

"Me," is all she says.

Everyone stares at her, trying to figure out whether she is kidding, but they all know Sloan doesn't have a funny bone in her body.

"This is insanity, Sloan," says Jensen.

"Look, like you said…" Sloan points at Tyler. "… He probably only has a dozen or so people since the majority of his army is scattered around the tri-state area looking for us. As far as I can guess, he will be in a weakened state, giving us the advantage. We make our presence known; we get back down to ground level, draw him to the beach, and make our final stand there, where the rest of you will be waiting for him."

Jensen speaks up. "OK, say that the whole thing goes according to plan. Say you cushion your fall; Liam follows you out, and we start fighting for our lives. How the hell do you get up there in the first place and make it past a dozen Empyreans without being caught or killed?"

Aiden smiles. "I may have a solution to that."

"What do you mean? What solution?" Jensen says.

Still smiling, Aiden replies, "It happened a little over a week ago. Pretty much when we all started training like our lives depended on it.

"Because our lives do depend on it," says Sloan.

"Right. Anyway, it was a complete accident. Zoe and I were working on being able to make others become translucent along with us. Non-Translucents invisible."

Tyler and Jensen look over at Zoe, who is smiling ear to ear, paying no mind to them.

"Wait," Jensen says, holding up his hands. "You can make anyone invisible along with you now?"

"Well, yes, but I'll get to that. This is much better."

"What's better than that?" Jensen asks.

"What's better than that?" Aiden says. "I'll show you."

Aiden steps away from the table, gesturing the others out of his way to create a path.

"Just in case something goes wrong," he laughs, moving Hannah safely out of the way and giving her a wink as he does it.

"OK. Now watch closely because it happens fast." Aiden kneels down into the position of an Olympic sprinter.

Jensen, who is standing off to Aiden's left, looks up at Tyler and shrugs.

"Hey! Eyes on me. I told you this is going to be over in the blink of an eye."

Jensen says nothing and returns his attention back to Aiden. Aiden pushes his fingers into the ground, his knuckles turning white, and his back foot twists back and forth as he tries to get more traction. His front foot starts to move; his shoe's heel breaks contact with the cement floor of the warehouse.

A small popping noise echoes through the warehouse as if someone just popped a piece of bubble gum. Aiden vanishes, as a soft breeze hits the crowd. Jensen's hair moves ever so slightly, and before it settles, in less than a second, Aiden appears at the end of the warehouse as another pop echoes through the air.

Silence follows. No one says a word; everyone just looks from one person to the next.

"Did you just teleport?" Jensen finally says in a whisper—as if he is afraid to sound like a lunatic.

Pop! Then another. Aiden is now standing right next to Jensen.

"What was that?" Aiden asks.

"Did you just teleport?" he says again.

"Sort of. Zoe thinks that I am breaking down my atoms even more than I already could when we go invisible. But they are being broken down, even more, allowing me to move faster than sound."

"Because he no longer has any wind resistance and is running at terminal velocity," Zoe says from behind the crowd. "Or at least, those are my thoughts on what's happening. That's why we've been referring to it as going subsonic."

"When I *teleport*—or go subsonic, as we like to call it—I am actually still running normally, but everything else is slowed down," Aiden says. "I haven't quite perfected it yet."

"You say you've been able to do this for about a week?" Tyler asks.

"Roughly."

"Can any of the other Translucents do it?" asks Sloan.

"Not yet, but we will get there. We have been concentrating on just Aiden, so at least one of us can do it. And as soon as he perfects it, he'll teach the rest of us," Zoe says.

"So I'll be the one to ask," Tyler says. "How does that help us with our current issue of getting into Liam's room?"

"I'm so glad you asked," Aiden says as he steps closer to Jensen. "Now, I haven't quite perfected that, but I have perfected this." Aiden brings up his arm; he goes translucent and then touches Jensen's shoulder.

Gasps fill the warehouse as Jensen stands next to Aiden, confused. Jensen looks to his left; Aiden is invisible. The only tell-tale sign that he's still there is the distortion in the air where he still stands. Jensen looks down to see that he, too, is just a wavy image floating in the air. The shock causes Jensen to jump back, breaking Aiden's grip on his shoulder and bringing him back to his full normal self.

"You really can make others Translucent with you!" Jensen exclaims, patting himself down to make sure he's still whole.

"Who else can make others translucent?" asks Tyler.

"Just Aiden and I so far," Zoe says.

"Oh, that's not it," says Aiden as he puts his arm over Jensen's shoulder.

A louder pop strikes the group's ears as both Aiden and Jensen vanish; half a second later, Aiden and Jensen reappear half the distance Aiden had traveled before.

"Wait. What?" Jensen says, trying to regain his balance. "That was weird. I don't like that."

"Like I said, I haven't perfected it yet, and I have a hard time bringing people with me. It really wears me out right now. But when I first started doing it, I could barely get two feet."

"This is really incredible, Aiden. It truly is," says Tyler. "But I fail to see how this helps our current situation."

"If I can perfect it, I will be able to subsonic myself and Sloan down the hallway and into his room without having to fight a single person."

"I don't even know if I can stop myself from falling four hundred feet, and now you think I can stop both of us?" Sloan questions.

"Well, if you can't, you better start practicing. Because if anyone can do it, it's going to be you," Aiden says with his smile still painted across his face.

Sloan shakes her head. "This is insanity."

Tyler says, "All right, let's all take a break and think on this. Especially you two." He points at Sloan and Aiden. "Since you will be the ones risking your lives."

* * *

Jensen walks down the steps leading into the bunker, following the line of people, Sloan leading the way. Sloan continues straight down the hall toward the bedrooms. Jensen turns right into the training facility to work on some of his abilities. He obviously needs to practice cushioning his falls. Launching himself into the air is the easy part. Stopping himself from hitting the ground too hard and twisting an ankle or worse is the hard part.

He starts off with a few force pushes, knocking over some practice dummies in the distance, then creating a shield in a ten-foot diameter around himself. He pushes himself harder, trying to create a bigger, stronger shield. The glow of the energy around him grows brighter and brighter. He can feel the energy flowing through and out of his body.

To think, a few weeks ago, he was just another ordinary person. He keeps pushing the shield harder until it fails, making a cracking noise that reminds him of a piece of wood splitting. Sparks rain down around him.

Next, he holds his hands at his hips, palms facing outward. They begin to glow, white at first, then a dark blue, and finally a lighter bright blue. A handle appears; he wraps his fingers around it. A hilt forms up against the top of his forefinger and thumb. The blades start to grow. Slowly at first, then it shoots out as if shot from his wrist. They reach their full extension with enough force to sway his arms.

Jensen waves them around, amazed at the weightlessness of them. He walks over to a metal target, striking it once with each sword. Sparks explode and rain around him. Two black marks scar the target's center, creating an X.

He holds the swords parallel with the ground, bringing them together; they begin to glow then start to merge. The weapons move and shift in his grasp, growing in length. The weapon finishes in the shape of a spear. The same spear he saw Mason wield before he was struck down.

He lets go of the spear, allowing it to fall with gravity and watches as it turns back into nothing, as it once was.

Jensen finishes his personal training session with the one thing he has neglected since he became a Transcendent. Jumping and stopping his fall. He practices over and over, pushing himself farther and higher into the air.

He starts off small, only going up twenty feet. By the end, he is nearly hitting the three-story ceiling with some attempts. With each attempt, he grows in confidence. Launching himself into the air, falling, and then cushioning his landing.

"One more," he says to no one.

He builds up the energy inside, feeling it and pushing it out through his palms. This explosive leap is more potent than any of the others. He travels upward faster than he expected, hitting the ceiling with more force than he wanted. Using his hands to soften the collision. Jensen falls at an odd angle, catching himself a meter from the ground. But still, it wasn't enough to keep him from injury. His left ankle hits first, taking the brunt of the impact. Collapsing and rolling onto his back, he allows a silent expletive to escape his lips as he grabs his ankle.

Sitting up, he examines his leg, his ankle, then finally his foot, making sure nothing is broken, which he didn't really expect given his new unleashed mutation. Standing, he slowly puts pressure on his left leg, feeling a sting rise up through it. *It'll be healed by tomorrow, I'm sure*, he thinks as he hobbles out of the training room.

As he enters the hallway, Jensen's neck tingles. Goosebumps shoot up and down his back, so strong he arches slightly from it.

"What was that?"

He has felt his sixth sense many times at this point. But this time was different; this time didn't feel like a friend or foe warning. This felt personal. It hits him again, this time almost directing him. Pushing him in the direction of it.

Jensen can't quite explain it. It isn't dangerous; it isn't joyful; it's misery. Somebody is in pain.

He rushes into the bathroom, looking everywhere as he enters—no one in sight. In the distance, he hears the distinct sound of water splashing onto the floor. The pain he feels is coming from the coed shower area. He picks up the pace as the strange feeling runs a marathon up and down his back.

He passes between the rows of bathroom stalls and the sinks lining the walls. He does a quick glance beneath the doors of the stalls and sees no feet.

"Where are you?" whispering to himself.

Jensen reaches the double-wide door leading into the open bay shower area. It has always reminded him of a typical shower room in a military movie or in the cult classic *Starship Troopers*. Six pillars running up from the floor to the ceiling in two rows of three with multiple shower heads wrapping around them. No sense of privacy here, and you get really comfortable with your body really quickly when you live in the bunker.

As Jensen enters the room, he scans left to right, looking for someone injured or in pain. He sees nothing, following the sound of water raining onto the tile floor. He tracks it to the back-right pillar. He sees the shower head running right before he spots Sloan.

His eyes fall to Sloan as she sits naked on the floor, her knees pulled up to her bare chest, her arms wrapped around them. Her head is buried into the crook of her elbows; the water runs along with her hair to her body. The fluorescent light from the bathroom reflects off the water as it travels down her. She looks up at the sound of him enter, and even with all the water on her face, he can still tell she's been crying. Her mascara is done running, any lipstick she had on is now just a memory, and her face is still beautiful but plain from the lack of makeup.

Her face twists with agony dropping back into her arms. Jensen rushes over, dropping to his knees to help in any way he can.

"Sloan, what's wrong? What happened?"

She tries to speak but can't make her words work. She releases her hold on her knees, wrapping her thin arms around Jensen's neck, pulling him in close. Her lips press into his; they are warm and supple. Her emotions flood Jensen's mind; her pain becomes his—her loss and her happiness now his. She misses Mason and fears the thought of what may happen to the rest of them. To Tyler, to Aiden, and to the person she loves most of all. Him.

He wraps her up in his arms, the water from the shower soaking through his clothes, making them heavy against his skin. He pulls her in close, and her soft, warm skin feels soothing against his. Their kisses become firm and passionate.

Jensen loses himself; his mind races with thoughts and feelings from her mind as well as his.

CHAPTER 27

A week has passed. Their training has gotten more intense as their plan has started to come together. Sloan and Aiden work every day on their suicidal plan to get in and out of Liam's hotel room. The news reports of the attacks have started to die off, without any leads to follow. And Jensen has never been happier.

He opens his eyes and lies motionless under the covers. Watching her shoulders rise and fall with every breath. *How did I get to this point?* He thinks as his and her breathing synchronize.

Jensen sits up on an elbow, leaning forward slightly to kiss the back of her head before sliding his legs out from underneath the covers. Throwing on a shirt and a pair of gym shorts, he slips on his flip flops and heads to the kitchen to start his morning ritual of coffee.

From down the hall, a buzz of conversations echoes toward him. A crowd has formed in the kitchen, looking excited about something. Jensen grabs a mug from the drying rack before stepping over to the coffee pot.

"What's going on?" he asks no one in particular.

"Eli's a turncoat," Eric says.

"A turncoat? You mean, like he's a traitor?"

"Yea. That son of a bitch. It's amazing we haven't been attacked yet," Zoe says.

Jensen can't believe what he's hearing. "Eli has been with us since the attack on Soteria almost three weeks ago. Why would he turn now?"

Eric shrugs as he answers, "Who knows? But Tyler is upstairs, attempting to find out what he's told Liam, if anything, as we speak."

Jensen sets the mug down without filling it up and starts toward the stairs at a slow jog, the group from the kitchen in tow.

They climb the stairs leading out into the warehouse in record time. Jensen pushes the hatch out of the way, turning as soon as he exits, just in time to see Tyler's fist connect with Eli's chin.

"Whoa! Wait for a second, Ty!" Jensen yells as he runs toward the huge group surrounding Eli and Tyler.

"What? This guy is a narc," Tyler says as he turns to deliver another punch.

Jensen grabs Tyler's arm as it begins to travel forward to send another blow.

"Do we have any proof? How do you know?"

"Heard him on the phone talking to someone named Luis," Tyler says, shooting Jensen a furious look.

"He's an old family friend, asshole," Eli splutters as he spits blood from his mouth onto the floor beside him.

"Liar. He was talking in code, and as soon as he saw me, he hung up," Tyler says.

Jensen looks at Eli then at Tyler. "I don't know, Ty; this all seems circumstantial. Also, he's a Translucent.

Wouldn't he be able to just slide right out of those restraints and leave if he wanted?"

"I have Hannah holding him in place right now until we figure this out."

Jensen looks over and finally notices Hannah, whose hand is perched slightly upward by her hip.

"I'm sorry, Tyler, I can't allow this until we have undeniable proof."

"You can find out which side he is actually on, Jensen." Everyone turns to see Sloan exiting the hatch.

"What are you talking about?" Aiden asks.

"Jensen. He has the ability to feel people's emotions, their feelings, their inner thoughts if he wants."

A confused look falls upon Jensen's face.

Sloan reaches the crowd and approaches Jensen. "Babe, it's true. It's one of the reasons Mason wanted to keep you from Liam. We never felt the need to tell you. There was no need to," she says, taking one of his hands in hers. "You are just like Liam in more ways than you would like to admit."

Chatter within the crowd begins to rise. The noise begins to drown out everything around them. Jensen's mind races; he doesn't know what to believe at this point.

"Remember when he unlocked your ability? Remember when he touched his hands to you? You possess the same ability. I know you have felt it. That's how you can tell if someone means you harm or not. How you can sense an attack coming. How you knew something was wrong with me that day."

"You've never told me..." Jensen's voice trails off.

"I didn't want to scare you. You are just like Liam in so many ways. You even have the natural ability to wield two powers without any training—even if you are very terrible at one of them."

Jensen allows a smile to spread across his face.

Sloan smiles back. "If you don't believe me, you can test it. Remember, when Liam took control of your body, how you were unable to move?" Jensen nods slowly. "You should be able to do that. And if you can do that, you can look into his mind, feel his thoughts, feel his emotions, tell if he's a liar and a traitor."

The crowd grows silent; the only sound is Eli's heavy breathing as he struggles against Hannah.

"Just give it a shot, Jen," Aiden says.

Jensen shoots him a furious look for using that nickname. He turns back to Sloan. His eyes say it all. He turns to Eli, giving him an apologetic look as he raises his right hand.

"What are you doing, man? Easy! You don't know how to control your powers yet!" Eli yells as he struggles.

"Concentrate," Sloan whispers. "I know you can."

Jensen's arm goes limp and falls to his side. "This is dumb. I feel ridiculous."

Sloan looks at Tyler and gives him a look as if they can read each other's minds. Without missing a beat, Tyler begins corralling the crowd of people away from Eli—except for Aiden and Hannah.

Sloan takes Jensen's chin between her thumb and forefinger, shifting his gaze away from the group and back to her.

"You trust me, right?"

"Of course I do," he says back to her.

"Good, you better. Now I believe in you, so believe in yourself. You can do this. If you could feel my emotions like you told me you could that day in the shower, then you can do this. Try actually putting your hands on him; maybe you aren't strong enough yet to control someone without touching them."

Jensen approaches Eli, a wave of guilt washing over him. As he steps behind him, placing his hands upon his shoulders, he leans down and whispers into Eli's ear, "Sorry about this, Eli."

"Go to hell," Eli responds with disgust.

Jensen grips his shoulders and closes his eyes. He sees nothing but the blackness from his eyelids. Then a small blue dot begins to appear, growing in size; his hands tighten on Eli's shoulders, causing Eli to writhe within his grasp. The glow fades and starts to take form, and a few seconds go by before Jensen realizes what he is seeing. The shape is of a human skeletal system, Eli's skeletal system. Just like when he fought that Empyrean soldier in Soteria, but this time, it is more than only a hand. Soon veins fill in around the skeleton, then nerves. It is a road map of the human body.

Jensen's eyes open wide, and his grip loosens. The image fades into nothing as he steps back.

"What the hell?" he says to himself as he looks down at his hands, expecting to see something.

"What? What'd you see?" Aiden asks.

"Everything. I saw everything. I could tell you he broke his left arm at some point in his life. I could tell his left leg is slightly longer than his right. He has a fractured rib—recently probably, from the battle in Soteria or from Tyler." He continues to look at his empty palms.

Sloan places a hand within Jensen's. "I told you. You can do this; believe in yourself."

He steps forward, placing his hand on Eli's shoulders once more. His eyelids fall; the skeleton appears, faster this time. Jensen concentrates, thinking of the right hand, *the right hand only*. The vision zooms in, focusing on the right hand of Eli. In his mind, he begins turning the handover, making the palm face upward.

"No way," he hears Aiden say.

Jensen opens his eyes to see Eli's hand rotating just as he wanted it to.

"This is unbelievable," Jensen says.

Keeping his eyes open now, he thinks hard about what he wants the hand to do next. The hand bends upward at the wrist. *Now the fingers*. The fingers curl inward, making a fist. *And the final touch*. The middle finger extends.

"Nice, very mature Jensen," Aiden says.

"Just a test," Jensen says, grinning.

Jensen removes his hands from Eli's shoulders. Eli's hand falls limp as he is given control once again. Jensen brings his hands up, placing two fingers on each side of Eli's temples.

They both go rigid as if struck by lightning. Jensen's eyes spring open; his irises are no longer brown with a hint of gold. The brown of his eyes has been replaced with a blueish gray cloud swirling around his pupil.

The group watches as Jensen's eyes wander, continually looking, as if searching for something and not finding it. It reminds Sloan of someone who's asleep and has entered the rapid eye movement phase—but with their eyes open.

"He's on the phone. I don't know who with," Jensen says suddenly. His eyes stop moving as if finally finding what he's been searching for.

Jensen watches as the blueish gray image of Eli walks around the same warehouse they are in now, talking into his phone. His mouth is moving, but Jensen hears nothing. Eli's image brings the phone away from his ear, and Jensen steps forward to look at the screen. He looks over the blue mirage of Eli's shoulder at his phone, seeing a timer of how long the call was with one word above it: *Riley*.

"He was talking to Riley. I just don't know when," he says as the image in front of him fades, and his eyes begin searching for something new. He searches and searches. Unsure of what he is supposed to be looking for. Suddenly stopping.

This time, it is as if he's inside of Eli's head, seeing what he saw. It's the fork in the hallway leading to the bedrooms. He takes the right side, stopping at Sloan's door. He watches from Eli's point of view as Eli goes transparent and passes through the door with ease. In front of him lie Sloan and himself asleep in bed. Jensen can see the outline of their bodies against the sheets.

"The son of a bitch was watching us sleep." The image passes back through the doorway and into the hallway. Jensen watches as Eli retrieves his smartphone from his pocket, using his thumbprint to unlock it. His thumb taps on the messaging app, types Riley in the contact line, then writes the message, *I'm ready.*

Jensen releases his touch on Eli; the swirling in his eyes fades back to a steady brown. His heart beats like a drum, his breathing labored as if he just finished jogging.

"Get his phone; it should be in his right front pocket."

Sloan finds it then presses the home button.

"It's locked," she says.

Jensen grabs Eli's shoulder, and the same hand he moved before curls into a fist. The thumb extends like a hitchhiker's. Sloan immediately understands without Jensen having to say anything. She places the home button against his thumb, unlocking it.

"Look at his messages," Jensen says as he releases Eli.

Sloan presses the app and scans the contacts, finding the one she was looking for. She taps the screen where it says Riley.

"The last message to Riley was sent today about two hours ago. All it says is 'I'm ready.'"

Tyler steps forward to see the screen better. "We've got to go, and I mean right now. Aiden, go get everyone; we have to get out of here now. It's a thirty-minute drive from the Hard Rock to here on a good day. Grab only the necessities. Money, phones, credit cards. There is no time to pack anything!" Tyler yells. "Sloan, take care of Eli."

Sloan points her right hand toward Eli in the shape of a C. Eli begins to cough as he struggles to fill his lungs with air. His lips have turned a shade of blue in seconds, and the color has faded from his face. Within seconds, his eyes close, and his head falls limp. Sloan steps forward, placing her first two fingers against his neck.

She looks up at Jensen. "Don't worry. He's still alive."

The hatch leading down into the bunker springs open, and a herd of people file out—one after the other, carrying only what they could grab as they left.

Tyler does a quick headcount, ensuring everyone is there, and no one is about to be left behind.

"All right, everyone is accounted for. We have little to no time." Tyler is cut off by the sound of a bell ringing from his back pocket. He retrieves his phone, glancing at the message displayed on the home screen. "We have even less time. The front gate was just activated. Someone is already here. Everyone into the tree line. Now!"

The group turns and scatters into the overgrown woods.

"Head for the water!" Tyler shouts as they make a run for it. "Aiden, Zoe, you two take the group to the water's edge and then travel east. You will come to a clearing. There you will set up a defensive line and wait for us. If we aren't there in thirty minutes, assume the worst and get as far away from here as possible. Understand?"

They both nod in unison as they turn, chasing after the rest of them. Tyler whistles toward Jensen and Sloan just as two cars round the bend, heading to the warehouse. They shuffle over to where Tyler is hiding, making sure to stay low, not wanting to give away their position just yet. No one says a word; they watch as the two blacked-tinted Lincolns roll to a stop with a dust cloud trailing behind them.

"What's the plan?" Sloan says as she continues to peer through a gap in the bush, hiding their position.

"Let's see how many there are first," Tyler says.

The dust cloud settles as all eight doors open in unison as if the passengers practiced it. Eight people emerge from the Lincolns. They begin to spread out, looking for something or someone.

"There's only one way out of this," Tyler says.

Jensen drops down onto his haunches, taking his eyes off the eight people and looking at Tyler. "Unfortunately, I agree. Spread-out?"

Tyler nods. "Jensen, you stay here. Sloan, go right, and I'll go left. We will go on my signal. Understood?" They nod back at him as Sloan turns to take her position.

Jensen watches as Sloan as Tyler head off in their respective directions, keeping low, trying not to silhouette themselves with the sun at their backs. *Eight versus three*, he thinks as he looks back through another gap toward the trespassers. His mind races with thoughts and scenarios. *Have I trained hard enough? Could I have trained harder? Will this be enough to stop them? Is this how it ends? After everything we have done to prepare, this is it.*

He can feel his heart beginning to race. His palms start to sweat, so he wipes his hands against his jeans. He looks up to see Tyler in position; he looks right and sees the shadowy figure of Sloan leaning with her back against a tree. *This is it.* He looks back to Tyler, waiting on the signal.

Tyler and Jensen make eye contact; Jensen gives him a thumbs up. Tyler shifts his focus to where Sloan is. He holds up three fingers. Two fingers. One finger. He starts to stand as the last finger falls into place.

Jensen doesn't hesitate; he stands along with Tyler, letting the buildup in his chest grow. He assumes Sloan is doing the same, not taking his eyes off the eight individuals who stand before him. The pressure continues to build, and he pulls his right arm back like an Olympian about to launch a shot put.

He glances at Tyler, then at Sloan; both are stepping forward, getting ready to unleash whatever power they have. Jensen's hands shake with anticipation, wanting to be relieved of the energy it has stored within it. Now is the time. Jensen brings his hand forward, stepping with it like a pitcher on a mound.

"Hey, Ty! Where you at, fool?" says one of the eight. The man is a very tall black man dressed in jeans and a green-striped button-up with the sleeves rolled up to his elbow.

Did he just call Tyler's name? Jensen thinks as he tries to stop his attack, but it's too late. He glances in Tyler's direction as a smile forms on Tyler's face; his hands, which were ready to fire energy projectiles, fall to his side. Jensen looks toward Sloan as she steps out from her hiding place.

But it's too late for Jensen; he is past the point of no return. He has never practiced this before; he has never had to stop mid-attack. His arm continues pushing his hand forward. A bright glow starts to appear from his palm.

"Elias?" Jensen hears Tyler say.

The ground shakes, and bushes around Jensen bend away from the force. Bark from the tree next to him peels away as the edge of his attack passes. The wave of power kicks dust into the air as it barrels toward Elias. The blue surge heads for its intended victim, it thunders, echoing in the distance and alerting him of the danger.

At the last possible second, he throws up a hand, creating a shield. Jensen's attack hits the shield with enough force to throw the two-hundred-and-twenty-pound man he now knows as Elias into his car door. Part of the attack misses Elias's shield and impacts the side of the Lincoln. The windows shatter with ease, the side crumbles, and the front left wheel snaps off, falling limply to the side.

"Sorry," is all Jensen can get out as the wave finally dissipates with a trail of destruction in its wake.

The person next to Elias helps him up as he looks from Jensen to Tyler back to Jensen. The smile that spread across Tyler's face has been replaced by a look of shock.

"Good God, man," Elias says as he gets back to his feet. "You could've killed me."

"I know. I'm so sorry. I tried to stop it, but to be honest, I haven't exactly trained for that," says Jensen as he jogs over.

"No, you're good. That's exactly what we need in this war. Next time, just aim it at the right person, will ya?" he says, dusting himself off before sticking out a hand for Jensen to shake.

Jensen takes his hand. "Jensen Atwood."

"Elias. So you're Jensen. The whole cause of this mess. Good to meet you. And these are the Philly Boys—well...and girls," he says, gesturing to the seven Transcendents standing behind him.

"Good to see you, Elias," Tyler says as he approaches, throwing his arms around him for a hug. "This isn't going to be easy or fun."

"As long as he brings that kind of power with him to the fight, I think we will be OK," he says, shooting a smile in Jensen's direction.

CHAPTER 28

The enormous man named Elias from Philadelphia, who is a part of the group known as the Philly Boys brought a decent group for the war. Elias is an obvious Force Transcendent; along with him are four men and three women. Two of the men are Force, and two are Energy Transcendents. On the women's side, they are split equally across with power. One Translucent, one Energy, and one Force. With their eight and the Knights' thirteen, their force will rival what Liam has in Atlantic City currently.

While Tyler walks around, shaking the hands of the few Philly Boys he doesn't know and hugging the ones he does, Jensen makes a phone call to Aiden.

Jensen holds the phone to his ear as it rings over and over before going to voicemail.

"Come on, Aiden," he says as he looks at the screen, pressing the red phone icon to end the call. He presses the green phone icon twice to redial the last number and again to initiate the call. Aiden's name appears on the screen as Jensen attempts a second time.

"Hello?" Aiden's voice says, at almost a whisper. "Did you already kill them?"

"No. Well, almost one, but that's beside the point. It's the Philly Boys; they came to help."

Aiden lets out a short laugh. "Tell me you almost took out Elias."

"Just get everybody back here, will you?" he replies.

"You did, didn't you?" Aiden says, still laughing as he hangs up the phone.

As the line goes dead, he hears Aiden beginning to yell out to everyone that it was a false alarm. Jensen slides the phone into his pocket and walks over to rejoin Tyler, Sloan, and Elias.

"How's it going, Jensen. I'm Elias. I've heard a lot about you for the last few months from Mason." Elias turns to Sloan. "My condolences, by the way, Sloan. I know he was like a father to you. We'll get that bastard."

"Thanks," Sloan says back as Elias throws one arm around her shoulder, pulling her close in a sideways hug.

"So, Ty, what exactly is the plan here? We just going to go in, guns blazing, and take that son of a bitch out?" Elias asks.

"I wish it were that simple. We will wait for Aiden to get back. Part of the plan you won't believe unless you see it for yourself; trust me."

A few minutes go by as they wait for the rest of the Knights to return from their tactical retreat into the marshland. While they wait, Elias, Sloan, and Tyler reminisce about things they did with Mason and events that happened way before Jensen even knew what a

Transcendent was. Jensen hangs back, leaning against the damaged car.

Elias walks over to Jensen. "Heard you have a natural ability like Liam. You were even able to move Eli against his will and to see into his memory."

"Sounds crazy when you say it out loud," Jensen says.

"Yea, it does. This whole world is a crazy ride. I'm just glad you're on our side."

A rustling in the trees grabs everyone's attention as Aiden, and the others start to file out. Friendly faces are smiling as they recognize friends from another group, just like theirs. People yell and wave back and forth as they approach.

Aiden turns and does a headcount to make sure no one got lost on the way back before turning toward Elias.

"Elias! Want to see a new trick?"

"I heard you have some grand plan to help get us to Liam. They wouldn't even tell me what it was. Said I wouldn't believe it until I saw it for myself."

"Oh, you aren't going to believe it when you see it either." Aiden pushes off with his back foot like a runner at the starting line. The signature popping sound follows as Aiden disappears and then reappears behind Elias in less than a second.

Elias spins around, baffled.

"What the hell?" is all he can think to say.

"Pretty neat, right?" Aiden says.

"Did you teleport?"

"Kind of, but it's more complicated than that. We think." Aiden goes into detail about the new ability while Zoe stands behind him, adding in anything he forgets to mention.

After the initial shock wears off and Elias is able to form full sentences again, Tyler starts in on the details of the plan to take Liam out.

"So, let me get this straight," Elias says, standing up and pacing back and forth as if it will make him comprehend the plan better. "You two…" He points to Aiden and Sloan. "…Are going to go Translucent and just pop into Liam's hotel room, bypassing all the guards and other Empyreans that are littering the place. Get Liam's attention and then jump out of the forty-first floor of the Hard Rock Hotel, together. Then Sloan is going to be able to hopefully slow y'all down enough not to become stains on the boardwalk. Then hopefully he follows you down and to the beach, where we are going to be waiting and have a very public battle for everyone to see?" Elias stops walking and takes a breath. "And after all that, if we survive, then what? We just go back to being a secret group of super-power-wielding humans?"

"Well, yea," Aiden says, nodding, unfazed.

"We don't expect to go back to being in the shadows after this. Our kind is going to be outed one way or another. This way, at least we can possibly stop Liam," Tyler says.

"This is insanity. You know that, right?" Elias says as the Knights all nod in unison. "Good lord. And you better hope that the Empyreans are stretched thin like you think they are; otherwise, they will destroy us simply with numbers because the DC Charter isn't going to make it. I talked to them on my way over here, and they are dealing with their own Liam-style issue. Rumor has it, Liam's grand plan to take the government by storm has been pushed into overdrive. DC, Atlanta, and New York are all dealing with a similar problem."

"All the more reason to get ahead of this and try and catch him off guard," says Sloan.

Jensen nods. "And to be honest, we are going to get outed one way or another. I think if we come out as dangerous to the public, which is what will happen when the battle on the beach goes down, Liam will have a tougher time selling the Transcendent idea to the masses."

"All right, does anyone else have any questions?" Tyler asks, looking around at the group of Transcendents. No one moves. "OK, that's it then. We will continue to modify the plan as we see fit and or as things come up. We still need to get out of here, though. Hannah's cousin Emily was nice enough to help us out again, and she reserved thirteen rooms at the Knights Inn on Pacific Avenue across from the Hard Rock Hotel."

"Knights Inn?" Aiden says with a chuckle. "The irony."

Tyler continues. "There, we will stage our final offensive. The only people who will be able to leave the room before the attack without a good reason will be Translucents. There will be a lot of growing pains, but we will have to adapt if we want to have a chance at winning this war. Now let's get out of here."

The army of Transcendents piles into the remaining cars and heads toward Atlantic City. Each vehicle is quiet as they drive down Longport Somers Point Boulevard. Each person thinking of a different scenario, a different outcome, the different ways they could win or lose. How they or someone they care about could die during this battle. But one thing is the same for every-one—not just for the Knights or the Philly Boys but for every Transcendent across the country. In a few days, the war will start, and life as they know it will end.

CHAPTER 29

"**A**re you kidding me?" Liam screams at his cell phone just before throwing it. It sails through the air, shattering as it makes contact with the wall. "We had them. We fucking had them, Riley," he says, turning to face her.

Riley is standing against the wall with her hands tucked behind her back like a soldier at parade rest. She doesn't flinch or move. She says nothing, not wanting to upset him any further.

"The coffee was still warm in the kitchen of that damn underground bunker of theirs. And now they're back in hiding."

"How could they possibly have known we were coming?" she says hesitantly.

"They somehow figured out Eli was working for us. He was found unconscious and tied up in the building above the bunker."

Liam leans against the window overlooking the pier, anger boiling from the inside. The back of his neck is flushed, and it stands out against his silver hair.

Unsure what to do with his rage, he begins pacing back and forth, his fists clenched by his sides.

Riley watches from afar, remaining next to the door of the room just in case she needs to make a hasty escape. Riley has never been afraid of anything or anybody, especially after becoming a Transcendent—except for Liam. She has seen Liam do things in the past to people that would make the devil himself blush. She sidesteps, putting the opening side of the door closer to her, just in case.

Liam's pacing stops; he stares straight ahead at the wall as if seeing something for the first time. His head-turning slowly toward Riley.

"It's over. I don't have time for this. I have a campaign to finish. This race for Senate is much more important than chasing these peons around Atlantic City. How much time have we wasted?" he asks, not expecting an answer. "Almost a month?"

Riley remains silent.

"Yes. To hell with it, Riley. We are getting out of here. I need to get back to New York. The future of our race depends on me taking my seat as senator. All of this will have been for nothing if I don't win."

Liam steps to his left, picking up the phone next to the couch, punching in three numbers, and staring at his broken cell phone as the line rings into his ear.

"Ezra. It's Turner. We are leaving. Let everyone know and get the cars ready. We leave in thirty."

He drops the phone into the cradle then looks up at Riley.

"Go pack. I'm done with this."

* * *

It's been two days. Two long days of sitting in their cheap, terrible motel rooms at the Knights Inn. No one has left their rooms, except for the Translucents, for obvious reasons. Forty-eight hours of constant surveillance of the Hard Rock Hotel and Casino.

"How on earth do cops do this for weeks on end?" Jensen says, looking at Sloan, who is stretched out across one of the two queen beds in nothing but a t-shirt.

All the Translucents have been on eight-hour shifts, taking notes and photos every time any of Liam's people exit the hotel. Aiden, being Aiden, went subsonic through the hotel all the way up to the fortieth and forty-first floor. He said he went for reconnaissance reasons, but they all knew he went just to test himself and prove it was possible. He came back with some excellent intel, though, so no one could really be that mad.

After he had popped in and out, he saw that, for the most part, there was no security, except for the hallway leading from the elevator to Liam's suite.

Jensen's phone vibrates against the table as it emits a bell chime. The screen reads, "Tyler." He answers the call, then activates the speaker function so Sloan can listen.

"All right, everyone," they hear Tyler say through the speaker of the phone. Jensen looks down at the screen displaying everyone's names who are part of this conference call. "Last chance. Does anyone have any questions or anything to add to the plan?"

Jensen begins to open his mouth to say something, but he is interrupted. "And, yes, Jensen. Sloan is the only one still capable of making that jump from the forty-first floor." His mouth closes without saying anything. Sloan giggles from her position on the bed.

"With the information from Aiden about how lax security is, I think tomorrow is going to be the day. One last time, I'm going to go over the plan, and then the next time you hear from me will be to start the attack," Tyler says as he takes a breath. "Sloan and Aiden will go subsonic all the way through the hotel, taking the stairs to avoid being trapped in the elevator."

"Oh, goodie," Aiden says sarcastically.

Tyler continues, "Once in the hallway leading to Liam's room, while still Translucent, Sloan will take out any of the guards still in the hallway. Aiden and Sloan will pass through the door. Knowing Liam, he will sense you coming. Once in the room, you will become visible before making your escape out the window. We will all be on the beach to the left of Steel Pier awaiting your arrival."

Tyler finishes the sentence as the call goes silent, except for the slight hum from the phone's speaker.

"Then what?" Elias asks.

"Then we fight for our lives, I guess, is the best way to put it," Tyler says after a brief pause.

"Perfect," Sloan says, rolling over onto her stomach. "What could possibly go wrong?"

"Look, is it the best plan? No. But we don't have much of a choice. The main purpose of this attack is to make the public aware of us and keep Liam from manipulating the government. This isn't about being safe; this is about stopping the Empyreans at all cost."

"This is insanity is what it is," Jensen says as he leans back in his chair.

"It's better than waiting for him to find us," says Tyler.

No one answers. They all feel the same way, but they all know Tyler is right. If they allow Liam and his fellow Empyreans to follow through, to enact laws enabling Transcendents to become open and a part of everyday society, who knows where it will end? Within a few years, Non Transcendents will have no way to stop them. The wicked will push out the virtuous; anyone not with them will be destroyed. The world will become a giant game of king of the hill. Everyone fighting for a position at the top, killing whoever they need to in order to rise up the ranks.

Jensen's phone vibrates, dancing across the table. A joyful ringtone chimes from behind him; he looks to see Sloan shifting to grab her phone.

"Hold on. I just got a message," Tyler says.

"So did I," Jensen answers.

"Me too," says Sloan.

"I think we all just got the same message," Aiden's voice says from the speaker.

Jensen leans forward, swiping his finger across the screen, bringing the message into view.

"We may have a problem," Jensen hears Sloan say from behind him.

The message is from Hannah. The message reads, *Em just called me. They r leaving. Like right now.*

"Shit. We've got to move. Aiden, Sloan. It's now or never," says Tyler.

CHAPTER 30

Liam looks down at his watch, pushing his cuff out of the way. 1342. It's been a little over thirty minutes since he ordered everyone to get ready to leave. He called down to the front desk, notifying them of his early unannounced departure. Riley took care of funneling down the information to the rest of the Empyreans. He told Riley he wanted to be out of the hotel and on the road by two. His eyes glance back to his watch. 1345. Fifteen minutes to go.

He hasn't brought much with him. Liam didn't expect to stay this long searching endlessly for Mason Knight's people. All he brought were four pairs of suits, shirts, and shoes. Enough to change his ensemble regularly, so he didn't wear the same thing twice. Then four days turned into a week. A week turned into two. Two turned into three. And three was apparently his breaking point. As much as he wants to find them, mainly Jensen Atwood, he doesn't have time for that. He has much more important things to do, to prepare for. What's the phrase? *Bigger fish to fry?*

He knows he will eventually get his hands on them, and when he does, he will make them pay. Specifically that blond-haired kid and the light-skinned black girl with the piercing blue eyes who ruined his chances of getting his hands on Jensen. Even if Jensen had fought back or seen the world differently. He would've been too weak against Liam at the beginning and would have been disposable. But now, who knows how strong he is?

Liam knew from the second he entered Jensen's mind what he was, who he was. What he was going to be and what kind of powers he possessed. That's what really made Liam nervous. It wasn't Mason or his kids. It was the fact that Jensen was now on their side, against him. The unknown abilities that Liam saw were downright unique. He dreamed about having half of what Jensen had. The boy is one of a kind. The next level of Transcendent. At his peak, he will make the rest of them look like mere mortals. As if he was cast from the bloodline of Zeus himself.

Liam exits his bedroom, does a final sweep for any items he may have missed, and closes the door behind himself. His rolling suitcase sits next to the coffee table, with his garment bag full of suits draped over it.

He grabs the bottle of scotch off the table, holding it up at eye level.

"I mean, there's only one, maybe two, glasses left in here. It would be sacrilegious to just throw it out."

He pours the glass then strolls over to the window to give the Steel Pier one last look.

"As terrible as this state is, this view isn't half bad," he says to his reflection staring back. "Maybe I'll come back here after I win my Senate race. Maybe this is where I will make my announcement. Bringing us out of the shadows and into the light, where we belong."

He watches as the Ferris wheel spins, sending its riders upward for the same view and downward, to where they belong. *Below me.*

His phone vibrates within his coat. Liam shuffles his glass from one hand to the other, freeing it to retrieve the call.

"Hello?"

No answer. The only noise is the sound of shuffling as if the caller's phone is in their pocket. He pulls the phone away to look at the caller. "Luis." *That's strange. He should be right outside,* he thinks.

He puts the phone back to his ear, a little harder this time as though it will make him hear better. "Hello? Luis?"

Nothing. Just the sound of wind rushing past the microphone. Heavy breathing can be heard now. A thud sounds from the phone's speaker and from behind him on the other side of his door.

Another thud. This time louder and more audible. Heavier, like somebody fell.

Boom! The door shakes in its frame. The noise catches Liam off guard, making him lose his grip on the glass. He watches it fall and shatter as it catches the corner of the table. Scotch explodes in all directions—a good portion of it landing on his newly polished dark brown double monks.

"What in the hell is going on out there?" he yells as he kicks his feet, ridding his shoes of the scotch.

"So much for the subtle approach," a man's voice says from the other side of the door.

The door explodes from the wall, taking bits of the frame with it. One hinge remains intact, acting as a pivot point. The door arcs through the air, coming to rest against an end table next to the couch.

Liam looks on in shock at the open doorway with nobody there. On the floor with his head leaning against the wall is Luis. Alive or dead, Liam can't tell.

Sloan and Aiden materialize in front of the doorway, in full view.

"I was just thinking of you two," Liam says with a smile.

He flicks his wrist, sending a sharp blue wave crashing toward Sloan and Aiden. A pop is audible through the room, followed by another pop. The two Knights disappear then reappear five feet to the right of where they were.

"That's a neat little trick. If I don't kill you, I'll be sure to have you teach me that one," Liam says.

Aiden holds onto Sloan's shirt in case he needs to make them translucent or go subsonic again. She brings her hands up and sweeps from right to left. The TV and the dresser both crash into Liam, knocking him off balance and into the dining table. Liam catches himself by grabbing one of the chairs.

"I've had enough of you two," Liam growls.

"It's going to be a long day then," Sloan says as she sweeps her hands, now from left to right.

The whole room begins to shake. The couch, its end tables, and the coffee table begin to shift and slide over the carpet. A picture frame above the sofa releases from the wall and hurtles toward Liam. Liam's suitcase launches into the air and rockets toward him. The furniture in the room has created a tidal wave of hotel accessories. The couch rolls end over end as it pushes everything with it. The wave slams into Liam, pinning him against the table.

Sloan bends at the knee and pushes forward with her hands like she's trying to move a huge entity. The couch cracks and groans as it continues to move against Liam. The table's traction gives way as it's forced into the full-length window overlooking the boardwalk.

Liam fights back, pushing with everything he has, but Sloan is too strong. He was caught off guard, and he can't create any force to fight back with.

The window begins to crack under the pressure of the wave. Sloan takes a step and pushes against nothing. The couch fractures in the middle, collapsing onto Liam, pinning him even further. The window, no longer whole, spiderwebs from top to bottom. The view of the pier no longer there, distorted by the cracks.

Sloan prepares for one last push. She brings her hands in next to her waist then pushes forward with a grunt. The air between them turns a shade of blue as the window finally gives. Sloan and Aiden watch as Liam rides the wave of furniture out of the Hard Rock Hotel and towards the boardwalk.

They stand silently, staring out of the window. The room is eerily quiet without the furniture, and a slight breeze pushes past the opening. The smell of the sea air fills their nostrils. Aiden looks from the open window, then scanning the room before stopping on Sloan.

A smile spreads across his face. "That was the coolest thing I think I've ever seen," he says as a chuckle begins to form deep in his belly. Within seconds, the chuckle turns into a laugh rivaling a hyena's. He doubles over, putting his hands on his knees. His laughter forces tears from his eyes. "I'm so sad no one else was here to see that," he says through it all. He stands upright, wiping the tears free with the back of his hands.

Sloan has moved to the edge of the broken window, and she looks down at the boardwalk. Passersby stand pointing and taking photos of what they just witnessed. She scans the impact area, not seeing anyone who was injured. Not seeing anyone, not even Liam.

"Shit. Where is he?"

"Who? Liam?" Aiden says as he joins her.

"Yea, I can't see him."

"Well, hopefully, he's under that pile of crap."

Sloan looks up toward the beach, where the Knights are supposed to be waiting. It's a reasonable distance away, but she doesn't think she can see anyone.

"You ready?" she says, now looking at Aiden.

"You sure you can do this?" he says, still looking down the side of the hotel.

"Well, if I can't, it won't be your concern for much longer."

"That's not funny." He snaps his head up to look at her.

"We don't have a choice anyway. We can't go back the way we came. I'm sure they are looking for us and heading in this direction as we speak. We weren't exactly covert coming in here."

Aiden groans, glancing back down the hallway they came from. No one insight. He wraps his arms around Sloan. One arm under her armpit, the other one over her shoulder. Then he clasps his hands together against her back, as tight as he can.

She turns so her back is facing the ocean. Wrapping her arms around Aiden, she leans back. A slight resistance from Aiden is felt, but her body weight counters him.

"Shit. Shit. Shit," she hears in her ear as they become parallel with the ground. She feels gravity take over, pulling them faster and faster towards their possible demise.

Aiden's grip tightens as she wraps her legs around his waist, releasing her hands and letting them hang freely. The wind whips past them, hissing loudly in their ears. Her fingers feel cold as the air races over them.

"Don't let go!" Sloan screams, bringing her hands behind her back.

"You think?" Aiden yells sarcastically over the sound of the wind.

She lets out a push. It exits her palms, jolting them into an upright position. She continues to push with everything she has left in the tank. Her hands are no longer cold as they warm up from the energy being forced from them. Sloan pushes wave after wave downward toward the fast-approaching surface. With every wave, she can feel their velocity slowing. But will it be enough to not kill them? That's the only question that matters.

"We are almost there, Sloan!" Aiden screams.

Sloan raises her hands to give herself a little more room to move. She feels the pressure in her chest build. She has to let it grow until the last moment. This will be the last chance. The weight inside her is so intense, it almost knocks the wind out of her. She pushes her hands down; the burden in her chest exits through her. There is so much of it, she feels it leave through her feet, pushing her shoes off. The surge causes Aiden to lose his grip slightly as he scrambles to secure himself. The wind subsides, and they hit a grass patch next to the pile of hotel-room furniture, bouncing away from each other.

Aiden sits up, running his hands over his limbs, up his torso, and up to his neck and head. "You did it!"

Sloan is already on her shoeless feet, searching through the pile of rubble. No Liam.

"He's not here. Shit! Come on. We've got to go."

Aiden springs to his feet, following Sloan's steps leading them to the boardwalk. Crowds of people have formed, pointing, talking, and taking photos of what just occurred. They point and stare at Sloan and Aiden as they scan the beach. The view is better from down here, and there are definitely no Knights over there waiting for them.

"How the hell did you just do that?" a person says from the crowd.

Sloan ignores them as she looks frantically around for anyone. She is unable to see anything through the horde forming around them.

They hear screams to the left of them.

"Come on," Sloan says, grabbing Aiden then using her hands to force a gap in the crowd so they can escape. Once free of the onlookers, they look in the direction of the cries—Ezra with Riley in tow.

"We grow tired of these games, peasants," Ezra says as he force pushes another tourist out of his way. He tosses one after another into the air and out of his path as if they are dolls.

Riley sidesteps to get a better view of Aiden and Sloan. Her hands hang stiffly by her sides, glowing brightly. A blue handle forms in both hands as she wraps her fingers around them. Her whips grow like two tails dangling behind her along the boardwalk, emitting sparks.

"Our time has finally come. Liam won't stop me now. My cage has been unlocked, and I am free to do as I please," Riley says as she launches the end of a whip toward an innocent bystander, hitting him in the back.

Sloan grabs Aiden's shirt and begins to pull him. "We've got to go now."

Luis appears from the crowd, falling in behind Riley, rubbing his neck with a displeased look on his face. Then Liam. Liam emerges just in front of Luis, taking his place next to Riley. He wipes off his sleeves, glowering at Sloan.

"Very clever," he says over the screams of the crowd. "It was a solid plan. Poorly executed, though. I don't think it's going well for your friends either." He points past them.

Sloan and Aiden turn to see the Knights already battling the Empyreans. They are at the entrance to the Steel Pier.

Blue light flashes in every direction from the ongoing battle. People scream, running in all directions. Parents scoop up their children, doing their best to shield them from danger as they head for safety. They watch in horror as people push and pull to save themselves. A young girl trips, losing her grasp on her mom's hand and is trampled by the stampede of people. A wheelchair-bound man is pushed over onto his side by an overweight gentleman trying to make room for his family to get by.

Panic has overtaken the pier. Laughter is replaced with screams. Lines replaced by rioting. People no longer hold cotton candy and stuffed animals. They now arm themselves with anything that can be used as a weapon. Anything to get them away from the supernatural war that has begun in the middle of their vacation.

Transcendents are no longer a secret, and any chance of people not being afraid is long gone. The people will forever remember the Battle of the Steel Pier. The day they lost their innocence.

CHAPTER 31

Jensen turns away from the battle, looking toward the crowd gathered at the base of Liam's hotel. Pushing their way through the mass of civilians are Sloan and Aiden, followed by Ezra, Riley, Liam—and Luis bringing up the rear. Ezra is grabbing and throwing the civilians around with his strength as well as his force ability. They tumble through the air, landing as gently as one could after being thrown by a monster like Ezra.

Liam saunters by Riley's side, face frozen in a cruel grin. The look on his face is a cross between a demon who just escaped hell and a child who just arrived at Disney World. He knows his plan to slowly release the knowledge of Transcendents is over, but now he gets to do what he's been yearning for. Kill every last Knight.

Jensen turns back to the battle, pushing his hands out in opposite directions, sending one Empyrean into the side of a food truck. The other is sent somersaulting over a table used by patrons of the same food truck.

Screams of terror fill the usually pleasant air of the boardwalk. Explosions echo up and down the street;

sirens can be heard as first responders try to help in any way they can.

"I can't believe you started without us," says Aiden as he and Sloan finally make it to them.

"Not much of a choice," Jensen says as he creates a dull blüe sword, blocking an attack from a staff-wielding Empyrean. "They found us before we even made it to the beach." With his free hand, Jensen pushes his attacker's feet out from under him. The Empyrean rolls to dodge Jensen's follow-up attack.

"Well, this is it, gents. We either write the history or become it," says Tyler.

Tyler has formed his patent two revolvers, one in each hand. They are a bright blue, almost too bright to look at, reminding Aiden of the pistols he always saw in Clint Eastwood movies. Tyler fires them one after the other at the never-ending wave of attacking Empyreans. An enemy Force Transcendent creates a shield protecting two others as Tyler's energy projectiles ricochet off in different directions, dissipating in the air after a few feet. Ty turns slightly as he puts the gun in his right hand under his left forearm, like a classic wild west gunfighter, and fires another blue projectile. It sails through the air at lightning speed toward another Empyrean.

Elias is on the ground with an Empyrean straddling his chest, knife in hand, pushing down. The blade inches from his chest. Elias struggles to keep the knife from penetrating his sternum. Tyler fires another bullet at the Empyrean, but their enemy's torso goes transparent, allowing the bullet to crash into the wall behind them in a shower of blue sparks and brick. Elias rolls away and jumps back to his feet, spotting the apparent sign of the Translucent moving toward him. He fires a wave of force, grabbing the oncoming attacker's visible knife-wielding hand, launching him over the edge of the pier to the beach below.

"Thanks, Ty!"

Aiden uses his newly found and perfected ability as he pops in and out, striking one foe after another, laughing as he goes. He leaves a path of angry and confused Empyreans in his wake; they wonder what just happened and what just hit them.

Eric and Sloan team up, fighting multiple people at once. Sloan uses her force as a blocking power while Eric employs his dual katanas. He blocks the attacks with unmatchable speed, slicing through the air, catching an unsuspecting Empyrean off guard. The blade hisses and cuts cleanly through an enemy, whose back is turned to Eric. The blade enters the man's left side, spraying blood as it exits. Eric spins on his heel, bringing his other sword around and plunging it deep into his back. The man gurgles and spits blood out as the blue blade exits his chest. The blade retracts into the hilt before extending out the other side, allowing Eric to quickly change his stance.

The monster known as Ezra towers over the battle, only using his power to block. He seems to prefer the old-school method of fighting. Pure hand-to-hand combat. He grabs a fist thrown from one of the Philly Boys in midair, crushing it with his brute strength. The man's agonizing scream is drowned out by the war around him. Tears raced down his cheeks as he attempts to take Ezra out at the knees. Ezra sees the attack and counters, batting it away before grabbing ahold of the man's leg and lifting him above his head. Ezra uses the man as his weapon, launching him into a group of three Knights.

The battle rages on. Multiple people have been killed, but no one can tell which side they were on. One thing is for sure. The Knights and the Philly Boys seem to be on the losing side. Even if they outnumber the Empyreans, the Empyreans have more practice and more skill to bring to the table.

Riley uses her whip, wrapping it around the neck of a Knight. She pulls with all her might, digging in her heels to give her more leverage. The Knight spins as he stumbles toward her. They come face to face, the Knight's face painted with shock while Riley stares back with a genuine smile; her tongue slides across the front of her teeth. The shocked man looks down to see that Riley has traded one of her whips for a blade, which has entered his stomach. She pulls away, letting him fall onto his final resting spot.

"Tyler, this isn't working! We have got to move. Now!" yells Jensen over the noise from the battle.

Liam has been strolling along, watching the battle from afar. He reaches the Steel Pier opening, where the crowds rushing out trying to get past the war that rages on around them unharmed. He raises his arms slowly, extending them outward and bringing his palms up. He closes his eyes, concentrating a little harder. The ground shakes beneath him; the boards behind him splinter as a clear blue wall rises up into the sky. It begins to rapidly expand to his left and right. The ground rattles from the sheer power of Liam. Spraying cement and wood into the air. The new wall curves slightly inward toward the pier, hugging the guard rails. Civilians running to escape collide with the invisible wall. They begin to bunch up as they search wildly for a way out, to no avail.

He has created a force field that spreads more than halfway up the pier; it is thirty feet tall. Everyone is trapped now on the infamous Steel Pier. The Knights, the Philly Boys, the Empyreans, and the helpless civilians who just weren't fast enough. Liam begins walking toward the ongoing battle, bringing his wall with him. It grinds and groans against the wood, pushing anything in its way, including the people. The people climb over anything they can, beating against the wall, searching desperately for a way to safety.

Some have given up and accepted their fate. Their backs leaning against the moving wall as it slowly forces them to walk forward to the death and destruction that lies before them.

Jensen blocks an attack with the spear he saw Mason use, then he grabs the rival with his force, lifting her ten feet into the air before smashing her into the ground. The ground collapses from the power as the woman lets out a groan, along with what air she had left in her lungs.

"Tyler! We need to go. Now!" Jensen yells.

"I know! Looks like there's only one way to go," Tyler says, pointing up at the wall Liam has created.

They watch as the trapped population of Atlantic City rolls over each other like a wave of human begins as Liam slowly walks forward, dragging his wall as he goes. The smile on his face has spread as far as his skin will allow.

"Sloan, we've got to move. Echo it to the rest," says Jensen.

Sloan echoes the command to one Knight, who echoes it as well. The order continues down the line until all of them are on the defensive and begin to move. They move as one toward the end of the pier. No longer are they trying to attack; now they are just trying to find some breathing room, a chance to think.

Tyler makes his way to Jensen and Sloan.

"I have a plan; it's going to be dangerous, so make sure every force person is ready with a shield." They nod in unison back at Tyler.

As they walk backward, blocking attacks from the Empyreans, they stare in awe at what they've left behind. Buildings lay in piles of rubble. Rides and attractions have been destroyed almost to the point of being unrecognizable. A merry-go-round has been completely destroyed. The horses that have carried many smiling faces around in circles are no longer attached, and they lie charred and broken.

A hundred yards behind the line of enemy Transcendents strides Liam, who is slowly herding the innocent toward them. On the other side of the barrier, behind him stands a line of bewildered police officers and some of the people who escaped before Liam could trap them. They touch the wall, confused as to what's going on or what it is. One cop even discharges his weapon into it, amazed when the bullet stops dead and falls to the sidewalk.

Jensen looks left; towering into the air is the well-known Steel Pier Ferris Wheel. They have gone as far as they can; behind them is the roller coaster and then the helipad at the end of the pier. This is it; this is the final stand.

Tyler puts a hand on Jensen's and Sloan's shoulders. "Be ready. I have to do this before the civilians get here. We can't allow anymore to die."

"We will be ready," she says, looking up and down the line as other Force Transcendents nod in return.

The lines are drawn and formed. On one side, the Knights and Boys, the Empyreans—with Riley and Ezra in the middle—on the other. The battle ceases for a moment. The silence creeps down the pier. No more explosions. No more screaming. No more death.

Riley steps forward. "This is your last chance, *Knights,*" she says with noticeable disgust. "You give up now, and I promise I'll make your deaths quick and clean. Otherwise, I'm going to drag them out as long as possible."

Jensen notices a bright light coming from behind him. He turns to see Tyler creating something in his hand. It's brighter than anything he has ever seen before. Tyler looks up, a worried look on his face, stepping forward, pushing through the line. The heat from the energy within his hands radiating as he passes. Sloan and Jensen exchange a look; Sloan takes Jensen's hand, and they return their focus to Tyler.

"Not today, Riley," Tyler says as he brings his fist up. The object glows within. He whips it at Riley like a second baseman looking for the out.

It arcs through the air, glowing bright like the sun. Jensen realizes that Tyler has just thrown the biggest energy bomb ever created by a Transcendent. He squeezes Sloan's hand as if it might transfer his thoughts to hers. He doesn't have time to say it. He just hopes Sloan knows what it is as well.

CHAPTER 32

E zra sees the attack and creates a shield big enough to protect himself and Riley. The bomb erupts upon contact, emitting a light bright enough to rival the sun and a high-pitched noise that sounds like tinnitus on steroids.

The sound fades, and the light dims until it is nothing. Jensen blinks multiple times before his vision returns with spots. His attention goes straight to Sloan, who is still at his side, then to the line of Knights. Every Force Transcendent has done as Tyler asked, creating a shield together. Combining their powers, creating one unbreakable line of defense.

Jensen's eyes drift out toward the Empyreans. The surface of the pier is charred and broken everywhere, except for where their shield is. Buildings are dust. The roller coaster is now just a mangled, twisted maze of metal. The Ferris wheel, what is left of it, was pushed over the edge by the explosion's force. What pieces didn't disintegrate float in the ocean, dancing upon the waves. The wheel's biggest part sticks out of the water forty feet in the air as the surf rushes around it.

Tyler has collapsed just inside the protection of the shield onto his hands and knees. Drained from the amount of energy needed to produce the weapon that caused such destruction.

Their eyes follow the ever-growing trail of devastation to where the Empyreans are. Ezra and Riley were the only ones protected by a shield; still, they were blasted into what is now the remains of the ticket booth for the Ferris wheel. Luis lies dead, his body in two pieces, burned down to the bone. One half is leaning against the foundation that the Ferris wheel stood on, while the other lies ten feet away, still smoldering. Three more unidentifiable bodies are scattered around the area. Some Empyreans still remain alive, although in unbelievably bad shape. Some have burns from head to toe, barely breathing, while others look lucky enough to have escaped with only a few broken bones.

Riley stirs from where the blast hurled her, struggling to her feet. Unsure of herself as she stands. She finally regains her balance and immediately retaliates, running straight for Tyler.

Sloan dives through the crowd, intercepting Riley, whose whips have already manifested behind her. Sloan releases a devasting force blast, which hits Riley square in the chest. It knocks the wind from her lungs but doesn't slow her down. She continues her attack, bringing one whip after another. Sloan dodges and ducks each attack as she stays on the defensive. She gets in close, too close to be effective with her ability but close enough for fists.

She swings right to left, catching Riley in the jaw with one fist in the abdomen with the other. Riley stumbles back, bringing one of the whips around before sending it forward. It finds its intended target, wrapping tightly around Sloan's waist.

Jensen makes a move while Riley is focused on Sloan. Riley brings the other whip back, and Jensen catches it in one hand as she tries to bring it forward. The whip wraps all the way up Jensen's right forearm, stopping just shy of his bicep. Riley turns when she is met with resistance. She snarls before increasing the power of the whip connected to Jensen. The whip glows with intensity, the heat growing with it.

The sound of his skin blistering fills the air; the smell of burnt flesh and hair fills his nose. The pain is excruciating, and all he can think to do is pull her off balance.

Sloan takes the open opportunity to close the distance between herself and Riley, grasping the hand containing the whip around her waist. Focusing on Riley's hand. Concentrating. Seeing the individual bones, the ligaments, the veins, the muscles. She squeezes.

Riley lets out a shriek that could shatter glass. Both whips dissolve into nothing as everyone watches Sloan break and twist every bone in Riley's hand. Riley pulls back, trying to get away from Sloan's grasp, trying to end the agony. Finally breaking her grip, Riley retreats back to Ezra.

Ezra, still fighting to regain his balance, stumbles and falls. Riley takes Ezra, throwing one arm over her

shoulder, forcing the giant man onto his feet. They stag-
ger off, taking their place beside Liam, who has finally
joined them. The scared, tired, and hopeless people
fall to their knees, not needing to walk any longer now
that the wall has stopped.

Elias holds Tyler up so he can stand.

"It's over, Liam. You've lost. Everyone knows who
you are now. Your future in politics is over, and you
have no army left. Let us end this," Tyler says weakly.

"True, my future as a senator is probably gone with
that Ferris wheel. But I still have a vast army."

The evil smile on Liam's face turns into a sneer. His
right arm comes up, level with his face; his hand opens,
stiff like he's palming a basketball. His eyes travel to
each person individually.

"Now you can fight them." His hand closes with
a snap. His eyes turn a cloudy blue. Just like they did
with Jensen so many weeks ago. Just like Jensen's
did with Eli. The clouds swirling around his pupils.

Along with the worn-out Knights and Philly Boys,
Jensen, watches in horror as the civilians Liam dragged
down the pier stiffen as if struck by bolts of lightning.
Their heads look toward them simultaneously, their
eyes glowing blue just like Liam's. They stand together.
They begin to move in a cadence like they practiced for
weeks to get it right. They get into five columns, more
than twenty in each row. They stand tall, quiet, and at
attention. They look like an army ready for morning
inspections—a hundred people. Two hundred glowing
eyes staring back at them.

They take a single step forward, in sync. It sounds like a single footstep. One giant step. It was a test, a test to make sure he had full control.

"The question is, are you willing to hurt these innocent people to stop me?"

CHAPTER 33

Liam roars with laughter, his head tilted slightly back as if he's laughing at the gods themselves.

"So what are you going to do, *Knights*?" he says with disdain. "Are you willing to kill these innocent people who don't have any control in order to get to me?"

Jensen steps toward Liam, only to have the army of civilians shift to block his attack. They move as one. The perfect army. They are willing to die for Liam. Not because they want to. Because they don't have a choice. He slowly backs up, holding his palms forward in case he needs to create a shield at the last minute.

"Ty, any ideas?" Jensen says over his shoulder, keeping his eyes on Liam and his army.

"I got nothing. I know you don't want to admit it, Jensen, but we may have to kill them."

"Kill who?" he says, anger flooding his face. He points at the helpless crowd with the glowing eyes. "Them? We are not going to harm them. I would rather die."

Jensen turns to Sloan, hoping that maybe she has an idea. She doesn't. Her eyes give it away. She is at a loss. They all are.

"Goodbye, *Knights*. Say hi to Mason for me." Liam opens his hand and pushes it, palm out, toward the line of Knights and Boys.

All at once, the civilians let out a scream rivaling a banshee's. They storm forward, running madly with their arms flailing wildly.

"Shield!" yells Jensen.

Like a well-trained phalanx of Spartans, the Knights create a shield around themselves. It is the strongest shield any of them have ever produced. It shines bright with a thick blue tint and makes a humming sound similar to power lines.

The mass of people hit the shield. Each creating a soft, resounding thud as their bodies stop suddenly. The screams make it almost impossible to think clearly. Jensen watches as the crowd of people begins fighting and climbing over one another, trying to find a way in. Within seconds, the entire shield has been covered by bodies. Inside, the shield goes dark as they block the sun like an eclipse.

"Jensen, we may not have a choice. I don't know how much longer we can hold this," Sloan says as she struggles to help protect them.

"Jensen, we have to do something," Tyler says, grabbing him by the shoulders.

Jensen stares into his eyes, seeing fear. He knows he doesn't want to, but they don't have much of a choice.

"Give me one chance. Aiden, get ready to go subsonic," Jensen says over the noise. "Sloan, I'm going to need you to make a hole here in a second." He moves to the middle of the group so everyone can hear him. "Listen carefully. When I say so, I need a gap in the shield right here," he says, pointing two feet up. "When that happens, Sloan, I need you to push the people away to give me and Aiden space. Aiden and I are going to pop out of here right into Liam. Now, once we are on him, you just let me go and continue away from Liam until you're at a safe distance."

"But…"

"No, Aiden. If this doesn't work, you may be the only one who can safely get people out of here. You hide until it's all over, or I'm dead."

"Jensen, you can't," Sloan says, a tear forming at the corner of her eye.

"You know as well as I do if anyone can stop him, it's me. He and I are the same in more ways than one," Jensen says, wiping the tear from her cheek. "This is it, boys!" Jensen kisses Sloan long and hard. Letting the feeling of her soft lips imprint itself onto his brain one last time. His eyes open as he releases his grip on her. "Now!"

Aiden grabs Jensen by the shoulders, kneeling down like a runner. A gap in the blue around them appears; a thump resounds from Jensen's right as Sloan lets out a powerful blast knocking away a group of the attackers. The pressure from the blast is intense, causing his ears to pop, then everything goes quiet. He feels a pull as Aiden makes him move. They move as quickly as possible, squeezing through the gap. Aiden making sure to keep a hold on Jensen the whole time.

While going subsonic, to Jensen, it just looks like Aiden stops time. But if you watch closely, everything is moving in super slow motion. Jensen can't help but smile at the peacefulness of it. Even as he stares at the mound of bodies trying to kill his friends, his family, his lover. It's still the most peaceful scene he has ever seen.

He brings himself back to reality, focusing on the cause of all this. Liam. He remains in the same spot. His hands at shoulder level, his fingers spread wide, dancing along like a puppet master controlling his marionettes. The same smile draped across his face.

Jensen looks at Aiden as they run toward their mortal enemy at full speed. They nod, then turn their attention back to Liam. Jensen tucks his shoulder just before catching Liam in the stomach. Liam's feet leave the ground as the full force of Jensen takes hold. Aiden releases.

The sound of screams and violence erupts again, filling his ears. Jensen stumbles as he takes Liam to the ground, sliding on his back to a stop. Jensen sits up, straddling Liam's chest. He swings right then left. Each time, Liam goes transparent, causing his punches to sail freely. Jensen sits back, bringing his fists up, clenching his hands, and interlocking his fingers. He brings them down like a hammer. This time, Liam shifts right, and the attack misses, shattering the ground. Liam counters, wrapping his arm around the back of Jensen's neck. With his head in Liam's armpit, he loses his advantage. Liam uses his weight to bring him down, forcing his head against the pier's boardwalk.

"Nice try, Jensen," Liam says as he uses his free hand to clobber Jensen's ribs.

Jensen struggles to keep his lungs filled with air as the punches come one after another. Liam uses the opportunity to roll his hips, putting Jensen on his back, but Jensen tucks his knees too and pushes off, sending Liam backward and giving himself more space to stand up.

"Come on, Jensen. I have nothing left to lose. This is why I am here now. The public will know about our kind in less than twenty-four hours, and then I will lead my army of Transcendents to Washington DC, where we will take our rightful place as kings."

"This is insanity. You had everything. Money. Power. Fame. You destroyed all that for what? To fight us? You could have just let us go! Stayed in New York."

"That will always be my downfall. I just can't let things go. I hate to lose."

Jensen sighs. "Then come on. Let's end this."

They both send a wave of force toward each other. The waves crack upon impact, causing the ground where they collided to split with ease. Jensen creates the Leonidas spear and charges for an attack. With a single movement of his arm, Liam deflects the attack and steps forward, closing the distance between them.

He grabs Jensen's shirt collar and pulls him in tight and fast. Liam's forehead connects with the bridge of Jensen's nose. Jensen feels it give way as tears blur his vision. His nose pops like a grape. The metallic taste of blood fills his mouth. He feels his knees go weak and give out underneath him. Yet he doesn't fall.

Jensen blinks through the tears and blood to see Liam holding his lifeless body up with one hand. Liam lets him fall to his knees.

Jensen sits upon his haunches, a defeated man. His head hung low, dripping with blood. Nothing left to give but his life. He feels Liam's hand grip his right shoulder. Shaking him to cause his limp head to fall back. Liam looks him in the eyes.

"You just had to be the goddamn hero, didn't you? Should have just joined me, Jensen. I could have made you something to be feared. People would've bowed to us." Jensen watches as Liam holds his right hand up in front of his face. It goes clear with the distorted look of the typical Translucent. "I bet you remember this little trick, don't you?"

Liam brings his arm back before pushing it forward toward Jensen's chest. Just like he did to Mason. Images of Mason dying flash through his mind. The haunting look of his face as his eyes struggled to remain in his skull. *This is it. After all of it, this is how I die. I love you, Sloan.*

Jensen feels his arms come up as if his body is instinctively trying to protect itself.

Goodbye, Sloan. Jensen hopes for a quick death. To feel Liam's hand enter his chest and stop his heart. His eyes close. Waiting.

But death doesn't come. No pressure. No pain. He blinks, trying to rid his vision of blood. He looks up to see Liam staring down in surprise. He shifts his head, allowing the weight to carry it forward. That's when he sees it—or in this case, he doesn't see it.

His hands have gone transparent at the wrists. Within his hands, he can feel Liam's still-invisible hand.

"This is impossible. How can you have all three abilities already? I saw you were capable, but how?" Liam stutters quietly as if talking to only himself.

Jensen digs deep inside, finding the only energy he has left. He grips Liam's hand more tightly, not wanting his opportunity to slip away. He sees the blue from his shield form around him like a protective blanket through his blurry vision.

The screams from the puppet army subside and are replaced by a single isolated cry. Jensen falls to his back as Liam's grip on him releases.

He feels a forceful surge pass over him before hearing a crash in the distance. In seconds, Sloan is by his side, wiping the blood from his face. He can finally see clearly. Jensen spots Riley and Ezra sprinting over to their boss, who is stumbling to his feet. Looking back, Jensen sees the army of the unwilling participants no longer possessed by Liam. The entire army of civilians rests upon their knees, confused, trying to find relief as they recall what had just transpired.

"What was that? How was he doing that?" Jensen hears multiple people from the crowd say.

Jensen returns his gaze to Sloan before looking down to see what he's been gripping. He opens his hand, and four fingers roll out of his palm and into his lap.

"What in the hell?" Jensen says, frantically swatting the fingers away before noticing the hand and forearm of Liam's left arm lying next to him. "Jesus Christ! I chopped his damn limbs off with my shield."

"It did the job," Aiden says, strolling up.

"Where did they go?" Tyler asks as he approaches.

"They were just over there." Sloan points in the direction she last saw them.

"Hey, how was that guy doing all of that?" a civilian yells.

"To hell with that. How were any of you doing any of that?" another yells.

"We have to get out of here, gents," says Aiden as one hundred helpless people begin to surround them.

CHAPTER 34

They push past the crowd. Aiden continually apologizes as they retreat from the pier.

"Man, are they going to be pissed off for a while," laughs Aiden.

"They aren't the only ones," says Tyler as they notice the wall of angry civilians and tourists lining the width of the destroyed pier.

They break into a jog, searching for an exit.

"We are going to have to jump," Aiden says, gesturing to the edge of the pier leading to the beach.

They look around, for the first time noticing the level of destruction they just caused. They all glance up at where it started. Four hundred and thirty feet up in the highest room of the Hard Rock Hotel. Then at the destruction behind the angry mob, which is slowly approaching. Buildings lay in ruin. Food vendors, carnival games, and rides are nothing but a mess of broken brick and mortar. Food litters the pier as seagulls rush in to get their fill. Prizes from the games scatter the ground, covered in dirt and blood.

Bodies lay everywhere, twisted in final expressions. No one can really tell who is a Transcendent and who is just a regular person. To them, they are just the dead.

This is not what any of them wanted. They wanted a battle. But a battle in the safest place they could find. It ended up being a war in one of the most populated areas in New Jersey. In Atlantic City. They might as well have fought in the lobby of the casino.

With Liam gone, they don't even have anything to show for it. They lost friends, people they thought of as family. Tourists came here for a good time and lost friends, family members. And for what?

"Hey! You! Freeze!"

They look up to see a line of boys in blue. Atlantic City Police, pistols drawn. Some even have rifles pushed into their shoulders, up and ready to fire at any moment.

"What the hell just happened here?" one of the police officers says.

"Easy, officer," Tyler says, stepping forward as if to say, *I'm in charge. Talk to me.* "We did not mean for any of this to happen. We were trying to stop another group, and it got completely out of control."

"What got out of control? What the hell are you people?" the officer says.

"What do you mean you…" Aiden says before being elbowed in the stomach by Sloan.

"Not the time," she whispers.

"Look, this can all be explained if you just put your guns down. We mean you no harm," Tyler continues.

"I'm not putting shit down, but you," the man in blue says.

Jensen looks right and spots a young police officer who looks way out of his depth. His hands shake as his eyes dart from them to the destruction behind them.

"I just watched you guys have a massive war, and none of you has so much as a stick to fight with. And what caused that small nuclear bomb back there?" the police officer says.

"Nuclear bomb?" Aiden questions.

The officer points his pistol at Aiden. "There was a bright light, then a mushroom cloud appeared. When it cleared out, everything was gone. Only one thing I know of that can do that kind of destruction."

"Holy shit, Ty. A mushroom cloud," Aiden says quietly.

"Like I said, it can all be explained. But please, first the weapons," Tyler says, nodding at the guns.

Jensen continues to watch the young police officer. Sweat has started to form on the young man's brow.

"Easy, kid," Jensen says, hands up, turning toward the young cadet.

"Hey!" the kid screams as he pulls the trigger, firing his gun.

The shot rings out, echoing around them. Every police officer releasing his nervous energy all at once, thanks to the new blood on the force. The firing ceases, and the smoke clears. Sloan stands in the middle of the group with one hand up; Jensen stands to her right, doing the same.

The officers stand, shocked, no one saying anything. Jensen and the rest of the Knights exchange looks as if to say, *Well, now what?*

A collapsed bullet rolls away from the shield and into one of the police officer's boots. He bends over, picking it up, unable to speak as he turns the bullet over with his fingers. Another officer steps forward, putting his hand against the blue tint.

"What are you?"

"We have to go, like right now," Jensen says, backing up toward the group.

Without another word, the Knights turn toward the side of the pier, jumping to the sand below. Shots ring out behind them; Jensen and Sloan continue to protect them as they retreat down the beach.

"Now what?" says a Knight from the group.

"First, let's get to the cars. Then we do our best to get out of here. We leave no one behind," says Tyler.

They arrive at the cars—located in a parking garage adjacent to one of the many casinos. As they scatter, Elias turns to Tyler.

"We are obviously going back to Philly. Where are y'all going to go?"

"There's a small town right on the Virginia–North Carolina border," says Jensen. "We'll probably head there. See if it's safe. I'll text you when we know."

They wave at each other as they slip into their respective cars. With Tyler, Aiden, Sloan, Hannah, and Jensen piled into one car, Tyler looks back at Jensen.

"So, where is this small town?"

"If we make it out of here, head south on I-95. Then just head to Raleigh, North Carolina. Once we make it that far, I'll know where I'm going. Old family land should be safe. I'll text everyone else as we go."

CHAPTER 35

Just outside of Richmond, the five Transcendents cruise down I-95 towards North Carolina, keeping their speed just above the speed limit to keep from getting pulled over. The car has been silent for hours; no one knows what to say, nor does anyone want to be the first to speak. While thousands of Empyreans had been wiped out, so had so many of their friends. Each one was in too much shock to able to process the pain just yet. Is the war over? Not even close, and they all know it. If anything, this was merely the beginning of a global disaster. It is only a matter of days, if not hours, before the country and the world learns of their evolutionary gene's existence and their kind; in turn, some will discover they have the same gene. This would most likely end just as Mason predicted: in complete catastrophe.

Aiden, who had been behind the wheel for hours, wipes the sleep from his eyes as they continue down I-95. Tyler rides shotgun, and Hannah leans against a window in the back. Jensen has the other window seat, with Sloan asleep from exhaustion, her head on his lap.

"Alright," Tyler finally says, breaking the silence. "Jensen, where the *hell* are we going?"

"We're almost there, I believe. It's been a long time since I've been here, but we take the I-85 exit next, then look for signs leading to Virgilina, Virginia."

Aiden looks into the rearview mirror at Jensen. "Virgilina, Virginia? That sounds completely made up."

"Technically, all town names are made up, Aiden," Jensen retorts, stretching his back out and waking up Sloan in the process.

"Touché," Aiden concedes.

"So, what is this place?" Tyler asks.

"I don't know if they still live there," Jensen replies. "Regardless, this place is super remote. I wouldn't be surprised if they are the last ones to find out what happened in AC. The place belongs to my aunt and uncle on my mom's side. We used to be pretty close until..." he trails off.

Tyler glances back at Jensen but doesn't inquire further, sensing the old memories flooding back into Jensen's head.

"They are my cousin Ryan's parents, er, *were* his parents..." he pauses and continues tentatively. "He committed suicide like five or six years ago, and then everything happened with my parents, and well, we just kind of drifted apart. I haven't talked to them in years. I don't even know if they'll help us in any way, but I mean, no one else had any ideas." Jensen says.

"No, you're right," Aiden says. "We have nowhere else to go. What's the worst thing that could happen?

They send us on our way? Anyway, what else do you remember about them?"

"Not much, really. Wayne is an old war vet. Desert Storm or Falklands or something like that. It's been so long. The only thing I truly remember is that they were the most kind and welcoming people I have ever met. Nothing ever made them mad. Oh, and they have a shit-ton of land. Like dozens of acres, if I remember correctly."

"That could be useful if they decide to take us in," Tyler says, turning his head slightly.

"Oh, this is it! The next exit," Jensen exclaims, leaning forward between Tyler and Aiden as he points at a green exit sign ahead of them. "S. Boston/Danville."

"This place is so small that it doesn't even have its own exit sign?" Aiden jokes.

They slow down, take the exit Jensen indicated, and follow the small signs leading to Virgilina. The town of Virgilina was the true definition of a one-horse town. A single stoplight lazily blinks yellow at a cross street with a General Dollar on the corner and a car wash adjacent. They pass a fire department that looks like it was built in the '40s, and they all wonder wordlessly if the firefighters still use a horse and carriage.

"Oh my god. What in the hell is that?" Aiden says as they pass a small, run-down bar with a sign above it that reads, *Cowboy Up*. "If we stay here, we are checking that place out. I may need to go get me some cowboy boots, though..."

Aiden drives right through an intersection without stopping as he stares at the only bar in town. Almost instantly, the loud alarm of a police siren fills the silent air around them, followed by the flashing of the blue-and-red lights of a cop car, signaling them to pull over.

"Dammit, Aiden," Tyler says, sinking into his seat, as Aiden halts the car on the side of the road.

The sheriff saunters over slowly from his brand-new Dodge Charger. "Evenin', everyone," the sheriff says with a massive Southern drawl. "I'm sure you can guess why it is I pulled you over on this lovely day."

"Uh...yes, sir. I accidentally drove through that intersection without stopping, and for that, I'm so sorry," Aiden responds apologetically. "We're from out of town, and I've never seen such a redneck town in my life," he continues bluntly.

"A *what* town?!" the sheriff exclaims with a look of outrage.

"I'm sorry, sheriff..." Jensen interrupts quickly, flashing a glare at Aiden to silence him.

"The name's Jeb."

"Jeb. Yes, sir. I have family that lived here years ago, and I wasn't sure if they still do. We were driving south and thought it would be nice to stop by and see them. The Baileys? I don't remember where they live exactly...I just remember that their house was huge and had stone pillars on either side of the driveway as you enter."

"The Baileys?" Sheriff Jeb exclaims in recognition. "I love the Baileys! Tell you what, kids, I'll take you over there, and if Wayne recognizes you, I'll let you off with a warning."

"That would be amazing, sir, thank you," Jensen says with a nod of gratitude, leaning back.

As soon as the sheriff walks away, Hannah gives Aiden a slap on the back of the head. "Idiot."

They follow the sheriff down a country road that seems so narrow that it could only be one way. Pines trees loomed high into the sky on both sides the fluffy green shrubs that thickly cover the base of the trees slowly transform into the bright green of soft field grass. They soon see a gravel driveway curving to the right and sloping slightly uphill. The field opens up all around them; it seems to go on forever before a house appears on the horizon.

The house seems massive from afar and only gets more prominent as they close the distance. Two roofs, grey on either end, come together in the middle, building up to a second story. The house is perfectly symmetrical all the way around. Off to the right is another building that closely resembles a barn but made from steel. A giant flag pole, which appears to be way bigger than necessary, holds atop it the American flag. It flutters in the wind towards them, almost as if waving at them in welcome.

"Holy shit, this place is huge," Aiden says, squinting into the sunlight as if helping him see.

They stop behind Sheriff Jeb's squad car as the front door of the house opens up. A tall man steps out first, at least six feet tall. His silver hair gleams in the sunlight as it flows lazily to his right, a full beard and a set of glasses lay across the bridge of his nose. A woman follows, roughly five-foot-tall, with curly, brown hair, so curly it was as if she were wearing a cotton ball on her head. She steps out from behind the giant of a man, and a smile of delight spreads across her face as she catches sight of their car. She hurries forward towards them as fast as her little legs would carry her. Before the door to the house could close, two small red-haired dogs race out from behind her, beating her to the car and barking excitedly at its occupants.

"I think she recognizes you, Jensen," Sloan says.

Jensen steps out of the car and gives a friendly wave. "Hi, Betty, Wayne."

Sheriff Jeb exchanges greetings and converses with Wayne and Betty before giving Aiden his warning and leaving the way they came. Wayne then turns to Jensen and shakes his hand.

"Jensen, it's been so long. What brings you down here to our little piece of heaven?" Wayne asks.

"It's a very long story. How much time do you have? I don't want to be a burden. We were just in the area," Jensen says.

"Family is never a burden, except when they stay too long," Wayne lets out a laugh as he holds the door open and waves them all into the house.

Sloan is cautious about moving as the two dogs dance around her, barking with enthusiasm.

"Oh, don't mind them, dear," Betty smiles warmly. "Henry and Jethro are as sweet as they come. Just start walking; they'll get out of the way." Betty walks ahead, taking Sloan by the elbow to help.

As they file in past Wayne, Jensen introduces them one by one and finally gestures at Aiden.

"Aiden," Wayne says. "Stop slouching and stand up straight."

Aiden doesn't retort as he usually would have; instead, he straightens his back so fast he may have pulled something as he continues into the house.

On entering the house, they realize that the second story wasn't another story at all: it was just a high ceiling. The whole place is made of wood and the interior smelled like it. The aroma of cedar filled their nostrils as they moved in, making room for them all to stand. The living room was the house's center point along with an enormous kitchen; a ten-foot island countertop separated the kitchen from the living room. A staircase to their right led up to what seemed like a balcony overlooking the living area.

"Your house is gorgeous," Sloan says to Betty, who's still holding her by the elbow.

"Why, thank you, dear."

"So, sit down and tell me a story," Wayne says, motioning to the chairs while taking a seat.

* * *

Jensen spent the next thirty to forty minutes narrating what had happened in the past leading up to the present. Wayne and Betty sat silently next to each other the entire time, nodding and never interrupting. When Jensen finally finished the story, they all sat there, no one speaking. Betty wiped a single tear from her eye and getting up from her chair before disappearing into a room behind the kitchen. Wayne, too rose from his

seat and walked towards the fireplace, picking up a picture. He stared at it for a while before running a thumb
across it and handing it to Jensen. Everyone shifted so
they could see the photo in Jensen's hands.

"Ryan?" Jensen asks, confused. "I don't understand."

"Ryan was one of these, *Transcendents*, as you call
it. He found out about it a year before he took his life.
Ryan had accidentally killed one of Betty's chickens
outside while collecting eggs. He couldn't explain how
he did it, and we had nowhere to turn to for help. For
months he tried to figure it out, *these powers*, but I guess
the burden was too much for him."

"Is that why he...he did it?" Jensen asks tentatively,
placing the picture on the coffee table.

"We believe so; we think he just wanted peace,"
Wayne said, choking back tears as he talked.

"I'm so sorry," Jensen hangs his head.

"Anyway," Wayne clears this throat, standing up,
his height looking even more impressive from their
positions on the couch. "I'm sure Betty will agree but
feel free to stay here and also reach out to anyone
you need to if they need a safe place to take refuge
in. Especially your friends, *the Philly Boys*. If what the
news said is true, Philadelphia will not last much longer, and they may need a place to stay. We will help in
any way we can."

"Wayne, are you sure? This is going to be a huge
burden on you two," Jensen says.

"Look, son, this place is quiet, and that's why we
moved out here. But at the same time, we would never
turn away people in need, particularly family. And if

these people are your family, then they are our family as well. I would also think it may have saved Ryan if he knew there was a group like y'all out there."

* * *

Weeks have passed since they arrived in Virgilina. The rest of the Knights have since arrived, and so have the Philly Boys.

Jensen, Sloan, Wayne, Tyler, and Elias stand around the dining table, a map of the area spread out in front of them and the TV blaring news of the country's destruction in the background. As they knew it, the government was collapsing; this was the start of a new era.

"So, what's our next move?" Elias asks.

"I think we should start setting up defensive positions here, here, and probably here," Wayne points at the map of his property.

"We?" Tyler asks.

"I am just as much a part of this as any of you. My country is being torn apart right in front of me, and even if I don't have the fancy powers that y'all have, I have what y'all lack," the rest of them look at each other. "Life experiences," Wayne continues. "Remember, I was in Desert Storm, and I know how to defend an outpost. While you kids work on your abilities, I will help design and set up an early warning system in the woods and on the road out front around the property to help us in the long run."

Jensen smiles at his uncle and his tenacity. "He's right. Thankfully, we are so far from civilization; this will probably be one of the last places to feel the war. We need to build houses for all of us to live in. Wayne, if you could call your guy, the one who helped build your workshop outback," Wayne nods with a smile. "And then we need to build places to keep an eye out for trespassers."

"Like listening posts in the woods," Wayne suggests as he picks up a pencil and begins marking places he thinks would be appropriate.

"Aiden get on Amazon, Wal-mart.com, and any other websites, and find anything and everything that may be used as home security that we may be able to use," Jensen says. "Tyler, work with Aiden and Wayne to figure out the best place for the listening posts and whatever Aiden finds on the internet before it shuts down. Sloan, you and Betty figure out where everyone can sleep till we get some houses made."

"And what are you gonna do, Jensen?" Aiden asks.

"The rest of the Knights and I are going to train for this war."

EPILOGUE

The Knights found safety and solidarity in the small town just north of the border. The news stations rained hate onto the Transcendents for weeks. Nowhere was safe for them or for the ordinary people of the country.

Every day, more and more people were discovering they were these Transcendents. And with no one to show them how to control their powers, thousands were killed within the first month. Big cities were a dangerous place to live between people trying to learn and people just naturally filled with evil tendencies.

New York was turned into ruins in a matter of weeks. The first incident was a thirteen-year-old girl who had just discover she was a Force Transcendent. She lived on the twenty-first floor of a thirty-story building. Unable to control her ability, she collapsed the building and two adjacent buildings to rubble, killing most occupants.

The collapse led to an immediate ban on all Transcendents. But how do you ban a group that has the power to level the building that created such a law?

Exactly. Two days after the law was authorized, a group of rogue Transcendents destroyed New York City Hall in Manhattan. Among the dead were most of the New York City Council members, including the mayor. One week later, the same group claimed responsibility for destroying the Manhattan Municipal Building, one of the world's largest government buildings and housed thirteen of the city's municipal agencies. These agencies had taken control after the mayor's death.

There was nothing Jensen, or anyone could do at that point but sit and watch it all unfold. Everything Mason had preached and warned about was coming true. Governments around the country were imploding, and the president was struggling to stay ahead of it. Two blocks around the white house were evacuated, and the first Transcendent-led task force was created to protect the president.

The country was in shambles, and it had only been a few months. Every day, people realized who or what they were. Nine times out of ten, those same people went down the same road Liam had. At this rate, Jensen and the Knights will be fighting this war on the ashes of the country's greatest cities.